MISTRUST

MISTRUST
Sam L Cox

CONTENTS

PART THREE

Prologue

It's mid-April and the sun is shining. I'm sitting in the garden in a spot that's sheltered from the breeze and can feel the warm rays on my skin. I have a can of ice-cold cola in one hand and I'm scrolling on my phone with the other. Instagram is showing me photos of the party I've missed. Here is one of Leonie, doing a posy pout in the mirror before going out. Lipstick matching the shade of her new dress. *Hmm, nice colour.* Here is another, with Joanne and Daisy leaning against a kitchen counter at the party, each holding a jelly shot. *Cheers girls!* And here is my bestie Lil, gazing up at the very handsome Charlie. *Wow - good for you Lily!* I should have been there. I mean I would have been there if I wasn't stuck here. If I wasn't forced to give up my life and move to this boring dump.

"Trust me," he said, "once you've made new friends you'll never look back." *Well, trust me, Dad, I'll never trust you again!*

My moment of self-pity is interrupted. I am hit by some sort of shock wave that rips right through my body. I literally jump. My muscles and nerves are all ablaze as if every cell in my body has been flicked awake. It lasts only for a second or two but I'm left with pins and needles in my hands and feet. The skin on my arms and legs is starting to sting, just like sunburn. I feel weak. Then, adrenaline kicks in and my heart starts to pound. Beads of sweat trickle down my forehead. I can't figure out what happened but I can feel a rising wave of nausea. My mouth fills with saliva. *Head*

1

between your knees, quick! I lean forward and throw up on the grass. A slight but dull thud makes me glance to my right. Laying there, twisted and broken, is a buzzard, which has fallen mid-flight. Metallic thuds echo in the distance; a single horn bellows. A plane roars overhead, rapidly losing altitude. As it disappears over the tree line an explosion rocks the earth sending a fireball high into the sky. Shadows start to creep from the corners of my eyes. I slip from the chair, unconscious.

PART ONE

Chapter 1: A new start

My name is Madison, Maddie for short. I'm 14 years old and the youngest of three. Jake is the eldest, he's 21 and then there's my sister Molly, who's nearly 19. However, now that they're both at university I am effectively an only child.

I remember when Jake left home. Everyone was so sad. Mum cried, dad moped around, and Molly started resenting any time she had to spend looking after me. A couple of years later when Molly left, mum didn't cry and dad didn't mope around. Instead, they talked about how my turn would come and what a great time I'd have at uni. It was like they'd accepted that their children were leaving the nest and couldn't wait to get shot of me too. They both work long hours during the week and when they're not working, they're busy doing chores. Most of the time, when I'm home, I'm either alone or ignored.

My world took a turn for the worse when we moved house. Dad had got a new job as a sales director but the job was a long way from home and the commute was too much. So we moved away from everything and everyone I knew to some tiny village in the middle of nowhere. I had to change schools and leave all my friends behind.

The plan was to move house during the February half term. I'd leave my old school and start at my new school with 'minimal disruption'. However, it didn't work out like that and we eventually moved only three weeks before the Easter school holiday.

My first day at school was truly awful. It seemed much bigger than my old one; a confusing collection of buildings with coloured walkways, surrounded by fields. I had been told to go to reception where I sat for ages waiting for someone to take me to my tutor room. When I finally got there I was introduced to everyone by my new tutor, Miss Lacey, with a sea of faces staring at me.

"So please make Madison welcome everyone," she ended.

A trio of blond girls at the back said, "Hello Madison," in a sarcastic chorus, one boy wolf-whistled and then there was a lot of laughter. I saw a few sympathetic faces and one smile. It was humiliating and I was furious. *I hate you all already!*

I was given a timetable and assigned a 'buddy', who was an annoying girl called Anna. She talked non-stop in a high-pitched whine. She must have volunteered, hoping to make a new friend. I had nothing really bad against her, just nothing at all in common. Every lesson I went to seemed to be full of different faces, none of them very welcoming.

Mum dropped me off and picked me up on that first, dire day at school, but after that, I had to get the school bus. The bus stop is about five minutes walk from our house. Only two other kids get on at my stop, both of them younger than me. We are one of the last pick-up points on that bus route and there are never many spaces left to sit. The poker-faced bus driver always lurches off before I've had a chance to work my way down the aisle. I have to clutch the headrests and try not to trip over any feet that get stuck out as I'm passing.

The spare seats are always next to kids that no one else wants to sit with. Most days I've had enough by the time I get to school.

The first week went so slowly and nothing much improved. At my old school, I was popular and had plenty of friends. But here it was like everyone was already part of a little group and they didn't need anyone extra. No one seemed prepared to try, except for Anna. I didn't imagine it would be so hard. Mum and dad were quite concerned but didn't have any suggestions other than to try harder.

At my last school, I used to go to after-school clubs. That might have been a good way to make new friends. However, I used to be able to get home on my own, either by walking or getting a lift from a friend. My new school has clubs too, but there's no way for me to get home. It's too far to walk, there is no bus, and I can't get a lift because I don't know anyone.

The start of the second week seemed even harder than the first. The blond trio at the back still whispered and giggled when they saw me. Anna was still trying very hard to fulfil her role as a buddy, much to my irritation. I was also getting some unwanted attention from a nerdy boy called Robert who for some reason thought he might stand a chance. *Weirdo!* Then Miss Lacey asked me to stay behind after tutor time, which didn't help. She was a little concerned that I seemed unhappy, which only made matters worse. I heard a girl calling me an attention seeker as she left the room.

During the second week, I found out that there were some lunchtime clubs, so I decided to go along to a fitness session. They called it circuit training, which involved various activities like sit-ups, short sprints, and push-ups. People started at intervals and you kept going until you needed a break. I came close to making a new friend. A girl called Emma said hello and that she'd seen me in her Geography class. We chatted for a bit and I thought I might get on quite well with her. There was another session a couple of days later so I went along, hoping she would be there, and she was. We spoke again and everything was going fine until a boy from the year above introduced himself to me. His name was Josh. He was tall and athletic with a crop of dark curly hair. We didn't speak for long, or about anything much, but when I looked up I got a death stare from Emma. She didn't speak to me again. At the end of the session I got changed and as I was walking out of the changing rooms I saw Josh and Emma chatting. Josh raised his hand to wave and Emma turned around to face me. I got another death stare. She must have thought I was trying to muscle in on Josh. He was good-looking but a boyfriend was the last thing on my mind. I had other priorities. So, I gave up.

In the third week, I didn't bother going to circuit training and Anna gave up trying to be my buddy. Most days I just went to my lessons and spent break times messaging my old friends. However, as the days went by they took longer and longer to respond. I felt invisible, a real nobody. I was completely miserable during the day and by the time mum and dad got home from work, I was really angry. I knew why they'd wanted to move, but they hadn't given me a choice. I was simply ripped away from everything and everyone I knew and dumped into a horrible new life that was no life at all.

The Easter holidays finally arrived and there I was, 'Billy no mates'. Jake didn't come home because he was swatting for his finals. Molly found a reason to spend the first week staying with friends. I had no one to talk to, nowhere to go, and nothing to do. That's how I ended up sitting in the garden with a can of cola, scrolling on my phone. Just when I thought things couldn't get any worse, they did. That shock wave ripped what was left of my life to shreds and turned my whole world upside down. That was just the start of it and this is my story.

Chapter 2: The aftermath

A cool wind blew, making me shiver. As I opened my eyes, I could see a green haze. I blinked once or twice, focusing on blades of grass. It took me a moment to realise where I was and several moments more to remember what I'd experienced earlier. I had no idea how long I'd been lying in the grass but the sun had moved and the house cast a long shadow over me. I pushed myself up onto my hands and knees, pausing to wait for the dizziness to subside. I tried to concentrate on a patch of grass in front of me, counting daisies until I got to twenty. My phone lay next to my knee. I picked it up and slowly headed for the house. My body ached. I felt like I'd swum a marathon. What had happened felt like a dream but the buzzard was still motionless on the lawn. In the distance, several plumes of smoke drifted up into the sky. I couldn't make sense of anything. All sorts of questions and possibilities raced through my mind. I needed to call my mum or dad but when I tried to turn my phone on, it wasn't working. I thought perhaps the battery was dead or the phone had broken when I dropped it. I walked into the house, intent on using the landline.

In the kitchen, I noticed that the LED clock on the microwave was blank. So, I checked the power by flicking on the kitchen light; nothing. I walked out to the hall and picked up the desk phone. There was no dial tone, which was odd because landlines usually work in a power cut. According to dad, telephone lines take electricity from the local telephone exchange, which has backup power supplies. So either things worked differently here or the telephone exchange must be in trouble too. The only noise I could hear was the ticking of a clock; an old mechanical clock that mum had inherited from grandma. It was four o'clock in the afternoon, which meant I'd been unconscious for around three hours. *No way!* I still felt pretty rough, so I went up to my room to lie down. I tried to stay calm. Mum and dad would be back later. If they'd been affected by the shock wave they'd already be making their way home. If they hadn't, they'd be home at their usual time.

When I woke up the house was silent. I lay still, eyes shut, recent memories hovering like a bad dream. I stretched, a dull ache travelling through the muscles in my arms and legs. I didn't feel myself at all; my head was sore and I felt slightly nauseous. I opened my eyes but shut them quickly. Bright light poured into my bedroom. I squinted, taking in my surroundings. Why hadn't I pulled the curtains? Why was I fully dressed? The digital alarm clock by my bed was blank. *No electricity! God, it was real, all of it!* The shock wave was real. It made me ill and I went to bed. The sun shone into my bedroom only in the morning, so somehow I had slept through the night. Fear gripped me. Was I still on my own?

I ran to my parent's bedroom to find that their bed hadn't been slept in. I ran to their window to discover that there were no cars in the driveway. They hadn't made it home. The lane was quiet. Normally I'd be able to hear road noise in the distance, but there was only silence. I tried not to panic but I already had a knot in my stomach and my hands shook. Tears welled in my eyes, blurring my vision. What had happened yesterday? Birds fell from the sky, cars crashed, and a plane exploded. I had survived whatever it was but been very unwell. What if I was the only person alive?

I took a few deep breaths to calm my nerves and gave myself a talking-to. *Stop panicking, it's pathetic! There will be a sensible explanation for all this. Just get a grip and find help.*

Our house is one of three houses down a steep but narrow lane on the outskirts of our village. I hadn't met any of our neighbours. I'd seen the people who live in the house above us on my way home from the school bus but they didn't say hello to me, so I ignored them too. At the top, the lane leads onto the main road through the village. That road has a lot more houses, including a pub. I didn't know anyone up there either but I thought I might find someone who could help. First, I had to summon up the courage to go outside. After what had happened yesterday, it didn't feel safe. I decided not to walk up the lane in plain sight but to make my way through the fields instead.

I locked the back door behind me and ran across the garden to the side fence, climbing into the neighbouring field. From here, I walked around the edge until I came to the boundary fence of an old disused railway track. The track runs in a cutting under the lane with a steep embankment on each side. I climbed over the fence. I tried to move down the embankment as quietly as possible but small twigs broke under my feet, sounding like rifle fire. My nerves jumped every time a twig snapped. I went slowly, looking carefully around me until I reached the bottom. I stared into the distance, first left, and then right. It

11

was deserted. The rails on the track had been removed years ago, leaving only the cinders. The track is now a bridle path, which stretches for miles in both directions.

I crossed the track quickly and climbed the embankment on the other side. At the top, I pushed my way through a gap in the bushes into the field beyond. The lane, which passes over the track via a bridge, was on my right behind a tall hedgerow of hawthorn and brambles. On this side of the lane the field stretches all the way to the main road. I walked up the hill, hugging the hedgerow. My back started prickling as if something was watching me from the treeline. *Get a grip!* I tried to stay calm, resisting the urge to run.

When I reached the top, I crept towards the road, hiding behind the hedge that runs beside it. I looked across at the row of houses opposite. All were quiet, doors and windows shut. I peered left and right. In one direction I could see a blue car that had crashed into a garden wall, crumpling the bonnet. The driver's door was open and the car was empty, abandoned. In the other direction, there was nothing to see. No people, no signs of life. I didn't know what to do. Should I try knocking on doors? I decided to wait and watch. Maybe someone would come out of their house. I wished I had some binoculars with me to get a better look.

After crouching for a few minutes, I heard a noise in the distance. At first, I couldn't make out what it was, but as it drew nearer I could hear a loud, tinny-sounding voice. Someone was speaking through a loudspeaker and I could hear the low rumble of a vehicle. My heart skipped a beat. *Thank God!* Someone was coming in a car, someone was passing on news, someone was coming to help. I resisted the urge to run out into the road, deciding to stay put until I could hear what was being said.

I could now see the car approaching, very slowly. It was big and black, some sort of Jeep or Land Rover, with a white loudspeaker mounted on the roof. The information was repeated over and over.

"This is the military. This area has been subjected to an attack that has destroyed all electrical devices. Cars and motorcycles will not work. Many people are injured or unwell. For your safety, please prepare to leave your houses. Transport will be arriving to take everyone to a shelter where you will be protected until the area is safe. You are permitted to take only one small bag with a change of clothes. Food and bedding will be provided at the shelter. Everyone must leave. No one is permitted to stay in their home. Please pack your bag and wait by your front door for further instructions."

The Jeep passed me and turned into our lane. It sped up until it was close to the first house, where it slowed again to deliver the same message.

I didn't know what to do. Should I rush back to the house, pack my bag and wait to be collected? What if mum and dad made it home and I wasn't there? I didn't know where they were going to take me, so I couldn't leave them a note. What if they couldn't find me? I hadn't seen anyone else, but if I wasn't alone, I'd end up in a shelter with a bunch of strangers. I didn't want to go.

The Jeep re-emerged from the lane and continued down the road in the opposite direction, repeating the instructions. Just then I spotted movement at a window across the road. Someone was peering out, watching the Jeep disappear. A few houses along, someone else appeared at their front door, looking apprehensively up and down the road. *Phew!* I wasn't alone after all, but these were strangers. I didn't want to show myself yet. My legs were aching from crouching, so I sat down, certain that no one could see me. I waited.

After about 10 minutes other vehicles appeared in the distance: a coach and another two Jeeps. A few people started to emerge from their houses, standing by their doors, clutching their bags. Some looked scared, some looked stunned, and some looked pretty ill. From quite a few houses, no one emerged at all. They were probably at work when the shock wave came, like my mum and dad. Simply no one at home.

At the first house I could see, the convoy stopped and two soldiers emerged from the first Jeep. I gasped with surprise. They were dressed in white overalls with a hood that included a full-length face mask. They had black gloves and black boots. At first, I thought of beekeepers but actually, they looked more like characters from a movie. The kind of movie where they need to protect themselves from radiation, chemicals, or lethal germs. *Oh no!* My heart started to thump and troubling thoughts raced around my head. What if I'd been exposed to something really dangerous? I hadn't been feeling great. What if I was about to get sick? Going with them might be the best thing to do. Then again, are they really the military? They don't look like the military. They didn't look friendly at all.

Another two soldiers, also dressed in white, emerged from the second Jeep and went to the next house. I watched, hoping to learn more. Maybe I could tell if they were OK or not.

The soldiers approached each house carrying clipboards. If the homeowners were waiting as instructed, they spoke to them, made some notes and directed them to the waiting coach. Then they wrote something on their front door. If there was no one standing outside, they knocked and waited and then wrote on their door too.

They slowly made progress along the road with the convoy following. There were more empty houses than houses with people waiting outside.

The soldiers were now almost opposite where I was hiding. I tried to slow my breathing and stay silent but my heart was pounding hard and suddenly I needed to swallow. *Why now?!* I gulped, trying not to make a noise. At the house opposite, no one was waiting outside but when they knocked, the door opened. In the doorway I could see an elderly lady, crying. Her voice was faint, but I thought I heard her say that she couldn't leave.

"No one's allowed to stay behind," barked one of the soldiers.

The lady continued to cry, shaking her head and trying to close the door. Then, one soldier forced the door open and went in. A few minutes later they both reappeared with the lady carrying a small bag.

"I need you to confirm your husband's name and date of birth," the soldier said. "His body will be collected and taken to the morgue where you can visit and make arrangements later. You can't stay here. It's not safe."

Body? Someone died? As a young and healthy person, I had lost consciousness and felt pretty unwell. The impact must have been too much for the old lady's husband. I couldn't believe it. *Dead!*

The old lady was led to the coach, still crying. Then, the soldier returned to write on the front door. It looked like they were using chalk and I could just make out what was written: '2/2 1D'.

As they moved on to the next house, one of the soldiers paused, staring in my direction. I froze, terrified that I'd been seen. The soldier muttered something over his shoulder and started walking across the road. *No, no!* I thought I was well hidden but maybe not well enough. I couldn't see through the facemask. I couldn't tell if he was staring straight at me or not. My heart was pounding. I had never been so terrified in my whole life. The soldier stopped, no more than two metres from where I was hiding. The mask tilted very slowly to one side, as if he was trying to peer through the bush. I held my breath. *Go away!* After what seemed like forever, the soldier turned and walked back to join his companion. I slowly let out my breath and silently sucked in more air to relieve my aching lungs. It had been a close call. The encounter was more than scary; it felt sinister.

By now, the other soldier had visited the next house. No one was waiting to be collected and no one answered the door. The numbers '0/4' had been written on the door. *Why?*

The soldiers got back into their Jeep and headed down my lane. Well, they weren't going to find me at home. I wasn't ready to go. Something didn't feel right. Besides, even if I started to make my way back now I would be too late and I certainly wasn't leaving without a bag of belongings.

I waited until the Jeep reappeared, some 10 minutes later. It turned right to catch up with the coach, which by now was almost out of sight.

As soon as the convoy disappeared, two military trucks came into view, stopping alongside the first house. I counted eight more soldiers, also dressed in the same white suits. However, these soldiers didn't carry clipboards, they carried rifles. My stomach lurched. *Why guns?*

One approached the first house and knocked. After a few moments they disappeared around the back of the house. Several minutes later they came out the front door. They must have broken in. Then, one of them attached something white to the door and moved on.

They didn't go into every house, which seemed odd. Several houses later I realised that they weren't going into the houses where people had been collected. Maybe they were checking to make sure no one was there. My thoughts were confirmed when I heard some commotion coming from one of the houses a few doors down. A man, presumably the house owner, walked out of the front door with his hands up, followed closely by a soldier prodding him in the back with a rifle. Behind them was a lady, maybe his wife, followed by another soldier with a rifle. The couple were made to stand with their legs apart and hands against the truck. They were searched, handcuffed, and roughly pushed into the back. I stared, open-mouthed. These were definitely not friendly soldiers. They were not here to help rescue people. They were here to remove people. A chill went down my spine. No way was I going with them. I decided to stay on my own, hoping that some real help would come sooner or later.

The armed soldiers and their trucks made slow progress along the road. Houses were searched, garages were searched, and gardens were searched. What they attached to each door was some sort of notice.

At the house opposite me, where the old lady had been forced to leave her husband, two soldiers entered the house. Five minutes later they came out carrying what must be a body bag and tossed it into the back of the second truck like a sack of rubbish. I was totally shocked. First of all, I'd never seen or been near a dead body yet I was staring at a bag with a dead person in it. However, I was also stunned by the way the body was treated. Surely the British military would have shown a little more respect? As the truck moved off I got a glimpse into the back. There were quite a few body bags piled up. *Jeez!*

I watched from my hiding place as one truck went down my lane. They would soon be searching our house. I waited, feeling agitated. After what seemed like an eternity, the truck re-emerged from the lane to make its way along the road. I kept quite still until the coast was clear. I wanted to know what the white notice said, but I didn't want to risk crossing the road. There was bound to be one pinned to our front door. After double-checking that no one was around, I retraced my steps.

Back at our house, I found '0/5' written on the front door in chalk. Now I figured it out. They knew that five people lived in the house but no one had been collected. On the top road, they wrote '0/4' at the other house where no one had been collected. Presumably, four people lived there. On the old couple's front door, they wrote '2/2 1D'. Two people lived there, both collected but one dead. The soldiers were keeping a tally and could account for the missing. I hoped I was wrong. If not, it meant that they intended to track people down.

Nailed to the door was the white notice. I read quickly.

This area has been subjected to an attack, which has destroyed all electrical devices. Vehicles will not work. Many people are injured or unwell. For your safety, you must leave your home. Transport will be arriving to take everyone to a shelter where you will be protected until the area is safe. You are permitted to take only one small bag with a change of clothes. Food and bedding will be provided at the shelter. Everyone must leave. No one is permitted to stay in their home. Please pack your bag and come to your front door when transport arrives for the next wave of evacuation.

You are forbidden to remain by order of His Majesty's Government.

Since when does His Majesty's Government break into people's homes and use guns to forcibly remove innocent people? And since when do they treat the dead like rubbish? I didn't trust them. *No!* I needed to avoid the evacuation.

I walked around the house to discover that the back door had been forced open. Knowing that armed soldiers had searched the house filled me with disgust. I decided to pack some stuff and find somewhere to camp out. Somewhere where I could keep a close eye on what was going on, without being found.

Chapter 3: Shelter

Camping outdoors isn't my thing. Why anyone chooses to sleep on the ground under a thin sheet of canvas with no bathroom is a complete mystery. However, I didn't have a choice. The soldiers were searching houses, outbuildings, and even sheds. If I wanted to escape the second evacuation, I needed to hide and find some sort of shelter.

My brother Jake was in the scouts for years and had loads of stuff that might be useful. I went to his room and rummaged around, pulling out anything I thought might be useful. I grabbed a wind-up hand torch, a Swiss army knife, an inflatable pillow, a rucksack, and two dry bags of different sizes. Tucked in a drawer, I spotted a waterproof mobile phone holder, which could be used to keep matches dry. I also came across a paracord bracelet and put it on. When unravelled, there would be a long length that might be useful for something. In another drawer, I found a hunting knife that mum and dad had argued about him owning. It had a serrated blade and could do quite a bit of damage in the wrong hands. Despite all the fuss mum made, it had never been used. I decided to take it with me.

A sleeping bag was essential if I had to sleep outdoors. Jake had a winter-weight bag, which was quite thin and easy to pack. It had cost quite a lot of money, but he had done his Duke of Edinburgh expedition in the Spring. They had to carry everything they needed during the trip, so mum splashed out to make sure he was warm at night but not overloaded for the trek.

I went to my bedroom to pack some clothing. I chose joggers, t-shirts, and fleece jumpers in dark colours to stay concealed. I collected underwear and warm socks, plus some thermal vests that I wore on ski trips. Everything went into the dry bags. I grabbed a few toiletries from the bathroom. I could skip a few showers but I had to brush my teeth.

Food was next. The fridge had been without power for more than a day and the interior was warm. I grabbed an open pack of sliced ham, some cheese, and mini sausage rolls. I intended to take a camping stove but I wasn't planning to cook anything that smelt strongly, so I left the bacon, eggs, and sausages. If I could only boil water, I needed to find things like pot noodles, pasta, or instant soups. I rifled through the kitchen cupboards to see what I could find. From the tin cupboard, I grabbed some lentils, baked beans, and rice pudding.

I would need drinking water but since it still flowed from taps, I didn't need to take much with me. We had an outside tap in the garden that I could use if careful. I took one large bottle of water and a few cans of cola.

Next, I went to the study to find the binoculars, looping them straight around my neck. I also grabbed my mum's khaki raincoat from the hat stand in the porch. It was long, almost reaching my ankles and had a large hood that fell forward far enough to keep the rain off, without needing an umbrella.

From the garage, I took the camping stove. It had a single gas ring, powered by a small butane canister. I also grabbed a few spare canisters from the shelf. Next to the stove was a camping cook set, which consisted of a couple of small saucepans plus plates, bowls and cutlery. The family tent lay on the shelf below. It was huge, bright-red and of no use whatsoever.

I took everything to the back of the garden and hid it behind a holly bush.

Next, I needed to find somewhere to camp. We have woods behind our house that run up to the old railway track, so I decided to investigate. The trees are mostly tall oak and ash mixed with smaller hazel and holly bushes. Although the tall trees were still in bud, the smaller deciduous trees had already come into leaf. I climbed over the garden fence and started to walk through the woods. Some areas were carpeted in bluebells and wild garlic while others contained brambles and ferns. Although it was quite dense and overgrown, it wasn't too difficult to get through.

After a while, I came across the fence that separates the woods from the old railway track. There wasn't much of it left. The concrete posts were crumbling and the twisted wires between them sagged, leaving large gaps. I ducked under the top wire and climbed through onto the embankment. In the distance, some movement caught my eye. Something was coming down the track at speed. I quickly hid behind a bush. Coming into view was a person on a bicycle but something looked really wrong. As they got nearer I could see why. A large man in a black beanie and grey puffer jacket was riding a child's bicycle. He was hunched over the handlebars and his knees were sticking out to each side as he pedalled furiously along. He reminded me of an overgrown frog. When he passed me I glimpsed his face. His expression was somewhere between grim determination and fear. At any other time, it would have been funny, but I was worried that he was being chased. I stayed behind the bush, scanning the track. No one was following. If he was trying to escape from someone, he'd been successful. I wasn't the only person who didn't trust the evacuation party.

Camping too close to the track was risky so I climbed back through the fence. I worked my way into the middle of the woods, looking for somewhere more suitable. Somewhere hidden but dry and large enough for me to sleep comfortably. Although the woods seemed promising, I struggled to find anywhere.

After a frustrating search, I reached a section of the woods where the ground dropped steeply down to a river. I made my way down the slope, looking from side to side. The bank was quite heavily wooded all the way to the river's edge. In the distance to my right, a fallen tree lay with its roots exposed to the sky. I made my way towards it. The tree was enormous and must have fallen a long time ago because the bark was partly stripped away. All of the trees along the bank seemed to tilt slightly towards the river, reaching out to compete with each other for light. This tree must have become too large for its roots to bear and simply toppled downhill. As I got close, I could see that a hole had been torn in the bank. The root ball was exposed, revealing large and small roots around the base of the tree trunk, like petals on a flower stem. I climbed through the gap between the bank and the bottom of the root ball to discover that the hole extended back into the bank. It was like a small cave with walls of mud, chalk, and flint. In many places, small roots stuck out where they had broken from the base of the tree, leaving areas of loose soil. Although the floor was uneven, there was enough space to move around and lie down. The overhang would also protect me from any rain. I decided that this was good enough. I wouldn't be visible from the top or bottom of the bank. With a few carefully placed branches, I would also be hidden from each side. I headed back to the garden to grab some tools.

Getting back to the house took about 10 minutes. I was further away than I wanted to be, but that couldn't be helped. Before climbing back over the garden fence I stopped for a few moments, watching and listening for any signs of activity. All was quiet. From the garage, I picked up a trowel, a small spade, and some secateurs. I also found a green tarpaulin on the garage shelf. After retrieving the hunting knife from my supplies, I retraced my steps through the woods.

Back at the cave, I pulled my hood up over my head and used the trowel to scrape loose soil from the roof. I got showered in small clods of mud, dust, and the odd creepy-crawly. *Ugh!* In the centre of the cave, I managed to increase the head height slightly so that I could stand up straight. Then, I used the knife to cut away some of the smaller roots that were in the way. Happy with the ceiling, I worked my way down the walls, clearing the loose soil away. In the far corner, a large protruding root formed a natural shelf, which would be useful for storing supplies clear of the ground. Some smaller roots to one side would serve nicely as hooks for the dry bags of clothing.

The floor of the cave was harder to deal with. The loose soil I had removed from the ceiling and walls lay in uneven piles. I started by flattening out the mounds of soft soil and then I trod carefully around the base of the cave to compact it. The floor was better but still uneven. I scraped soil from the top of small mounds into the hollows and trod down once more. By repeating the process a few times I created a level area with only a few roots sticking out. Some of them came out with the knife but other roots were too big to do anything about. I laid the tarpaulin down in the flattest spot at the back of my cave. Finally, I needed to return to the house to get the supplies I had collected. Before leaving, I pulled some dead branches up to the entrances on each side of the root ball, arranging them to look as natural as possible. I left myself a small gap for access.

An hour later I had arranged my sleeping bag on the tarp, blown up the inflatable pillow and changed into some clean clothes. Some tins of food, cans of cola, and a bottle of water were arranged on the shelf. A plastic bag containing the rest of the food hung from a nearby hook. Other hooks held the dry bags of clothing clear of the ground.

I hung the windup torch by the bed. It didn't work very well, but it was better than nothing. The gas stove was wedged between two roots on the floor of the cave and a pan of water was coming to a boil. I made myself some instant soup into which I dunked slices of white bread. Afterwards, I ate the sausage rolls and a tin of rice pudding.

Looking around, I was quite pleased with my efforts. It would do for a day or two. I was going to miss a bathroom but I'd have to put up with being grubby.

The daylight was fading fast and I was exhausted. I trudged down to the river for a pee, then returned to the cave for my first night in the open. Climbing into my sleeping bag, I pulled the soft fabric high around my neck. Through the cave opening, I could see the outline of the sun dipping over the horizon, enveloped in a red haze. *Red sky at night, shepherd's delight!* Good weather tomorrow. I lay awake for a while, worrying. I was scared. I'd never slept outside on my own before. Was I doing the right thing by hiding? Should I let the soldiers collect me in the second evacuation? I thought about the events of the day. They said they were the military. They said they were rescuing us. But the guns and the way they had treated people just wasn't right. No, I was doing the right thing. Sooner or later I would get some proper help. I really missed my mum and dad. I hoped they were OK, my brother and sister too. Eventually, I slept.

Chapter 4: Coping alone

I woke to a blood-curdling cry and a rush of adrenaline. It was pitch dark. At first, I had no idea where I was but as sleep retreated I remembered my situation with a feeling of dread. The noise I had heard was an owl, that much I realised, but hearing it so close at hand was chilling. I imagined other creatures of the night that might be out there right now. A fox maybe, or a badger, drawn by the faint smell of food or flesh. When cornered, I knew that both could be dangerous. What would I do if one came in? Fire would keep them away, but I couldn't possibly risk that. A weapon? The closest thing I had was the knife and a spade. I had no idea what time it was, but there was no getting back to sleep. I lay staring out at the dark sky. Clouds moved slowly, revealing stars in their wake, which were blotted out as other clouds moved in behind. The wind had also picked up. Although it was not blowing directly into my cave, there was a steady breeze circulating. It was cold and as my adrenalin subsided, I realised it was icy cold. The sweat on my skin chilled and I began to shiver. There would be a frost by dawn. Fearing death from hyperthermia I forced myself out of my sleeping bag and grabbed a dry bag full of clothing. After pulling on an extra layer, I got back into my sleeping bag. Slowly the shivers subsided, but I couldn't go back to sleep. Instead, I lay there, listening to the sounds of the woods. Anxiety ate away at me. I gasped at every rustle and swallowed hard at every click, no matter how small.

Finally, dawn began to break and darkness was replaced with a faint light. I felt desperate. Life was so unfair. First I was forced to move away from my friends, from everything I knew to this miserable place in the middle of nowhere. Mum and dad were never around, my brother and sister were away somewhere having a great time. Here I was, hating school, having no friends, and now thrown into a nightmare where everything that I had left was taken away from me. I was totally alone, scared, cold, and miserable. The tears started to flow. I knew I shouldn't be feeling sorry for myself because it wasn't going to help, but I couldn't hold back the tears. It was all I could do to keep myself from crying out loud. At that moment I felt the lowest I had ever felt in my entire life and I didn't even have a box of tissues. My cheeks were wet and snot was running down my face. I wiped the mess away with my sleeve. *Gross!*

A while later, I managed to regain some control. My eyes felt puffy and my nose was blocked, but my shoulders had stopped shaking. I lit the stove, my fingers fumbling with the controls, and warmed some water.

After a hot chocolate, I began to feel a bit stronger. I was determined not to give up. However, I had to do something to improve this camp or find somewhere else altogether. I couldn't put up with more nights like the one I'd just had. I needed to do something to make it warmer and safer. It occurred to me that another tarpaulin could be tied across the entrance to keep out the wind. If it was hung slightly back from the opening it wouldn't be seen. However, I wasn't sure if there was another tarpaulin at the house. If I used the tarpaulin I had slept on then I would have to find something else to keep me and my sleeping bag off of the mud floor. I racked my brains, trying to remember what I might find in the garage or maybe in the garden. *Cardboard boxes!* The garage had loads of cardboard packing boxes from our house move. Dad had tied them in bundles and left them in the corner, ready for recycling. A pile of those beneath me would be quite comfortable and warm too. Feeling a bit more optimistic, I ate a few biscuits and got ready to leave. Although I was still quite cold, I took off the extra layer of clothing. I'd warm up once I got going.

Back at the house, I crouched by the fence, waiting and watching. All was quiet. I quickly climbed over and went into the garage. From the pile in the corner, I chose four bundles of cardboard boxes. They were thick and sturdy and would make a good sleeping platform. Getting them back to my camp was going to take more than one trip. I moved them over the fence and into the woods so that I didn't have to go back into the garden again.

The bundles were light but bulky to carry and kept catching on tree branches and brambles as I went through the woods. I managed to transport them in two trips. Being a bit worried about leaving a trail, I varied my route slightly each time. Where possible I used tracks made by wild animals and avoided trampling the bluebells and wild garlic patches. By the time I had transported the bundles back to the camp, I was hot and sweaty and covered in scratches. I removed the tarpaulin from the floor and dragged in the bundles.

I laid two bundles end to end and placed the other two bundles on top. My new bed was plenty long enough for me to stretch out on and would lift me a good 30 centimetres off of the floor.

I took a break to contemplate how I was going to hang up the tarpaulin. Fortunately, it looked like a simple task because roots were sticking out of the ceiling, which I could hang it from. The tarpaulin even had metal-ringed holes along the edges through which I could thread some rope. I'd found a use for the paracord bracelet.

After a pot noodle lunch, I hung the tarpaulin and then surveyed the camp from outside. Thankfully nothing could be seen. At that very moment, I heard the distant sound of an engine and froze. Perhaps the next evacuation was underway. I quickly brushed some fallen leaves over the area immediately outside the cave and climbed in. Crouching down by the entrance, I could just about hear the vehicle. They were using a loudspeaker again but I couldn't catch everything that was said. What I did hear confirmed that it was the second trip to pick up anyone who had missed the first evacuation. The words were much the same; a warning about health and safety, followed by instructions for getting collected. I was going nowhere. I lay down on my new bed and listened. The only sounds I heard were those of the woods, which I'd now got used to. A bit later on, I heard the engine again, this time moving further away. I thought about going back to check on the house but I was so tired. Besides, the new bed was much more comfortable than the mud floor. Without intending to, I drifted off to sleep.

When I woke up, the sun was getting low in the sky. The thought of the night ahead reminded me of how scared I'd been in the dark. I decided to weigh down the bottom of the tarpaulin to deter anything from pushing its way through. There were lots of chunks of flint lying around that had been unearthed when the tree fell. They worked well. I also propped the spade next to my sleeping platform just in case something did get in.

I cooked some pasta and stirred through some cream cheese and ham. By now, the sun had set and the moon had risen to take its place. The air outside was chilled, but the tarpaulin did a good job of keeping the draught out. I put on an extra layer of clothing and climbed into my sleeping bag. After taking an unexpected nap in the afternoon, I wasn't ready for sleep. So instead I tried to come up with a plan for the next day. I decided to explore the area along the old railway track. I thought perhaps I might come across other people who were hiding out or who might know what was happening. I also realised that my food stocks would not last forever, so perhaps there would be a chance to replenish my supplies. Eventually, I fell asleep and although I woke once or twice during the night, I was warm, comfortable, and felt safe.

The following day I woke early and made myself a cup of hot chocolate. I spread some jam on a couple of slices of bread, noting that the bread was getting stale. I was going to have to look for food in other people's houses. It was wrong, I knew, but no one would blame me.

I decided to start exploring the track to the west of our house. I had been for a short walk in that direction a couple of weeks ago and from memory, it was quite heavily wooded. I remembered passing a few houses with back gardens that you could see straight into and being glad that our garden was not overlooked. I grabbed an empty rucksack, pulled on my mum's raincoat, and put the binoculars around my neck. I imagined returning with my rucksack full of supplies like crisps, biscuits, chocolate, and fruit.

First, I went to check on the house. Nothing seemed to have changed. The second evacuation had come and gone without any further notices being attached to the front door. Unable to resist, I cautiously approached the back door and peered inside. The hairs on the back of my neck stood on end. The shoe rack had been upset and a pile of shoes and boots lay in a muddle on the hall floor. I hadn't left it like this, someone had been in the house again. I glanced quickly over each shoulder and hastily retreated to the woods. *Idiot!* I didn't need to go into the house for anything. Being curious was plain stupid. I needed to stay out of sight.

I went back into the woods to find the fence that ran beside the old railway track. Climbing over, I headed west along the top of the embankment and soon came across the bridge that crossed our lane. I glanced quickly up and down, then sprinted over to disappear into the undergrowth on the opposite side. From there I continued to walk along the top of the embankment, ducking under branches and weaving between the trees and bushes. I had quite a good view of the track in either direction and there was no one around at all.

The first house I came to stood behind a tall prickly hedge. Through a small gap, I could see into the garden, which was mostly a lawn and borders with shrubs. They had a conservatory at the back of the house, which led to a patio with a table and chairs. The house looked quite secure. If the occupants had been evacuated, the house would be locked. It might also be alarmed although I wasn't sure that burglar alarms would work after the shock wave. It wasn't worth the risk. I decided that this house was too difficult anyway. There was no way I could get over the prickly hedge, so I moved on.

The next house was set a long way back from the boundary across a huge lawn. Although their fence was quite tall, a five-bar gate offered easy access to the garden. Peering carefully around the side of the fence, I could see a paddock and stable. A white horse grazed away at the grass, twitching its shoulders now and again to disturb the flies. I decided that this house was also too risky. That was a huge expanse of lawn to cover before reaching the back door. As I went to move away I accidentally stepped on a stick that made a large cracking noise as it splintered beneath my foot. The horse looked up and whinnied loudly, the noise breaking the silence. I darted over to a dense bush and crouched down, my heart thumping. The horse continued to make a commotion. It was probably used to a routine that had been disrupted. Stabled at night, let out during the day, extra oats to eat, and fresh hay for the night. Eventually, it quietened down. I sat still for a while longer before silently slipping away.

The next stretch of track had no neighbouring houses. I continued as quietly as I could, stopping every few paces to listen for noises. Eventually, I came across another house, much smaller than the last two. It was only a short distance from the track to the back door and there was almost no boundary fence to worry about. I stopped to take a good look at the surroundings. The front of the property faced a small road that travelled via a bridge over the railway track. I wanted to see the markings on the front door because it wasn't worth attempting if the occupants had been evacuated. I backed into the woods and made my way forward until I was next to the bridge. Through the binoculars, I could just about make out the chalk markings on the door, '2/2'. So both occupants had left and the house would be locked. My heart sank. All this effort so far and nothing to show for it.

I moved back to my original position and used the binoculars to look at the track on the other side of the bridge. All I could see was woodland, no houses. By now it was getting on for lunchtime and I was hungry. I decided to go back to my camp for something to eat and then set out along the track in the other direction. I retraced my steps.

Back at camp, I warmed some water and ate another pot noodle. Food was getting boring already. I'd never been a pot noodle fan and decided that if I ever got out of this mess I'd never eat another one again. I ate a few dry biscuits and drank the last can of cola. I was determined to find some supplies in the afternoon and not come back empty-handed.

I walked through the woods towards the railway track until I reached the fence at the top of the embankment and then turned east. As before, I stuck to the top of the embankment, weaving between the bushes and trees. On my left-hand side, the land started to fall away from the track and I could see across the fields to a distant treeline. I scanned the landscape with my binoculars but nothing stood out as unusual, except the silence. I moved on. The bushes screening me from the field started to thin out. Fearing I might be seen, I crossed the track to the other side where there was more cover. The embankment on this side extended upwards to join a field that sloped up to the skyline. Again, there was nothing to be seen. I knew there was a gap between our village and the next one and decided that I must have reached that point in my journey. I felt very exposed, believing that someone could be looking down on me from the top field. I hurried on.

A couple of hundred metres further on, the track was once again in a cutting with heavily wooded embankments. Although my journey was slowed by the undergrowth I felt calmer. I was well hidden here. I cautiously passed some steps that were cut into the embankment, linking the track with another pathway. A little further on, the track passed over a road that I recognised. The road was no distance from our house by car, but it felt like a very long way on foot.

Suddenly the landscape changed again. Rather than running through a cutting, the track was now on a ridge with the embankment falling away steeply on both sides. Luckily, this stretch was hidden by trees, heavy with ivy, which bowed across the pathway, blocking out the light. I passed a large foreboding house on my right. Tucked under the eaves was a bright yellow burglar alarm. I moved on. Beyond this point, the track levelled out once more and across a field to my right I could see the back fences of people's gardens. I had reached the next village.

Looking into the distance, the track seemed to be more exposed with just a few trees on the boundary and open fields across to a river. I didn't want to venture that far. However, just ahead, the track crossed over a small bridge. Underneath the bridge was a shallow path, lined with this year's new growth of stinging nettles. The sides sloped gently upwards and were covered with shrubs and small trees. The path looked as if it would lead up to the main road that ran through the village.

I pulled my hood forward to cover as much of my face as possible and started to work my way down to the path and then up towards the main road. I went slowly, pausing every few paces to listen for any sounds. Ahead, to my left, was the end of someone's garden. It was long and thin. I passed a vegetable patch, separated by a picket fence from an area with small apple trees. Beyond this was a seating area and finally the house. I paused for a short while, studying the house and immediate area for signs of movement. Nothing.

The path led straight to the main road. I edged forward far enough to get a view of the front door. The markings read '0/3'. *Good!* The soldiers would have entered this house to search for occupants. I should be able to get in with no fear of a house alarm. I moved back down the path until I was at the rear of the house. I scanned the windows with the binoculars and could see no sign of anyone being home. The fence was easy to get over and I was soon at the back door. I slowly pushed down on the handle and the door opened. I couldn't believe it was that easy!

I crossed the threshold, feeling scared but also guilty. *Burglar!* I was in an open-plan kitchen with a dining area that overlooked the garden and fields beyond, all the way to the railway track. I could trace the route I had taken precisely.

I didn't want to spend any longer here than necessary. Walking into the kitchen I opened a cupboard at random. Plates. Next cupboard, glasses. Next cupboard. *Yay!* I could see flour and sugar, plus other baking ingredients. I grabbed a bag of almonds and a tub of glace cherries. Not my favourites, but high in calories.

Suddenly I heard a noise and spun around. Before I could see what was happening, someone pushed me back up against the cupboard and shoved a hand roughly over my mouth. I was terrified. I tried to scream but the noise was muted by the hand. I tried again but the hand squeezed harder, forcing the inside of one cheek onto my teeth. I tasted blood.

"Shhh!" hissed the voice. "Don't make a sound!"

Chapter 5: Company

I shut my eyes, trying to block out what was happening. Waves of fear were washing over me. I was gasping for breath but the hand was clamped so tightly over my mouth that I couldn't breathe. Panic took hold. I thought I was going to die. I forced myself to open my eyes and look at my attacker. A face came into focus, which I recognised. *What?!* It was Josh from school. He looked different out of uniform but it was definitely Josh. I nodded to assure him I wouldn't scream. At the same moment, I saw that he recognised me.

"Maddie?" he whispered. "Jeez, I'm sorry!"

He took his hand away, looking embarassed. I gasped for breath. Before I could gather my thoughts I burst into tears. I didn't want to cry, not then, but I couldn't help it. Perhaps it was the shock and then the relief that followed. *I'm not alone!* I tried to force myself to stop but the tears kept coming and my throat ached with the effort to stay silent. This was embarrassing, but I just couldn't help it. Josh put a hand on my shoulder.

"Sorry. Honestly, I'm so sorry," he whispered. "Listen. It's going to be OK, but it's not safe here."

I pulled back slightly to look up at him. His face showed concern and he gave me a sympathetic smile. I managed a small smile and his face lit up. I could see that he was pleased to find me and I was pleased to find him too.

"I'm sorry about breaking into your house," I said quietly, finally regaining some control.

"It's not my house. It belongs to a friend. I was sleeping rough in some stables but these guys with guns spotted me and I had to leave everything behind. So, I'm borrowing some things. Listen. It's not safe here. We really shouldn't stay here any longer. I watched you coming up the path. Someone else might have seen you too."

I thought I had been so careful and was annoyed with myself. Josh mistook the look on my face.

"Honestly, I didn't realise it was you," he said, "not with your hood covering your face. I would still have had to stop you screaming but I didn't mean to scare you so much."

He looked embarrassed. I raised my eyebrows. I didn't want to struggle on my own any longer so I just came straight out with it.

"I'm camped out in some woods near my house. I think it's pretty safe if you want to come with me. I've made a shelter and I've got some food and access to fresh water. I reckon two pairs of eyes are better than one, you know, to stay out of trouble?"

"Really? That's great," he said enthusiastically. "If you're sure?"

I nodded, smiling.

"I'll just grab the stuff I'm borrowing." He looked down at my feet. "Don't forget the almonds and cherries. I love a good cake!"

I grinned, the idea of baking a cake seeming so surreal. *Really?* It was the first time I'd found something funny since this whole sorry thing had started. He smiled back, then turned and picked up a large holdall from the doorway.

"Come on, let's go."

At the back door, he suggested we move independently to cover each other, as they do on Quad. I had no idea.

"OK, you move and get over the fence. I'll keep watch. Then you stop and watch for me until I catch up. Then we keep going like that. It's easier to spot someone else who's moving if you're not moving yourself."

It seemed to make sense, so I agreed.

We worked our way back down the path to the track. This time I stayed a little further away from the fence line, but still tucked under the trees. When we reached the track, we moved through the undergrowth at the side, as I had done before.

After a while, we came to the section with the steps. Josh stopped.

"Wait," he said, "I've got an idea. A friend of mine lives in a house just through the woods at the top of these steps. We can get to his back garden without breaking cover. They have chickens and we might be able to get some fresh eggs."

"Eggs? Well, I've been careful not to cook or eat anything that smells too much in case it attracts attention."

"We can make hard-boiled eggs then."

"But they stink when you peel them."

"Not if you peel them under water. My mum does that all the time."

I'd never heard of that before, but it sounded feasible.

We climbed the embankment next to the steps and set off through the woods. After only a few minutes we came to a pathway that led down to a road. Running alongside the pathway was a small pink cottage and garden with a mesh fence. At the back of the garden, chicken wire enclosed a small coup where several fluffy brown chickens strutted around pecking at the ground. Josh dropped his holdall, climbed over the fence and opened a gate on one side of the coup. Without any hesitation, he walked to the hen house, unlatched the door and went inside. A small commotion of clucking broke out, with several more chickens rushing outside through their small side entrance and ramp. I glanced around, worried that we might attract some attention. All remained quiet. After what seemed like ages, Josh emerged clutching a handful of eggs. He had a big smile on his face and a few feathers in his hair. I breathed a sigh of relief. We quickly stored the eggs in his rucksack and retraced our steps to the railway track.

It took almost an hour to reach the embankment closest to my camp. I motioned to Josh to follow me through the woods but to wait at the top of the bank. I looked for signs of disturbance and found none. When we reached the cave, I could see that Josh was impressed. He hadn't seen it until we were right on it. He climbed inside to take a closer look, then poked his head out grinning.

"This is great," he said. "So where are you sleeping?"

I pushed him back inside, smiling. Josh wandered backwards and forwards, picking things up and putting them down, then poking his head out of the tarpaulin to look around.

"Wow! You did a pretty good job here Maddie."

Yes, I had. It was a lot of work, but I was proud of myself.

By now it was late afternoon. We sat inside on my makeshift bed. All four eggs had made it back without breaking and were safely stored on the shelf. Josh emptied his holdall to show me what he had picked up: a sleeping bag, a towel, some toiletries, and some clothes. He had also grabbed a few tins of food, some spaghetti, and a few bars of chocolate. As I heated some water to cook the spaghetti, Josh told me his story.

"The night before it happened, I'd been staying over at a friend's house. I got up late and started cycling home on the old railway track, around lunchtime. I'm really not sure what happened but the last thing I remember was cycling through some kind of invisible ripple, like there was a force field across the track. I lost control of the bike. The next thing I remember was waking up to darkness with a banging head and pains in my legs. I managed to shuffle into a more comfortable position but passed out again until dawn."

"I lost consciousness too," I explained, "without falling off a bike. Were you badly hurt?"

"Apart from a sore head, no. I think the pains in my legs were from lying in an awkward position. Once I'd moved, they were OK. Anyway, I was freezing cold and just wanted to get home. One wheel of my bike was buckled, so I started to walk. Apart from a bad headache, I just had a few scratches and bruises. Here," Josh said, taking my hand and placing it at the back of his head. "Can you feel that bump?"

"Crikey, that must be sore."

"I took a shortcut across the fields to my house and climbed over the back garden fence. Just as I reached the path that goes around to the front of the house, I saw our neighbour standing in the road with his hands up and a guy in white pointing a rifle at his head. My neighbour saw me but quickly looked away like he didn't want to draw attention to me. I ducked out of sight. I couldn't believe what was happening. They took him away in a truck!"

"I saw a similar thing," I said. "A man and woman on the top road who didn't go with the initial evacuation were forced out of their house and taken away. Those people in white suits claim to be soldiers in the military, rescuing people!"

"Soldiers? Really? Well, I didn't see the evacuation. It happened before I got there."

"They had a couple of coaches. They went door to door, checking people off on some kind of list and putting marks on their doors. I think the marks showed how many people lived there and how many they had picked up. Anyway, so what did you do next?"

"Well, once the coast was clear I went into my house but no one was home. I found a note on the kitchen table from my mum saying that they were being evacuated to a safe place and that she hoped to find me there. It's weird, I thought that they were evacuated to save them from those people in white suits."

"No, the people doing the evacuation were dressed exactly the same," I explained. Josh shook his head.

"What on earth is going on? This is like a bad dream. I wonder where they took my mum and brother?"

"They talked about a shelter of some kind where they would be kept safe and given food. Wasn't there a note pinned to your front door?"

"Not that I remember," he replied, "but I really wasn't thinking too clearly. I grabbed a few things that I thought I might need: a sleeping bag, some clothes, a little food and some drinks. I headed for an empty stable block at the bottom of the field behind where I live. My mates meet up there from time to time. I hoped that some of them might head there too. I knew it would be warm and dry with a good view up to the houses. It's also close to the old railway track for a quick getaway. But no one was there, just me. I stayed there all day, keeping watch. That night I slept badly but by the morning I felt a lot better. My head didn't hurt so much and I started to think more clearly.

"I realised that I needed more supplies if I was going to carry on sleeping rough. There was more food at the house, so I decided to nip back and grab what I could. The coast looked clear, but after I'd gone a few paces I spotted one of those soldiers across the field at the end of someone's garden. I rushed back but I'd been seen. Then, four of them appeared with guns and started to walk across the field. I got out the back entrance to the stable and managed to escape to the track without being spotted. I ran down the track and climbed a tree to hide. I could just about see the stable. Two of the soldiers went inside and two had their guns trained on the entrances. They took my sleeping bag, stuffed with all the clothes and supplies I had. Although they walked up onto the track and looked up and down, they didn't come looking for me. They went back to whatever they'd been doing on the main road.

"I spent another uncomfortable night sleeping under a bridge. I was so cold and so hungry but I didn't dare go back to my house. So I decided to go to Dan's house, which is where I met you."

The spaghetti was ready. I drained the contents and added a tin of baked beans. We shared the meal from the same pan. Josh ate faster than I did, but I didn't mind him getting the lion's share. It sounded like he'd had much more of an ordeal than me.

"You must be in the girl guides," he said, gesturing around the cave with one arm. "I can't believe you got all this set up so well on your own."

"I think I got lucky." I hoped I wasn't blushing.

Josh went quiet for a moment, deep in thought.

"So whoever these so-called soldiers are," he said, "they know who lives where and are trying to account for everyone. They could show up at any house that is marked as having missing people at any time."

"Yes, I think they could but they didn't get things completely right at my house," I explained, "because my brother and sister don't live at home. They are away at university."

"Yes, but they are probably shown as living at home on the electoral register, so that's what they must have been using as they went door to door."

"So do you think that makes them genuine British soldiers then?"

"Not necessarily. They might have hacked a database somewhere. They could be Russians."

"The ones I heard spoke good English. No accents."

"So if they are British soldiers, why are they wearing those suits and why are they trying to track everyone down?" he asked. "Do you think we've all been exposed to something dangerous?"

"That did occur to me but I feel fine now and you seem fine too. If they are British soldiers, I want to know why they had to threaten people with guns and why they're treating people so badly. None of it makes sense. I reckon we should lay low for a few days and see what happens."

"I agree. Compared with my last few nights, this place is luxury."

For the first time since everything happened, I started to feel more at ease. I was no longer alone. I had someone to share my worries with and talk through the many questions that ran round and round in my mind. Together, we were stronger.

I told Josh about my experiences. What the shock wave had felt like to me, how it had affected me, and how I'd cautiously investigated the top road and witnessed the evacuation. I went on to tell him about my trip to explore the area west and then east of the camp via the old railway line. He mostly knew the places I had been, the houses I had watched, and the routes I had taken. He had lived his whole life in this area and knew it like the back of his hand. I felt more and more at ease. Everything and everywhere had seemed so alien to me, but with Josh, I now had a companion and a guide.

Josh told me about his family. His parents split up when he was six. He lives with his mum and his younger brother Joe in an end-of-terrace house in the next village. His mum has to work hard to make ends meet and he feels like he's missed out on a lot of the things that his friends take for granted. A dad that gives a damn, for one! He's never had a family holiday abroad, for another. He's never been on any of the decent school trips either. His friends are always showing off their new trainers and iPhones whereas he has to settle for something cheap from Sportsdirect and a pay-as-you-go brick. He doesn't blame his mum though as she's doing the best she can. While a lot of his richer friends mess around at school, he's determined to do well. He wants to do A-levels and go to university so that he can get a decent job and earn lots of money. He wants to be able to treat his mum too. That's sweet.

I reflected on my own childhood. I had been much luckier. Whilst my parents worked hard and weren't around much, at least they were still together and there wasn't much I didn't want for. I felt a bit mean for all the grief I'd given them recently.

When Josh announced that he needed to nip out for a 'comfort break' I told him to go down to the river. I also pointed out the trowel, but he said that wouldn't be necessary. I chuckled to myself. If someone had told me that I would be living in a cave with a boy from school, stealing eggs, and peeing in the river I would never have believed them. What would tomorrow bring?!

When Josh returned, I popped out to do the same, noting that the sun was already setting. Back at the cave, I pulled the tarpaulin closed and weighed the bottom down with a few rocks. Then we got into our sleeping bags to stay warm. My sleeping platform was just wide enough for us to lie together on our sides. Josh lay behind, facing me with his knees bent. I lay with my back to him, mirroring his shape. *I'm spooning!* I blushed at the thought but smiled at the imaginary death stare I would get from Emma. She'd be furious. We chatted for a little longer but I was exhausted. It wasn't long before we both drifted off to sleep.

Chapter 6: Chester

In the morning we woke to the sound of rain splattering against the tarpaulin. Josh pulled part of it aside to reveal a grey sky with persistent light rain. In the gloomy interior of the cave, I boiled some water and we made hot chocolate to go with stale bread and jam.

"We'll need to get some more water today," I said, holding up a near-empty container.

"Where do you get it from?"

"We have an outside tap at the back of our garage, so that seems like the easiest place. This is the first time I've needed to get a top-up."

"I bet there are some standpipes in the fields around here too," Josh said. "Anywhere with stables will have something. But I'd like to see where you live, if that's OK?"

When the rain eased off mid-morning, we set out for the house. Josh followed me on the route through the woods until we got to the fence at the back of the garden. I crouched down and he crouched beside me. All was quiet.

Josh stared at the house.

"Blimey, it's enormous! Your parents must be really rich. And your garden is massive. I bet your dad has one of those ride-on mowers."

"He does," I replied, feeling slightly embarrassed. I'd done nothing but moan about this house since we had moved here, but compared with a lot of homes, it was really nice. I felt like a bit of a spoiled brat. Josh lived in an end-of-terrace house with a family that struggled to make ends meet. I had all this but hadn't stopped complaining since we left our old house behind.

We worked our way around to the side of the garden next to the garage. I climbed over the fence and quickly filled my container. I passed it back to Josh and we returned to the camp, just as the rain resumed.

"Now that I think about it," Josh said, "I must have passed your house loads of times over the years. When I was younger I used to go to a kids club in the Summer holidays. They did loads of craft activities, sports, that kind of thing. Every year we'd get to make little boats and we'd go to the river further down your lane to race them. There's a bridge there, do you know it?"

"Not been down there yet."

"Well one person in each team would lay flat on the bridge and when the starting whistle blew, they'd let the boats go. Everyone else would be lining the river and cheering for their boat. The team whose boat crossed the finish line first would get a bag of sweets to share. It was lots of fun."

Josh was smiling, deep in thought.

"I hope my little brother is OK," he added, his expression becoming more serious. "At least he and my mum are together, wherever they are."

I stopped to wonder about my family. Everyone had been somewhere different when the wave came. If it had affected everyone, I hoped my brother and sister were with friends. I hoped my mum and dad had been able to find one another too. I imagined them, sick with worry for all of us. I wished I could tell them I was OK. That I had found Josh and was not on my own.

A noise disturbed our thoughts and we quickly looked at each other, sitting up straight. There was a low humming noise in the distance, which got louder and louder.

"Helicopter?" I said, hazarding a guess.

Josh nodded in agreement. He quickly yanked on the tarpaulin and the part that he had pulled aside swung back down to seal us inside the cave. We sat motionless, listening. Josh pointed to where he thought the helicopter was positioned and moved his arm slowly as he traced its path. It sounded like it was across the river, travelling east. As it moved away the noise became quieter again. I was just about to speak when the noise increased once more. This time it was travelling west and came closer to our camp. Then, another change of direction. This time the helicopter flew more or less directly over us.

"They're searching," Josh said. I nodded in agreement.

We spent the next half an hour or more in the dark in complete silence, listening to the humming noise rise and subside. My stomach was doing somersaults and my throat was dry. What if they could see the camp or maybe some of the trails I had left in the woods? Josh sat with his hand over his mouth and his eyes following the sound of the whirling blades. Eventually, the noise dropped out of earshot.

"Sounds like a pretty thorough search," I said. "Glad we got back before they started."

Josh frowned.

"How come these people have working cars and helicopters when we can't even turn on a light bulb?" he said, shaking his head and running his hands through his hair. "How can they claim to be the good guys when they are breaking into people's houses with guns and hunting people down in helicopters."

"I know," I replied. "How could anyone possibly trust them? For all we know they've put people into concentration camps like they did to the Jews in Germany. Well first they'll have to find me and then they'll have to drag me kicking and screaming!"

"Me too!"

"What are we going to do though Josh? We don't have an endless supply of food, so we can't lie low here forever."

"We'll have to outsmart them," he replied. "We'll make plans, we'll go on raids. I know the area better than they do. Sooner or later something has to change and things will go back to normal. I'm sure it won't be like this forever."

I didn't feel so certain, but I liked his optimism. Josh got up to pull the tarpaulin aside once more. A grey light filtered into the cave. Outside, a faint mist hung in the air. Big heavy drops of rainwater fell from the roof at the entrance, bouncing onto the mud floor. Small pools of water had collected outside but thankfully they were draining away down the bank to the river. At least we were dry.

"I think we should stay put for today though," I suggested. "They probably have search teams on the ground as well as in the air. We have enough food for a day or so."

"Agreed. Sounds like it's time for lunch then!"

Lunch was a tin of chicken soup into which we added a tin of boiled potatoes. It wasn't too bad.

"This is good comfort food for a rainy day," Josh said. "We just need a couple of slices of toast swimming in butter and marmite and I'm in heaven."

"Ugh really?" I said, laughing. "Toast and butter, yes, but marmite, never! Can't stand the stuff. No, my version of comfort food for a rainy day is a bowl of steaming thick tomato soup with white bread and butter soldiers for dipping in. My mum used to make that for me when I had a cold. It was always so good."

Reminiscing about comfort food and talking about my mum made me feel a bit sad. Josh must have sensed my mood. He rubbed my shoulder and changed the subject.

"So tell me about your old school. What was it like?"

"Better," I replied, falling silent for a moment while I tried to justify my answer. "Well, I guess it's all about friends. I had some really good friends that I had to leave behind. I'd been at school with some of them since I was five years old. Starting all over again is a pain, especially when some of the girls here are so evil. They make me feel like an outcast."

"Well there are girls like that everywhere," Josh said. "I expect they feel threatened."

"Threatened? But I've done nothing!"

"You don't need to. They see you as a threat because you're good-looking."

I laughed out loud. Josh looked a little embarrassed.

"All the boys think so. Anyway," Josh continued, "I thought you were getting on OK with Emma?"

"Who? Emma, your girlfriend?" I asked. I didn't think she was, but I really wanted to know. Josh laughed.

"She's not my girlfriend," he said, chuckling, "although she does have a habit of ambushing me!"

I was glad. I did fancy him a bit and Emma wasn't in the picture.

"Well I thought I was getting on with her OK," I explained, "but she's been blanking me ever since she saw us talking. So yeah, maybe you're right. She wants you all to herself."

"Yikes, scary! You'll have to protect me when we get back to school."

"If we ever get back to school." I sighed heavily.

Actually, I did want to get back to school. I wanted things to be back to normal, even if my new life was a little different from before. Even if it meant trying harder to fit in. I'd be less aloof, less detached maybe. Smile a bit more. Yes, perhaps my anger at having to move had been showing through. I realised that since the move, I hadn't liked myself much either. No wonder no one wanted to make friends. I'd change all that if only I had a chance.

The afternoon passed by with us chatting about our families and memories of our childhood. Josh was really easy to get on with. The more we got to know one another, the more I was attracted to him. In other circumstances, I might have flirted to let him know. However, at times he treated me like a little sister, caring and protective. I didn't want to unbalance things or risk pushing him away. I was happy just to be with him and keep my feelings in check.

Josh seemed to be hungry all the time. Every hour or so he was looking for something else to eat. My brother was much the same. My mum used to say that he had empty legs. However, I was painfully aware that our limited supplies wouldn't last more than another day. Hopefully, the weather would be better tomorrow and we could venture out to search for more food.

"What are we going to have for our dinner tonight then?" Josh asked. "We could have some of those eggs that I collected and there is also a tin of spam from Dan's house."

"Spam?" I said, horrified. "Who eats spam these days? It's grim!"

"Well I wouldn't normally eat it, but I'm so hungry and it will go well with the eggs."

"Presumably it needs heating up? Won't it smell?"

"Let's try. If it smells we'll have to eat it cold."

I shuddered at the thought.

Josh grabbed the tin of spam from the shelf, opened it and emptied it into a pan. He cut it into slices and then cut the slices into cubes, ready to cook. Meanwhile, I put all four eggs into a pan of water and started to bring them to a boil. I let them boil for a good 10 minutes and then dunked them into cold water to cool. When the eggs were cool enough to handle, I put my hands in the water to remove the shells, as Josh had suggested. He was right, no smell! He was grinning at me.

"Good tip!" I said. "Although I'm not convinced they won't smell when we cut into them."

"I'll eat mine whole then," he replied, still grinning. I rolled my eyes.

I put the pan of spam onto the stove. As soon as it started to sizzle it gave off a really strong smell, like really greasy bacon.

"That is so grim," I said, removing the pan from the heat and tipping the contents onto a plate. I added a hard-boiled egg and passed the plate over to Josh. "Here you go. Slightly warm spam and egg."

I grabbed an egg for myself, leaving two for a picnic lunch tomorrow and sat down next to Josh.

A sudden noise at the entrance made us both look up. Standing in the gap between the root ball and the cave was a large dog, its lips curled back to reveal an impressive set of teeth. A low growl sent a stab of fear through me. I tried not to react. Josh also froze, wide-eyed. The dog was a German Shepherd with a big bushy mane of tangled hair. I could just see a collar, which gave me some confidence.

"Hey," I said gently, trying to keep my voice calm, "you look hungry. Did you smell the stinky spam?"

The dog stopped snarling and looked at me. It licked its lips, sniffed the air and started to growl again. I picked up a cube of spam from Josh's plate.

"Hey, you want some of this?"

I tossed it towards the dog, who caught it mid-air and swallowed it in one gulp. It looked at me expectantly. I tossed another piece, then another. The dog licked its lips again and then wagged its tail. I stood up slowly and walked over with another piece of spam in my hand.

"Sit," I commanded. To my amazement the dog sat, looking up at me. I held the piece of spam out and the dog took it gently.

"Who's a good dog then?" I picked up Josh's plate and tipped most of the spam onto the edge of the tarpaulin. The dog gobbled up everything in a matter of seconds.

I slowly sat back down next to Josh.

"Come here, come on," I said gently. The dog moved cautiously towards me. "Sit. Good dog!" I held out my hand and ruffled the fur behind its ear. Then, I carefully twisted the collar around until I found a name tag.

"Hello Chester, now I wonder who you belong to."

At the mention of his name, Chester met my gaze and then licked my hand. Josh laughed, which upset Chester all over again. He growled, baring his teeth at Josh.

"I think you'll have to give him something to eat too. He's trying to work out where he fits in the pack."

Josh looked down at what was left of his meal, picked up a small piece of spam and tossed it to Chester.

"Give him a bit more," I suggested. "Call him to you and hold the spam in the palm of your hand. Don't stare at him either. Just look casual."

Josh did as I said. Afterwards, he asked Chester to sit. When he obeyed, Josh praised him, looking pleased with himself.

"How come you know so much about dogs?"

"We used to have a dog when I was younger but I learnt about the food trick from my aunt. She got a rescue dog that took some time to settle. He used to snarl and growl at my cousin, who was only about eight. Anyway, she thought they were going to have to take the dog back but someone told her to get my cousin to feed him. After a couple of days, it worked. Dog psychology, apparently. Whoever gives you food is a step up from you in the pack."

Chester came back over to me and sat at my feet. I scratched behind his ears and he leant into me, one back foot tapping on the floor like he was doing the scratching himself.

"Looks like we've got another mouth to feed," Josh said.

"I think we've also got a guard dog. I bet he'll know if someone's creeping up on us."

"Good point."

We finished our meal, sharing small morsels with Chester. When it was clear that there was nothing left to eat, Chester lay down at my feet and closed his eyes.

"Poor boy," I said. "He must have thought he was abandoned. I wonder how many other pets are in the same situation?"

I was right about Chester being a good guard dog too. Later that evening I nipped down to the river for a pee and Chester came with me. Apart from straying to the river's edge to gulp some water, he didn't leave my side. When Josh left the camp for the same purpose, Chester stayed with me. When he returned, Chester growled softly but stopped the moment he knew it was Josh.

When we finally laid down to sleep that night, Josh was behind me at the back of the cave and Chester stretched out in front of me. He smelt a bit doggy but the extra warmth was very welcome.

Chapter 7: Hunted

The next day we needed to go in search of more supplies as there wasn't much left to eat. However, having Chester with us was a bit of a worry. He might sit on command, but we could hardly take him into people's houses. Josh thought that perhaps he should go alone, leaving me in the camp with Chester, but that hardly seemed fair. In the end, I suggested that we set Chester a test. I got up to leave the camp and when Chester jumped up to follow I told him to sit and stay. I went all the way to the river and back. To my amazement he was sitting in exactly the same spot, waiting patiently. I praised him and made a fuss of him, which he absolutely loved.

"What a star," I said. "I think we can take him with us."

Josh looked a little unsure, but I insisted.

"I think he'll be a help. He'll sense someone approaching before we do."

After a meagre breakfast, we set off, retracing the path we had made a couple of days ago from Dan's house. This time, however, we planned to check the neighbouring houses for supplies.

Chester was excited, which caused us both some concern. He presumably thought he was going on a dog walk. However, our careful movements through the woods soon altered his mood. He kept close to us, ears alert, nose searching for a scent. I breathed a sigh of relief, knowing that I could trust him not to give us away.

The journey back to Dan's house was uneventful. We took our time, kept a careful watch, and made slow but steady progress. Finally, we were crouching in the covered pathway, next to Dan's back garden.

"OK," Josh whispered. "If we climb into Dan's garden, we can then climb the fence into his neighbour's garden and work our way over until we find the right house for raiding."

As we stood up I told Chester to sit and stay. He obediently sat on his haunches. Getting into Dan's garden via the path was straightforward. Getting into the neighbour's garden was also straightforward because the fence was nice and low. We approached the back of the house cautiously, peering through the patio doors to see what lay beyond. The room appeared to be an open-plan kitchen with a dining area, similar to Dan's. Josh pushed sideways on one of the doors, attempting to slide it open. It wouldn't budge.

"We're not going to get in here easily," I whispered.

"I don't think it's as secure as it looks. I've heard of a few burglaries where they've got in through patio doors."

I watched nervously as Josh attempted to force the door. First, he yanked the handle up as he tried to slide the door open, then yanked it down. No joy. Next, he tried to pull the door outwards as if he could pop it off its runners. I didn't want to say anything but I could see this was going nowhere and he was making unnecessary noise with the effort. Finally, he gave up, breathing hard and pushing back his mop of unruly curls.

"Yeah, come on, let's try another house." Josh turned, leading the way. The fence to the neighbouring property was too high to climb. "Let's climb over the back fence and see if we can get into another one further along."

A warning bell sounded in my head because a field lay behind the houses and I didn't recall seeing any cover.

"Are you sure it's safe?" I said.

"What choice do we have? Come on," Josh replied, sounding frustrated.

We peered over the fence, looking left and right to make sure the coast was clear. Josh went first, then held out his hand, helping me over. Suddenly, a shout came from our left.

"Stop! Stop where you are! You, Joshua Haddon, stop!"

I spun around. I saw two soldiers in white suits emerging from the back of Dan's house, each with a dog on a leash. The dogs were Dobermann, the sort used by the military as tracking and attack dogs.

"Run!" Josh shouted. "Follow me!"

Josh took off across the field towards the old railway track. I followed, hot on his heels. I heard the dogs barking behind us. If they let them off the lead we would be caught for sure. I ran as fast as my legs could carry me, which was not as fast as Josh, but I wasn't too far behind. We reached the fence that bordered the railway track. Josh vaulted neatly over and then stopped to help me. He looked over my shoulder, fear in his eyes.

"Chester's helping," he said, panting. "Quick. Let's get to the river where the dogs can't track us."

I looked back. The soldiers were advancing across the field and had let their dogs off the lead. They were charging towards us. However, Chester was racing to intercept them and just at that moment, I saw them pause, distracted by his appearance. I swung one leg over the fence and Josh held my weight as I lifted the other one over. I thought I was clear but my raincoat had caught on the barbed wire. Panicking, I pulled at the coat to get it free but it wouldn't budge. Instead, I quickly slipped my arms out of the sleeves, leaving both the coat and my empty rucksack attached to the fence. An almighty uproar commenced from behind. Dogs barking savagely, men shouting orders. We scrambled up the embankment to the railway track, across and then down the other side into another field. As I started to run, my foot caught on a root and I fell sprawling to the ground. Josh stopped to help me up and pushed me on, looking back over his shoulder.

"Hurry," he said. "We need to get to the river before they cross the track."

"But what about Chester?"

"He's OK," said Josh, breathing hard. "I saw him get away. He did enough to save us."

With moments to spare, we made it to the river, slipped down the grassy bank and plunged in. I gasped at the freezing temperature, stiffening with the shock but adrenalin spurred me on. The river was waist-deep. With the bank above us, we couldn't see across the field, which meant that the patrol couldn't see us either. The binoculars were still around my neck, so I pushed them through the collar of my sweatshirt, hoping to save them. We started to swim downstream. I moved as fast as possible with a combination of breaststroke and pushing off the rocky riverbed with my feet. We started to make good progress and soon rounded a bend in the river that took us out of sight from our entry point. It was hard going. The depth of the river varied a lot. It was almost impossible not to come into contact with the bottom as I battled to keep up with Josh. I bruised both knees and my shins repeatedly and scraped my knuckles too. We kept going, entering a section under the cover of a few trees. It was shallower here and rather than swim we floated head first, using our hands to propel ourselves along the river bed. I grabbed whatever I could below the water, stubbing and bruising my fingers as I went.

"There's a bridge not far from here," Josh said, gasping for breath. "We can hide under there until it's safe."

The river became deeper once more and we swam as best we could. It was really hard going. The water dragged at my clothing and my arms and legs ached from the effort. My lungs felt like they were going to burst. Every now and then I accidentally gulped some water, coughing and spluttering. I wasn't sure I had the strength to go on.

"There, ahead!" Josh said, pointing. "The bridge."

I looked up, gritted my teeth and forced my arms and legs to move. With a final burst of energy, we reached the bridge. It was a low bridge constructed from brick that carried a narrow road over the river. I could see only a small gap between the water's surface and the underside of the bridge. It didn't look big enough to hide under without drowning. I hesitated for a moment but Josh grabbed my arm and pushed me in ahead of him.

"It's OK," he said, "we'll be safe here. It's too dark for them to see underneath and the dogs won't be able to detect us."

We scrambled through until we were more or less under the centre of the bridge. We sat in the river, side by side, with only our heads above water. I dug my heels into the rocky river bed to stop the current from pushing me but everything was slippery with moss. I shifted position a couple of times until I was secure. After a few minutes, my breathing returned to normal but as it did, I started to cool down. The water was icy and pulsed constantly against my clothing. It wasn't just dark and freezing under the bridge. I could feel the tendrils of something brushing against my face. I told myself they were just plant roots and didn't dare dwell on the alternatives.

"How long do you think we have to stay here?" I asked. "I'm going to freeze to death in no time." My voice was already starting to wobble as the shivering set in.

"I don't know," he replied, "hopefully not too long. Then we'll get out, find some warm clothes and some food." I wanted to believe him, I really did.

The minutes dragged by. I could hear nothing above the gentle lap of water against the sides of the bridge. Looking back up the river, I couldn't see anything beyond a short stretch of water and the opposite bank. My teeth started to chatter uncontrollably. I folded my arms, placing a frozen hand under each armpit.

"Not much longer," Josh suggested. "Too risky to get out just now."

I was now shaking all over. My head ached and I felt faint. Josh manoeuvred position, forcing one leg behind my back and shuffling across so that I sat between his legs. He put his arms around me and pulled me close. I felt a momentary reprieve from the cold water that pulsed against me.

"Thanks!" was all I could muster.

More minutes passed, huddled in the dark and frozen space beneath the bridge. Eventually, a strange sensation started to wash over me. I started to feel comfortable, acclimatised to the cold, drowsy even. My head stopped hurting, my teeth stopped chattering, and my muscles relaxed. I remember Josh squeezing my arms and asking me questions, but I was too sleepy to answer.

The next thing I remember was waking up to bright light. I opened my eyes, winced and squinted, then tried to focus. I was in a greenhouse, covered in some soft white material. It was warm, lovely and warm. Josh lay next to me, cuddled up under the cover. He was staring at me, looking concerned.

"You OK?" he asked. "I was really worried about you for a while there."

"Where are we?"

"We're in the garden just above the bridge. I had to drag you up here. You were totally out of it. All you wanted to do was go to sleep. I reckon you were starting to suffer from hypothermia. I got our wet clothes off and found this fleece in the corner. It's the stuff gardeners use to protect plants from the frost."

I peeked under the fleece to find that I was in my underwear. I nearly died of embarrassment as I pictured Josh getting me out of my joggers and hoodie.

"Sorry," he said, "thought it was for the best. If it makes you feel any better I'm not wearing my best pants either."

I laughed but cringed inwardly. Part of me wanted the earth to open up and swallow me whole. I took a good look around. The greenhouse itself was pretty bare. There were a few stacks of plastic plant pots of different sizes and a couple of watering cans. I looked through the glass. The greenhouse was in an enclosed, sloping garden with a high panelled fence running down one side. A large farmhouse stood at the top, surrounded by plant borders and a gravel driveway. Below the greenhouse were a couple of vegetable plots, mostly empty. At the foot of the garden were several tall willow trees, their branches reaching down to the ground like a fine curtain. I could just see the bridge that we had taken refuge under earlier. The garden was well-screened but I was glad to be hidden beneath the fleece.

"The good news," Josh said, "is that I've spotted a washing line full of clothes on the far side of the house and I'm going to pick up some dry stuff. I'm also going to see if I can get into the house and find some food. We both need something after that swim."

"What about the search party?" I asked, remembering our narrow escape from the patrol.

"All quiet," he replied. "I guess they gave up when the trail went cold, at least for now. I can't believe that they knew my name though. That's really worrying! They know I didn't get picked up with my mum and brother. They must have been looking for me. Maybe those dogs picked up my scent, which led them to Dan's house."

"What about poor Chester?"

"No sign of him, but he's a clever dog, Maddie. He'll be OK I'm sure. In fact, I wouldn't be surprised if he catches up with us! Anyway, we can't hang around. It's too risky. You wait here. I'll go to the house."

I pulled the fleece back over my head, grateful not to be venturing out into the cool Spring air just yet. I still felt tired and my arms and legs ached from the swim in the river. It occurred to me that if they knew Josh was unaccounted for, they probably knew that I was too. How long would it be before the search party arrived at my house? I had made so many trips between the house and the camp that the dogs wouldn't fail to find it. I realised with despair that we couldn't go back there, not even to collect anything.

After a while, Josh returned with an armful of stuff.

"Got some dry clothes for us. They're going to be a bit big but they'll do until we can get our clothes dry. Here," he said, passing over a small bundle. Josh had found me a pair of navy joggers that were several sizes too big, a grey T-shirt, and a dark blue woollen cardigan. I pulled them on. They were warm and dry, for which I was grateful, but I felt like a bag lady. I rolled the waist of the joggers over several times until my feet popped out of the elasticated bottoms. Josh had put on his dry clothes too. He wore equally outsized trousers, a checked farmer's shirt and a fleece gilet. We looked at each other and smiled.

"I don't think we're going to win any catwalk prizes today, farmer Giles!" I said, chuckling.

"I also found a couple of oilskin jackets. His and hers."

Josh held one out in each hand. They must have been gardening coats or something. They were dark brown and looked really grubby. They would be warm, however, and since I'd lost my mum's coat, I was grateful.

"Got another surprise for you," Josh said, smiling. "I didn't try to break into the house because there was a burglar alarm, but I did get into their garage. They had a chest freezer in there that was still cool inside. There was mostly meat, which wasn't worth risking, but I found a loaf of bread and some ice cream. One tub each. Do you want Baked Alaska or Chocolate Fudge Brownie?"

I suddenly realised how ravenous I was.

"Either. Anything. Wow!"

Josh passed me Baked Alaska, then ripped the lid from his Chocolate Fudge Brownie. The contents were liquid, much like a thick shake. He brought the tub to his lips and tipped it up, swallowing in great mouthfuls. I followed suit. The Baked Alaska was so sweet it made my eyes bulge. However, it went down very well. I drank half before pausing for breath. Josh had already finished his. I looked at him and laughed.

"Chocolate fudge moustache," I explained. He licked his lips.

"1200 calories," he said, looking at the side of the tub. "That should keep us going for a while. Come on, drink up, we should be off."

Josh had also found some plastic sheeting, a tatty tarpaulin, and a drawstring holdall in the garage. He wrapped up our wet clothes and stuffed everything into the holdall. He passed over my trainers to put on. They were still soaking wet but at least they were warm after sitting in the sunshine. I pulled them on and we set off.

Chapter 8: The shooter

The greenhouse that we sheltered in was on the other side of the river from my camp and Josh thought we ought to stick to that side until we had put more distance between us and the tracker dogs. We crossed the lane that ran over the bridge and entered some woods on the other side, then started to pick our way back towards the camp. We talked about the search party and Josh agreed that going back to the camp was too risky.

"Let's stay on this side of the river," he suggested. "There are some woods ahead that will take us past your place. If we give the river bank a wide berth, any patrols that find the camp and search the area won't pick up our trail."

"But where will we go?"

"I'm not sure yet, but we ought to get as far away from here as possible. I'll think of something."

"All that effort to build the camp and make it comfortable!" I said, shaking my head. "Now we have nowhere to sleep, hardly any food or drink, nothing except what we're carrying."

"We'll have to break in somewhere and help ourselves to what we need," Josh said reassuringly. "I know. There's a row of cottages not far from here. They are small places that probably don't have fancy burglar alarms. I'm sure we can pick up some supplies."

We moved slowly and carefully through the woods, using the binoculars to scan the surrounding area. Amazingly, they still worked, although there were a few bubbles of water that distorted the view. All was quiet. After a while, we entered an area where the river split into two smaller streams. Each stream meandered into the woods, following its own path.

"That left-hand stream is the one that goes past our camp," Josh explained. "So we should stay next to this one to give the place a wide berth. The streams join back up further down, so if we wade across this stream in a bit, we can walk across the island. I'm afraid we are going to get our feet wet again!"

We walked a short way along the bank of the right-hand stream and then waded across to reach the island. The area was quite swampy with patches of tall reeds, interspersed with shrubs. Quite a few trees also lay on their sides or were partly fallen but propped up against other trees. Remarkably, most were still alive, even though some of their roots were exposed above the ground. The area was certainly pretty, but very difficult to navigate. One minute we were climbing over tree trunks, the next we were knee-deep in cold slimy water. We disturbed quite a few ducks and other water birds, who must have started to build nests. Every time one burst out of the undergrowth, my heart skipped a beat. I'd recover from the shock but be left wondering if the commotion was drawing any unwanted attention. I was relieved when we came to the end of the island and were able to cross over the stream to firmer ground.

Knowing that we had passed the camp and wouldn't be going back left me feeling disheartened. I felt relatively safe there and since it was only a short distance from my house, I always felt that I'd be returning home soon. Now we were going to be travelling away from my home, to places I'd never been. If my parents suddenly returned, how would they find me? What if I never saw them again?

Josh seemed to sense my mood. He put an arm around my shoulder and squeezed, affectionately.

"Come on," he said, "let's find ourselves something tasty for dinner."

We continued our journey through the woods alongside the river.

"Just up here," Josh explained, "the river goes under the main road and out the other side. I think we are going to have to cross the road, but there's a sharp bend there, so it's not too exposed."

Through the trees, I could just make out what must be my neighbour's house. I stopped to take in the scenery. A small wooden footbridge crossed the river, connecting a footpath. Large willow trees stood on the banks, trailing their branches into the water. I could also see where the other stream rushed back through a narrow channel to join the main river. I hadn't realised it was so pretty and it was right on my doorstep. I wondered how long it would have taken me to discover it.

Josh tugged my arm.

"Come on," he said, "we ought to put some distance between us and this place."

We reached the road. As Josh had expected, we were on a bend and could see the tarmac stretch only a short distance in each direction. I pushed my head out to get a good look and gasped when I spotted the tangled wrecks of two cars. One white, one silver, both totally destroyed.

"Wow, looks like a head-on collision," I said. He peered out too.

"I can't see if there's anyone in them," he said, "but I doubt there'd be anything we could do for them now. This must have happened when the shock wave came."

"I can remember hearing what sounded like a car crash and a horn," I said. "I guess this is close enough to my house to have been where it happened. I wonder how many accidents there were? I wonder how many people got injured or died because there was no one to help them?"

"Yeah, there are probably some people we know. It doesn't bear thinking about. Come on, let's move on."

Josh counted to three and we made a dash for the bushes opposite. I tried to slow my breathing. Why was something as simple as crossing a road such a trauma? I set off after Josh who was already weaving through the shrubs to rejoin the river's edge.

We slowly made our way along the river bank, sprinting across short open gaps and taking cover beneath the trees. I was grateful for the trees, realising that they always do well where there's water.

In due course, we came across a weir where fast-flowing water spilt over a ridge before disappearing under a bridge. The water was dark and looked very deep and very cold. I shivered. As with the bridge that hid us, there was almost no headroom above the water line and neither of us fancied another dip. We were going to have to cross the road that ran over the bridge. A small gap between the wall of the bridge and the hedgerow gave us easy access to the road. However, on the other side of the road, the bushes were thick and thorny. There was no gap to get back down to the river bank.

"We'll have to climb over the bridge wall," Josh said. "You wait here and I'll see how easy it is."

The bridge wall was quite high and made of brick, which was partly covered in dark green moss.

Josh poked his head through the gap by the bridge and took a good look up and down the road, then ran across. He jumped up and swung one leg over the wall. Then he swivelled around, pulled his other leg over, and lowered himself onto his stomach. He looked over at me, grinned, nodded, and dropped out of sight.

Now it was my turn. The road was clear, so I ran across and jumped, trying to copy Josh. However, he was a good bit taller than me and I couldn't swing my leg over the top. I tried again, this time attempting to get a foothold on the face of the wall. However, my wet trainers slipped over the mossy surface and I landed back on the tarmac. My legs were still aching from our swim in the river and I wasn't sure I had the energy to try again. Panic started to set in as I stood there, motionless. I was in full view of anyone who appeared on the road or passed overhead. I crouched down, feeling helpless and unsure what to do. Should I go back and find another way? Suddenly Josh's head reappeared. He jumped up and straddled the wall, holding out his hand. I grabbed it and jumped again. Josh tugged really hard and I managed to get my foot over the top. He tugged again and I was up, straddling the wall too.

"Come on," he said, "let's go."

Josh slid over and I followed. He helped me down, supporting my weight until both feet were firmly on the ground. I was shaking, as much from fear as effort.

"Can we stop for a little bit?" I asked.

"Sure. Let's get to those trees over there," he said, pointing to some decent cover.

We reached the trees and sat down, resting our backs on the trunk of a large oak. I felt like I was letting the side down a bit.

"I'm sorry," I said, "I guess I'm still feeling a bit tired after the river. I got so cold and my arms and legs don't seem to want to work properly."

"You're doing fine," he reassured me. "That was my fault back there. I should have thought things through a bit more. You're shorter than me. If we had gone together I could have helped you over the wall first. I promise I won't leave you behind like that again." He reached for my hand and held it. "We'll be alright, you'll see."

After a break we set off again, sticking to the tree line beside the river. I guessed that it was mid-afternoon. The sun was dropping in the sky and the shadows were getting longer. Josh stopped and pointed.

"Do you see that row of houses across the river? Those are the ones I was talking about."

Six, maybe seven terraced houses stood alone in a short row at the back of a field. Each seemed to have a small back garden. However, separating us and them was a long and wide field that didn't seem to have much cover.

"How do we get to them without being seen?" I asked.

"I don't remember them being so isolated," he replied looking disappointed. "I've mostly come across them from the road at the front, which runs close to the old railway track. Hmm." Josh fell silent for a moment, thinking.

"If we follow this path by the river we eventually get back to the railway track and could double back from there," he suggested, "but it's quite a long way."

"Or maybe we can just take a chance across the field?" I said. "If we stick to the edge of that hedgerow to cross the field, we are screened from one direction. How long would it take? A one-minute dash? I'm just so tired and it's getting late. We've still got to find somewhere to camp as well."

"Are you sure, Maddie? I know you're tired."

"Yes, let's do it." I wasn't sure how much more I could take today. Finding food and somewhere dry and safe was all I wanted.

Another five minutes and we were standing directly across from the houses. Although a small bridge stood nearby, we decided to trek through the river in our damp trainers. With dogs potentially tracking us, it was good to break up the scent trail. First, I scanned the horizon with the binoculars, looking for any signs of movement. We dropped into the river, which was knee-deep, and waded diagonally to the opposite bank. From here we scurried to the hedgerow and crouched beneath a hawthorn tree. I scanned once more with the binoculars.

"Looks quiet," I said.

"OK," Josh said with some confidence. "Let's head for the back garden of the first house on the left. We'll stop at the fence to make sure it's safe, then hop over. If anything goes wrong, we retrace our steps and get back on this path to the railway track. Ready?"

I took a deep breath and nodded. We ran as fast as we could from the hawthorn tree to the first back garden, keeping as close to the hedgerow as possible. The distance was probably only one hundred and fifty metres but it was sloping gradually uphill. My heart felt as if it might burst through my chest and my lungs were gasping for air. Suddenly I ran straight into Josh's back, sliding past him to one side and falling heavily into the grass. He had stopped dead, several metres from the fence, and I hadn't seen him. I looked up, feeling annoyed. Josh had his hands raised above his head and a look of terror on his face. I slowly got to my feet. Someone was shouting.

"Off my property! Go on, get out!"

On the other side of the garden fence stood an old man with an untidy white beard and unruly hair. He wore a filthy green oilskin jacket over a threadbare checked shirt. He was holding a shotgun, which was pointed directly at us.

"I've been watching you two, sneaking around over there, planning to come here and steal my stuff. I ain't got anything, OK? Now get out of here before I shoot!"

As he spoke his eyes were darting everywhere. One second he was looking at me, then at Josh, then over his shoulder, then up to the sky. Unstable, was the word that came to mind, crazy even.

"Sir, please, we're sorry. We meant no harm," Josh said pleadingly. "We've nowhere to go and we just wanted to find some food and somewhere to hide."

"Well, there's nothing here and nothing in my neighbour's houses either, so don't go thinking you'll try their houses too. You people think you can just raid and steal whatever you like. Well, you ain't taking nothing from here."

The gun was still pointed directly at us. I was stunned, speechless, and terrified. I took one step backwards. Josh took one step to the side. Without warning the old man raised his gun and fired over our heads. I was rooted to the spot, a queasy feeling deep in my gut. Josh grabbed my arm and held one hand up to the old man.

"OK, OK!" Josh shouted. "We're leaving. We won't trouble you."

We started to walk slowly backwards, retracing our steps along the hedgerow.

"Faster, go on, get!" the old man screamed.

"That shot is going to attract some unwanted attention," Josh whispered under his breath. "Run!"

My legs felt like lead but the adrenalin got them moving. As soon as we got back to the river, Josh started to wade across.

"Which way are we going?" I asked.

"That way," Josh replied, pointing further down the river. "We'll keep going down that path and pick up the old railway track."

"Then let's stay in the water and not get on the path," I suggested. "If a patrol turns up and they pick up our trail here, they might end up going in the opposite direction."

"Good plan. It's shallow here too, so much easier than before."

We set off, wading as fast as we could. The rocky bed of the river was green and greasy, threatening to tip me off balance or twist an ankle. However, we were well-screened. Trees lined the river bank on each side and formed a canopy over our heads. I doubted anyone could see us.

Josh stopped to let me catch up. When I was almost level with him, something caught his attention. He held a hand up to indicate that I should stop. In the relative silence, I could hear an engine, maybe two engines. That would be the patrol that we were worried about. We both stood completely still, listening intently. When the engine stopped I heard some raised voices but couldn't make out what was being said. I could distinguish the voice of the old man because he was screaming in much the same way as he had screamed at us earlier.

Suddenly there was a single shot followed by return fire. The first shot was a bang, just like the one he fired over our heads. The return fire was more like a series of whiplashes, which must have been from a different type of weapon. Silence followed.

"I think they killed the old man," I whispered, taking in a deep breath. Josh nodded and dropped his head.

We continued wading in silence. I couldn't believe it. How many soldiers had there been in that patrol? At least two, maybe more. Sure the old man was a little crazy, but he was surely no real threat to them. And yet they had opened fire. I felt even more certain that these were not genuine soldiers. It just didn't make sense. We had to get away.

The river ran more or less in a straight line and apart from one short stretch it was screened from both sides by trees. Where we had no cover, we managed to climb up into the woods behind the river and loop around to stay out of sight. Eventually, we came to a section of the river where a large pool had formed before the water flowed under the arch of a tall brick bridge.

"That's the railway track up there," Josh said, "but since we're already wet, we might as well go straight under."

"Where are we going to go now?"

"Well, I guess we need to find somewhere to camp. It'll be dark soon."

We walked under the bridge, one hand on the wall to steady ourselves on the slippery rocks.

"I know," Josh said, "there's a tiny bridge not far from here that the railway track crosses. It will be dry under there at least. If we follow the embankment we should see it up on our right. It's not far."

The day was never-ending. We had started in such high spirits but lurched from one near disaster to another. I was exhausted. My feet were sore from walking in wet trainers. My legs felt battered and bruised. My arms ached from the swim in the river. I was also starving. Since breakfast time, all we had eaten was ice cream.

We made our way along the railway embankment, hiding and moving from bush to bush. Before long we came to the bridge that Josh had mentioned. It was a low bridge that ran under the old railway track, presumably just an animal crossing. Strands of ivy hung from the bridge like a torn curtain. Josh pulled a section aside and we went in. The floor was gritty but dry. Josh emptied the rucksack and spread the tarpaulin on the ground. We sat down, leaning against the wall. Between us, we ate most of the bread that he had found in the freezer. It was a bit mushy, but I was so hungry, I didn't care. Luckily we had some water left to wash it down. We'd have to find some more tomorrow.

I got our wet clothes out and hung them from some rusty hooks that protruded from the brickwork. They were unlikely to dry, I realised, but better to hang them up than leave them to fester in the plastic wrap. We curled up side by side on half of the tarpaulin and Josh pulled the other half over us. It had started to drizzle and I could hear large raindrops falling outside where the water had collected in the tree canopy. I tried to stay positive. At least a cloudy night would be warmer than a starry night. At least this smelly oilskin I was wearing would keep me vaguely warm. Maybe we'd survive. I wished that Chester was still with us. Some contrast with last night!

PART TWO

Chapter 9: The forest

When I woke up it was barely light. A grey mist hung in the air, blurring the outline of the trees and bushes that were just beyond the entrance. The world was monochrome, like a black and white photo, devoid of colour, and silent. I hadn't slept at all well and I was in a miserable mood.

Life seemed to have turned into a game of snakes and ladders. After the shock wave, I worked so hard to build a comfortable camp. I spent hours digging, clearing soil, dragging cardboard boxes through the woods, and accumulating supplies. I made a comfortable bed where I slept soundly in a nice warm sleeping bag, free from icy draughts. I had food, access to water, and plenty of clothing. Now I had nothing. All that effort, then everything gone, just like that! I'd just spent a miserable night under a bridge on the hard and uncomfortable ground, wrapped only in a tarpaulin and wearing someone else's clothes. I was so, so cold. Josh however was sleeping soundly and looking quite content, which really bugged me. I shuffled about, deliberately disturbing his sleep until he woke up. As he opened his eyes and looked at me, he smiled. Now I felt guilty as well as grumpy.

"Sorry," I lied, "I didn't mean to wake you."

"No worries," Josh mumbled, yawning and stretching his arms above his head. "Hey you look cold, come here."

Josh wrapped his arms around me and pulled me closer, burying his nose into my neck. My mood started to lift. I reminded myself that I hadn't lost everything. I still had Josh. I realised that if I had a choice of being back in my camp alone or here with Josh, I'd choose here with Josh. He was kind, he was funny, and he knew this area so well. I'd have lasted no time at all on my own. I realised that actually, there was no one else in the world that I'd rather be with. *Wow!* My heart was racing. But how did he feel about me? I wasn't sure. At times I thought he liked me, fancied me even, but then sometimes he treated me like a little sister. I wanted to roll further in towards him, wrap my arms around him and tell him how I felt. But if I got it wrong I'd make such a fool of myself and ruin everything. I closed my eyes and lay still, relishing the contact, not wanting it to end. When I opened them sometime later, dawn had finally broken and the monochrome world was full of colour.

Today we were heading for the forest, wherever that was. Josh thought that going any further west on the track was risky because we would enter a more built-up area. More houses, less cover, and potentially more patrols. The forest, he explained, was vast. People got lost there all the time. Parts were so heavily wooded that they were impossible to navigate. However, all around the edges were small villages where we ought to stand a good chance of finding food, water, and the sort of survival gear we had left behind in the camp.

We were both thirsty and hungry. There was no water left but we had saved a couple of slices of bread for breakfast. They were stodgy and difficult to swallow without a drink, but we needed something.

Josh packed everything away in the rucksack and we left the shelter under the bridge, slipping back down the railway embankment to the river. My feet felt almost dry for the first time in ages, so I was determined not to wade through the water again. We found a section of the river with a few large boulders protruding from the water and managed to get across without getting wet. Josh was a bit paranoid about leaving a trail, so he splashed water over the boulders in an attempt to wash away any scent.

We walked through the woods, away from the old railway track and the river. It was difficult terrain, with brambles and holly, but we were used to this sort of challenge now. Although the woods stretched all the way to the road, Josh's attention was drawn to a couple of paddocks and a stable.

"We need to find some water," he said. "This might be the last chance before we enter the forest."

I pulled out my binoculars and from the edge of the woods, I scanned the area next to the buildings. Sure enough, there was a standpipe, right next to a trough by the stable. I passed the binoculars over to Josh.

"To the left of the stable block, by that metal trough."

Josh slid the backpack from his shoulder and pulled out the empty drinks container.

"You wait here and keep watch. I'll creep along that hedgerow and go around the back of the stables."

It was a risk, but we needed water. I hadn't had anything to drink since last night, and even then, it was a tiny amount. Josh set off along the hedgerow, running short distances and then crouching to look around. My heart was in my mouth. At the end of the paddock, he slipped behind the stables, emerging on the other side to approach the standpipe. I trained the binoculars on him. Hiding as best as he could behind the trough, I saw him turn the tap and hold the bottle in the stream of water. He must have drunk some immediately because he held the bottle in the stream of water for a second time before going back behind the stables. I expected him to emerge on the other side almost straight away, but he didn't. I scanned the area through the binoculars, looking for any sign of movement. Perhaps he had seen something and needed to hide. I felt butterflies in my stomach. I willed him to come out, come back. I couldn't bear it if we were separated now. After what seemed like the longest few minutes Josh emerged, carrying something under his arm. I sighed with relief, realising that he had taken the opportunity to see what he might find in the stable. When he finally got back to me I threw my arms around him.

"I was so scared, I thought something had happened to you!"

He hugged me back.

"It's OK, I found a tack room. I grabbed a few things that we might need. Look."

Josh unfurled two slightly hairy blankets, some leather reins, and a few tools.

I had a good glug of water as Josh repacked the rucksack. He rolled the blankets and used the reins to tie them closed. He gave these to me to carry over my shoulder and we set off once more for the forest.

To get to the forest we had to cross a main road. In fact, it was the same one we had crossed the day before, near my house, but we were now further west. We had a clear view up and down the road in both directions. We were also able to run from a wooded section on one side of the road to another wooded section on the other side. So far so good.

Almost at once the woodland changed from deciduous trees such as oak and ash to evergreen conifer trees such as spruce, fir, and pine. The trees were tall and packed closely together, their branches sweeping downwards to the forest floor. The ground underfoot was a rusty light brown colour, soft, and spongy from fallen pine needles. The holly bushes and brambles were gone, replaced here and there by the odd fern or clump of bracken. I could smell pine in the air too. It wasn't unpleasant, but it did remind me a little of my Grandma's bathroom.

In the forest, the ground was a lot quieter and easier to walk on compared with the woods. However, we had to weave our way carefully between the trees because the needles on the lower branches were sharp. If we pushed the branches aside, they sprang back, stabbing us viciously. We made slow progress. The further we went, the quieter and darker it got as the canopy closed overhead to blot out the sunlight.

After twenty minutes or so we came across a path. Being so far in amongst the trees and screened on all sides, we didn't hesitate to use it, which made progress much easier. Soon after, we passed a trail marker, indicating that we were on one of the many pathways that hikers used in the forest. The path itself was quite narrow, so I walked slightly ahead of Josh.

"Have you got somewhere in mind to camp?" I asked, turning my head as I spoke to Josh over my shoulder.

When I looked back, I saw a tall, heavy-set man with a bald head standing a few metres in front of us, hands on his hips. Panicking, I turned around, as did Josh. Behind us another man stepped out onto the path. He was a muscular black guy with a top knot. I glanced left to see a third man approaching us from the side. Glancing right, an Asian-looking man blocked any escape.

"Hello strangers," the bald man said dryly. "Where are you going?"

None of the men smiled. Their manner wasn't immediately threatening, but they were deeply suspicious of us. I was suspicious of them too. I wondered why they had stopped us and not just let us go by without revealing themselves. They must want something. Maybe they were hoping we carried some food or something else of value. Josh clearly thought the same.

"We're just passing through," Josh said. "We don't have anything. No food, no drink, nothing of any value. We had to leave it all behind yesterday."

"On the run then," the man on the right said. "Hope you haven't been followed. We won't be too happy if you've got someone trailing you."

"We've been really careful not to leave a trail," I replied.

"I do hope so," the first man said. "You better come with us."

I hesitated, looking at Josh. He seemed unsure too.

"Thanks, but I think we're OK," Josh said. "We don't want to be any trouble."

"Well we won't take no for an answer, but if you need some persuading, we have food and shelter."

I looked at Josh trying to gauge his reaction. He looked at me too. After a moment he nodded and took my hand. The man ahead of us turned and started to walk along the path. We followed, the other men falling in behind us.

"Whereabouts are you camped?" Josh asked, trying to ease the tension.

"You'll know when we get there," came the response. We walked in silence. Every time I glanced at Josh he half-smiled back, trying to reassure me. However, I could tell he was uncertain too. On the one hand, we might have found a group of people who might help us. On the other hand, we might be robbed and abandoned deep in the forest. After twenty minutes or so I was beginning to feel more confident, but suddenly the man in the lead stopped and turned around.

"We leave the path here," he said, "but the route is secret."

One of the men behind us tapped me on the shoulder. I turned, just as he pulled something over my head. I was plunged into darkness and started to panic. I heard Josh call out.

"Hey, is this really necessary?"

"Of course," came the reply, "but don't be afraid. We'll guide you."

One of the men took my arm and guided me off the path. The hood over my head was loose but I couldn't see through it. Looking down, I could catch glimpses of my feet and the ground immediately around them. Trying to anticipate each step was difficult but necessary to maintain balance. Occasionally, my captor, as I currently thought of him, gave me a queue.

"Step up here," or, "hole on your left." Otherwise, he pulled or pushed me, steering me through the conifers. The hood was becoming stuffy and my breathing ragged. I stopped.

"Can you just give me a moment," I pleaded as Josh piled into me from behind.

"Sorry!" he said. I could hear the tension in his voice. He was finding this as unpleasant and annoying as me.

"OK, this part gets more tricky," the lead guy said. "Just listen to the instructions and you'll be fine."

The route we took started to zigzag wildly.

"Sharp left, now right, duck right down." My captor was now behind me pushing and pulling me as we went, forcing my head down from time to time. I had tried to keep a sense of bearing but I had to admit, I had no idea which way we had come from or which way we were headed. My breathing became more ragged still. I called out.

"Stop! Just give me a moment, please."

I bent over, putting my hands on my knees, allowing the hood to swing forward and pass fresh air in. I could hear Josh panting too. Did these people have any idea how difficult this was? I was now more angry than afraid.

We continued. I gave up trying to anticipate the terrain myself, relying purely on my captor's instructions. After a while, I fell into a routine. By listening and remaining calm, I was able to control my breathing. However, our fate troubled me. I wished we had never come across these men.

Eventually, we seemed to emerge into a less restrictive area. My captor loosened his grip but still guided me forward. I sensed that I had entered a room of some kind. The general noise of the forest was muted and the sound of my footfall dulled.

"Sit here," my captor said, pushing down on my shoulders. I put my hands down and felt a rough seat, like a log. Yes, I was sitting on a section of a tree trunk, like a stool. The hood was pulled off of my head. I blinked rapidly and looked around, my eyes adjusting to the light. I was in a tent, green light penetrating the ceiling. Several logs were dotted around for seating, some topped with cushions or animal fur. My captor was the man who had stood to our left on the path. He was tall and willowy with short dark hair. He stood with his arms crossed, looking me up and down, making me feel quite uncomfortable.

Chapter 10: The community

Josh wasn't in the tent.

"Where's Josh?" I asked.

"Next door, don't worry," came the reply. I was about to object when a woman entered carrying a cup. She was probably ten years younger than my mum with long brown hair, tied in a braid. She was slim and attractive, with olive-brown skin. She walked over and handed the cup to me, smiling and nodding in greeting. The cup contained water, which I drank down in one go. I nodded thanks and handed the cup back. Mentally I calculated that there were at least five people in this camp. I wondered how many more.

The bald man who had first appeared before us on the path entered the room. He sat on a log opposite me, looking serious. My captor stood behind him, still with his arms crossed.

"I have some questions for you," the bald man said, without smiling. He proceeded to ask me a whole barrage of questions. No sooner had I answered one than he was asking another. There was no friendliness in his manner.

"What's your name?

"How old are you?

"Where do you live?

"Which school do you go to?

"What year are you in?

"What's the name of the road your school is on?"

To this question, I had no idea.

"I don't know," I replied, "I've only been going there for three weeks."

"Where did you live before?

"Why did you move to the area?

"Where's your nearest post office?"

Again, I had no idea.

"I've not needed to use one," I said.

"So tell me where you have been?"

I racked my brains. What was this all about?

"Nowhere really," I said, which was the truth. "I started school here three weeks ago. We've spent every weekend unpacking and organising the new house. My parents have been so busy that they've not taken me anywhere."

"You must have been somewhere? Village shop? Fish and chip takeaway? Pub lunch?"

I shook my head, feeling more and more frustrated. I was telling the truth, even if it didn't sound like it.

"I'm new around here," I pleaded. "Ask Josh. He goes to the same school as me."

"OK, so tell me your story. How did you end up here in the forest?"

I took a deep breath and started to recount the events since the shock wave struck. When I told him about what I had witnessed during the evacuation, he interrupted me to ask questions. I went on to tell him about making a camp, exploring, and meeting up with Josh. When I got to the part where we had to escape from the patrol he listened intently. I also told him about our efforts to cover our tracks, which seemed to satisfy him.

When I had finished the man got up and left the room. *Ridiculous!* We should have insisted on going our own way. I felt like some kind of criminal.

My captor remained standing, arms crossed, saying nothing. I put my head in my hands, waves of despair coming over me. I struggled not to cry.

About half an hour later, the bald man came back into the tent followed by Josh, who he told to sit down beside me. Josh looked harassed but pleased to see me. He nodded encouragement, but I felt distinctly uncomfortable. My captor left and a blond-haired man arrived, sitting down on the stool opposite us. I guessed he was mid-thirties, maybe a little older. He was much shorter than the other two but he had piercing blue eyes and an air of authority about him. Unlike the bald man, he was smiling.

"Maddie and Josh, welcome to our camp. My name is Boss.

"First of all, sorry for bringing you here with hoods on and for all the questions. We had to make sure you were genuine locals, not a couple of spies, sent to find out who and where we are. I'm pleased to say that you both passed, although Maddie, you have Josh to thank for vouching for you."

I took a deep breath and exhaled, relief washing over me. I still wasn't one hundred per cent sure about these people, but what he said made sense. He continued.

"Now that we know a little about you, I'm going to tell you a little about us. Then you can ask me any questions. OK?"

We both nodded, staying silent. It was clear that he wanted to speak uninterrupted and we could speak when invited.

"After the event," he said, making quotation marks with his fingers in the air, "three of us chose not to join the evacuation. We set up camp here in

93

the forest, finding a couple more like-minded people along the way. Since then, we've been joined by three others, whose paths we crossed in much the same way as we did with you two today. What we offer here in the camp is a community that helps one another to survive off-grid. We have shelter, we have food, and amongst us, we have the skills to live comfortably out here in the forest. Everyone has something to contribute. Everyone works in some way to benefit the community as a whole. Of course, we do have rules, which everyone agrees to abide by. That way we can live in harmony without disagreements.

"Think of us as Robin Hood's merry men. We live in the forest, taking care of one another. We don't steal from the rich, but we do explore and acquire whatever we need to survive. In normal times we might be called looters, rustlers, or poachers, but these are not normal times. We are building a new life here, which we make as comfortable as possible, until normality returns. If normality doesn't return, we have started a foundation for a new way of living.

"So, some basic rules. In camp, we keep noise to a minimum. No open fires, no smoking. You respect everyone in camp. Any disputes, you come to me.

"Drinking water. Everyone who leaves the camp to forage has to take an empty bottle and return it full, provided it's safe to do so. It's the one thing we don't have easy access to and so far, it's the one thing we can still rely on from the old days. Whether you get it from a tap in a house, a garden or a field, it's a priority to keep the camp stocked up. We use that water only for drinking, cooking, and brushing our teeth. We use river water for washing and bathing. Think of tap water as the most precious resource in camp. It's liquid gold. If we do run low, we mount a special run to boost our reserves.

"Any patrol sightings whilst you're out and about are reported directly to me. I keep track of the numbers, their activities and the areas under surveillance. We have to stay under their radar and we have to know if they are getting close. Understood?"

Boss looked at both of us in turn and we nodded in agreement. He continued.

"Each evening we sit together and we agree which jobs need doing and who will do them. I make sure that there is variety for everyone and fairness in which tasks are allocated. Together, we figure out what supplies we need, whether that's food, toiletries, clothing or something for the camp. We also have a wish list, which everyone has the opportunity to add to. Maybe someone needs a hairbrush or toothbrush, wants chocolate or warm pyjamas. Then we prioritise the list and figure out how and where to explore. So, you see, we do what we can to provide for everyone, together.

"If you wish to remain with us, you follow the rules, you work hard, share your skills in whatever way you can, and you respect everyone here in the community. If you don't wish to remain with us, you leave by the same route you came and we say goodbye."

I felt positive, energised, and relieved. We had found help. We weren't alone. I glanced at Josh who was nodding and smiling. He looked at me and took my hand, realising that I was happy too.

"OK, now it's your turn for questions," he said, opening his arms out wide.

Josh started.

"Do you know what happened? What caused all this?"

"The honest truth? No, we don't, but depending on who you talk to here you'll get wildly different answers. Anything from aliens to solar flares, to a dirty bomb. What we do know is that it wiped out the national grid, at least around here, and destroyed anything electrical; cars, phones, and radios. Anything we might use to communicate or travel. Basically, everything that we used to rely on for our old way of life. How far the damage extends is anyone's guess, but the fact that there are patrols driving vehicles and flying helicopters, well, it can't be worldwide."

"By patrols, presumably you mean the soldiers in white suits? Who are they?" I asked.

"They claim to be British soldiers but we don't believe them. If they really are British, they might be involved in some sort of coup to overthrow the government. Or, they could be foreign and highly organised, using English speakers to gain people's trust. Whoever they are, they are enforcing their rules without any freedom of choice. We are supposed to live in a democracy, where citizens have rights. The right to live the way we choose, and the right to freedom of speech. We shouldn't be herded up like cattle and transported to God knows where. As you've witnessed, they aren't afraid to use force. Does that sound like the country we live in? Or does it sound like something you might expect in another nation like Russia, China, or North Korea?"

So we weren't the only ones not to trust the patrols. Everything he said made sense.

"Do you know where their base is?" Josh asked. "Or where the evacuation centre is?"

"Well, we've probably covered a five-mile radius from this camp and we've not seen anything that looks like a base camp or a centre for all the local people that got evacuated. So they must be coming in from further afield. We see patrols in the area nearly every day so we figure they must have some kind of base no more than 20 or 30 miles away."

The woman who had brought me a drink came back into the tent, this time carrying two bowls.

"Josh and Maddie, this is Barbara, Babs for short," Boss said. "She's an absolute star. Sorts out the meals for us day to day. We couldn't do without her."

Babs smiled and handed us each a bowl of something.

"Porridge," she said, "as best we can replicate it."

It looked and smelled delicious. We thanked her and tucked in. It was a little creamy and had some sweetness. It certainly wasn't like porridge at home but tasted great.

"When you've finished," Boss said, "I'll take you on a tour of the camp and show you what we've got. Not everyone is here at the moment, but you'll get to meet the rest later when we all get together to eat and talk."

We followed Boss out of the tent. The camp was cut into the forest trees, about the size of a tennis court. The trees were growing quite close together, forming a dense canopy. However, all the lower branches had been removed, a little over room height, leaving a space like a large hall with pillars. Tarpaulins were strung up beneath some of the lowest remaining branches to provide shelter, covering one end of the area. These tarpaulins, which were various shades of green, screened the tents below.

Boss walked us around, explaining things as he went.

"Considering that we've only been here a little while, we haven't done badly eh?!" he said, clearly pleased with himself. "We're slowly acquiring what we need to make this place as comfortable as possible."

"We've got another tarpaulin if it's of any use," Josh said.

"Perfect! One day we'll have enough to cover this whole area."

There were three main tents, two for sleeping and one for the camp residents to use as a day tent. The day tent was where everyone ate and where they had meetings. That's where we had just been to hear about the community from Boss. The smallest tent was for Boss and Babs to sleep in, so they must be a couple. That meant that everyone else slept together in the other tent, which didn't impress me too much. I didn't fancy sharing with those other men who found us in the forest. I hoped that would just be temporary. Maybe Josh and I could wish for our own tent sometime soon.

A small kitchen area had also been established beneath one tarpaulin. Babs was busy cutting up potatoes on a worktop, next to a couple of camping gas stoves just like the one I had. Overhead, a long branch had been tied underneath the tarpaulin. A few pots and pans hung from it.

In another area, a small man with a mop of sandy-coloured hair was bending over a small piece of wood, slicing off wafer-thin shavings with a knife. Next to him lay a small reel of wire.

"Meet Rambo," Boss said, "our resident survival expert."

Rambo looked up, flashed a brief look of annoyance at Boss and then nodded a greeting at us. His face was weathered and lined. I reckoned he could be about fifty, maybe older.

"His real name isn't Rambo," Boss said, laughing, "but he picked up that nickname early on and it stuck. But seriously, we couldn't do without him. He's spent his whole life waiting for an apocalypse to happen, so now he's in his element."

"What are you making?" Josh asked politely.

"Some more snares," he replied, "for rabbits."

I couldn't help staring at Rambo's hands. He was a small man but his hands were huge and calloused. He must have worked as a labourer of some sort for most of his life.

Boss pointed out four exits from the camp, all of which were in the uncovered area. None were very obvious unless you looked carefully. Two were opposite the tents on the far end and two were opposite each other on the sides of the camp.

"The ones on each side lead out of the camp. We only use the one on the left-hand side, which is where you came in. The other one is an escape route, should they find us. Both of them weave around so that the camp is very well hidden.

"Those two at the end. The right leads to the toilet and the left leads to a small stream for washing and bathing. Come, I'll show you the toilet."

Boss led the way down the right-hand path, which wove between the conifer trees, obscuring the destination. In a small clearing stood a tall wooden box with a door, underneath a tarpaulin. Boss opened the door to reveal a crude bench with a real toilet seat set on it. A toilet roll hung on the wall, suspended by a piece of rope.

"Luxury living," Boss said jokingly. "Underneath is a hole. At some point, we'll dig another hole nearby and fill this one in, then lift the cubicle across."

It looked pretty crude, but it was better than digging your own hole.

We walked back to the camp and then down the left-hand pathway to the wash area. A guy with jet-black hair knelt near the edge of a small stream. He had dug a shallow, semi-circular hole behind the river bank and was lining it with stones. He reminded me of someone, but I couldn't remember who.

"This is Mikolaj," Boss said. "Mikolaj, meet our latest recruits, Josh and Maddie."

Mikolaj jumped to his feet. He grinned broadly while brushing the grit and mud from his hands.

"Hi! Nice to meet you," Mikolaj said in a heavy Eastern European accent. He pointed to his work. "I make bath. When all stones are in hole, I dig out this bit next to stream and water flows in and out."

I was impressed, although the idea of bathing in the stream didn't appeal too much, not unless it was a lot warmer than the river. Maybe it was intended for washing clothes or dishes too.

When we returned to the camp, Boss asked what we had brought with us.

"Hardly anything," Josh replied, emptying the rucksack. "We were travelling light when we got chased. I did get a couple of blankets from a stable this morning. There's also the tarpaulin and our wet clothes."

"Babs can let you have some soap if you want to wash those clothes out."

"We have these binoculars too," I said. "They've been really useful. Hopefully, they're of some use here too."

"Definitely! We have someone on lookout high above the entrance each day. They'll be a great help." I handed them over.

"We operate the lookout on two shifts," Boss said, "one in the morning and one in the afternoon. The camp is so well hidden that once we are all back, we don't need anyone up there. The biggest danger is for someone to be spotted entering or leaving."

I went to ask Babs for some soap and we took the clothes back to the stream. Mikolaj was still busy making the bath. I crouched at the water's edge, doing my best to soap the clothes and rinse them clean. Josh started picking up smooth stones downstream, bringing them back for Mikolaj.

"Cheers my mate!" Mikolaj said, smiling.

When the clothes were rinsed we twisted them around and around until most of the water had been squeezed out. We also washed our hands and faces. The water was cold but I felt so much better for it.

Back in the camp I found a washing line beneath one of the tarpaulins and hung the clothes to dry. I hoped that they might be dry by tomorrow so that I could get out of my bag lady outfit.

Boss told us that Matt was in charge of supplies, so he could probably find a couple of spare sleeping bags later on. Just in case there were none, we beat the blankets from the stables to remove as much dust and hair as possible. They really needed a wash in the stream too, but not today.

Babs made some flatbreads for lunch and she put out a few tins and jars for a choice of filling. I made us a wrap with some tuna and sweetcorn. Boss spread his flatbread with peanut butter and persuaded Babs to let him have a couple of slices of cheese in there too.

"Just this once," she said smiling, but I got the impression that Boss always got what he wanted.

In the afternoon we tried to make ourselves useful around camp. Babs started preparing food for the evening meal, so I asked if she needed help. She gave me a basket of big green leaves with pink stalks. She said were chard and asked me to wash them in the stream. They must have been harvested from someone's garden and needed the mud rinsing off, plus the odd slug. When I brought them back, she asked me to chop some onions and then slice the chard while she browned some slices of meat in a pan. Before long she had created some sort of casserole, which she left simmering over a low heat.

Boss took Josh away to show him the lookout post, a job he said he'd like to give him tomorrow morning. I felt a little panicked as he left, but Babs slipped her arm through mine.

"Come on," she whispered, "let's get you properly washed up. We'll warm some water and shampoo your hair. You can use the suds to wash the rest of you. Then I've got some spare clothes you can change into."

An hour later I was sitting on a stool, wearing clean underpants, a pair of blue jeans, and a pale pink sweatshirt. Babs was a similar size and the clothes fitted well. Earlier, she had warmed some water from the stream and washed my hair for me, just like I was at the hairdresser's. Afterwards, she wrapped my hair in a towel and guarded the day tent so that I could wash with the bucket of suds. It was such a relief to feel clean and refreshed. Once I was dressed, she carefully combed through my wet hair to tease out the knots. We chatted and she told me a bit about herself.

Babs was married but separated from her husband. They had an eight-year-old daughter who had gone to stay with him for part of the Easter holidays. She was worried sick about her and missed her terribly, but hoped that she was safe with her dad. She asked how old I was and about my home life. Speaking about my parents made me feel so sad and I started to cry. She hugged me, rocking gently back and forth, rubbing my back.

"It's all so very sad," she said, "but don't worry, I'll help you. Anything you need, just ask."

I felt a real connection with her. I was so glad that we'd found these people. It felt like a weight had been lifted from my shoulders. We had adults to help us and I didn't have to be so brave anymore.

I was curious about the other people in the camp. Babs told me that there were eight people altogether, not including us. That meant that we had already come across all of them even if we hadn't been properly introduced. I was looking forward to the evening meal and meeting everyone properly.

By the time Josh returned to camp my hair was dry and brushed out. His eyes lit up when he saw me.

"You look really great," he whispered, hugging me. He made me feel so happy.

Josh found and moved two logs into the day tent so that we could sit with the others later on.

By late afternoon, the other men returned to the camp, carrying full rucksacks. Boss went to see what they had, congratulating all of them on getting such a good bounty. The guy who had been my captor was making notes in a small book as they sorted and stored the supplies. I guessed he must be Matt. I noticed how quiet everyone was; no one raised their voice and only one person spoke at a time.

Chapter 11: A meeting

Babs was busy with the final stages of the meal and she beckoned to me to help lay out the plates and start serving. The camp residents lined up to receive their meal and went into the day tent to eat. Josh and I picked up our plates and joined them. As I walked past Matt he looked me up and down again. When Josh passed him he said, "You girlfriend and boyfriend then?"

"Yes," Josh replied and winked as he sat down next to me. I wondered if he meant it. I hoped he did but thought he might be keeping me safe from Matt.

The meal was venison stew, with potatoes and chard. Rambo had caught a small deer in a trap. He had arrived back at camp with it already skinned and dissected, bringing only the tenderest parts. The rest he had left at the kill site for the wild animals to devour. With no means of storing fresh meat, Babs had cooked it all in one go. The potatoes and chard had come from someone's vegetable plot in a nearby village. While we had been cooking, she promised me that not every day would be as lavish as this and to make the most of it. I'd never eaten venison before and normally I would have refused to eat it. However, it was my first proper meal in days and it was delicious.

When the meal was over a few people helped to clear away the plates, which were left submerged in a bucket of water with the cutlery. Then, everyone returned to their seats for the daily discussion. All attention was on Boss.

"For Josh and Maddie's benefit, I'll explain what we talk about in our daily discussion. First up, we go around the room to hear what people have achieved today and gather any intelligence on local patrols. Then, we talk about what supplies we need. Afterwards, we all get to make a wish. That wish is for something achievable, like a new toothbrush or a new pair of socks, not something that requires a magic wand. Then we'll discuss what needs doing tomorrow and agree how those tasks are allocated amongst us. Just for tonight, as a way of getting to know each other, we will all tell our stories, Josh and Maddie included. Who we are, where we were when the energy wave hit, what happened next, and how we came to be together."

Boss looked around the room, smiling. "OK. Jerry, what did you get up to today?"

Jerry was the tall, bald man that had interrogated us. His update was brief and to the point.

"Out on patrol this morning, heading for the pub on the main road. We came across our two friends here, who we escorted back to camp with the usual formalities. Then I took over lookout duty from Mikolaj."

"Thanks, Jerry. Al?"

Al was the name of the Asian-looking guy, who had been part of the patrol.

"Out with Jerry on patrol this morning. Went back out again after we brought Josh and Maddie back to camp. Picked up some supplies from the village out west. A good haul today."

"Matt?"

Matt was the tall willowy guy who had been my captor. He was the one who kept staring at me and who was in charge of supplies.

"Yeah, I was with Al. We got lucky in that village. Brought back all sorts for our stores. We found quite a bit of food; pasta, rice, and tins, but also some cans of beer and cider. We grabbed a couple more sleeping bags, thinking of our new friends here, and two or three warm tops. Al got lucky with loo paper, but go easy with it guys because it takes up a lot of space in the rucksacks. For the wish list, we found some washing line and pegs, a saw, and two towels."

There were a few murmurs of thanks around the room.

"Cheers Matt. How about you Lester?"

Lester was the fit black guy. He spoke with a slight Caribbean accent.

"Got nothing to add except Matt forgot to mention the bottle of whisky he found. I expect he forgot to write that in his little book too." Lester chuckled. "A whole bottle of Bells, in case you're wondering."

"Something to celebrate the arrival of our new guests!" Boss said. "How about your day Mikolaj, my mate?"

Mikolaj was keen to talk.

"Well, in morning I was up tree on lookout. It was bit boring but I saw plenty birds, lots of squirrel, but no peoples except us. Then Jerry took over and I went to river to build bath. Now, bath coming on nicely. I finish digging hole, about knee deep in middle and gentle curve up sides. It is clay on bottom and bashed down nice and hard. Then I line with big stones from river, all nice and smooth. Josh here help me. Tomorrow I break through river bank to get water flowing in and once it settle and clear, you can all have bath or wash clothes or dishes."

107

"Excellent progress," Boss said. There were murmurs of gratitude around the room. "OK, Rambo, you're up next."

"Checked the traps this morning. Nice small deer, which Babs has done justice to tonight. Spent the afternoon making some rabbit snares and fixing up more tarpaulin under the trees. Spotted a patrol out east, about four miles away, sniffing around the sheep farm and outbuildings. Three men with rifles, one jeep."

"Duly noted. Thanks, Rambo. Babs, your turn?"

"Food, food, food," was all Babs said.

"And delicious it all was too," Boss replied. "So my day. Well, I spent some time thinking about the camp, what we need, where we could explore for our next supply run. Then our friends here arrived and we had the usual chat, followed by a tour of the camp. The opportunity gave me a moment to reflect on what we've achieved and we should all be really proud of ourselves.

"OK, so moving on. Let's talk about supplies. Babs, what do you need for meals?"

"Well, with another two mouths to feed we're going to have to bring in more basics. Dried foods store well and I can find all kinds of ways to turn those basics into meals. I'm talking flour, oats, lentils, split peas, stock cubes, and gravy granules. Anything like that. Just look in people's store cupboards and grab what you can. Tins are great, and we've done well with those, but they don't go so far in big meals."

"Yeah, and they're heavier to lug back," Lester said, interrupting. "Them pulses are good and healthy, right?"

"Absolutely," Babs agreed, "and if anyone finds dried yeast, I can try and bake some proper bread for a change."

A murmur went around the group. Proper bread sounded amazing.

"We could also use a few more dishes, bowls, and cutlery too. We've only just got enough for the group, so a few spares would be great."

Matt was taking notes for the next foraging trip. Boss looked over at him.

"Matt, how are we doing on other basic supplies?"

"I was looking earlier Boss, what with our new friends arriving. We picked some sleeping bags up this afternoon, so that's a start. In the store, we do have a couple of spare towels plus a new toothbrush each and toothpaste."

Matt glanced over at Josh and me and we nodded our thanks.

"We should also pick up some more toiletries. Shampoo, soap, washing powder, and loo roll."

"OK, thanks, Matt. So now we've covered what we need, let's start with wishes. Josh and Maddie, you go first." I looked at Josh, unsure of what we dared ask for.

"Well," Josh said, "Maddie and I had to leave our camp in a hurry, so we arrived with almost nothing except a set of dirty clothes each and some that we borrowed. Babs has lent Maddie some clothes, but I guess we both need some extra stuff."

"Sure," Matt replied, making notes and looking at his book. "There are a few things in the store that you can look through, but we'll add clothing to the foraging list. It's easy enough to find."

"Thanks, Matt."

I took a deep breath.

"I was wondering about sleeping arrangements," I began hesitantly, "only it looks like the main tent must be pretty full already. Would Josh and I be able to have our own tent? Just a small one, maybe?"

The request was met with a mixture of raised eyebrows, sniggers, and grins. I could feel myself turning crimson. Babs looked a little concerned and Boss sat there scratching his chin. Josh tried to justify the request.

"Maddie is right," he said, "I don't think there's enough room in there and it's also a bit awkward for her to be sharing a tent with a group of men. On the other hand, she shouldn't be in a tent on her own. It would be too cold and could be a bit scary."

Boss cocked his head to one side.

"Well, I'm not sure your parents would agree, but I guess the two of you have been sharing so far, so what's the difference?"

"I know where we can find one," Al said. "Remember the big house near the main road? The one with a pool and pool shed?" Jerry and Lester nodded. "I spotted one there. Dragged it out to take a look but left it behind when I saw it was small."

"Or," Jerry said, "we look for a bigger tent that has sleeping pods in it. Then the group can divide up more and have their own spaces."

This suggestion seemed to go down well with the rest of the men, who must be fed up with sleeping in a big group like a school dormitory.

"OK," Boss said, "we pick up the small tent that Al spotted tomorrow, but let's keep our eyes open for a better tent, now that the group has grown.

"So, moving on, Babs, what can we get for you?"

"Oh, I'd love some hand cream, please. All the cooking and cleaning is taking its toll."

"Rambo?"

"I could do with a new chisel or some fishing line if you come across any. We've got more mouths to feed so we need more traps."

"How about you Lester?"

"I want a new pair of trainers 'cos these ones are messed up! All the wet and mud is rottin 'em. Size 11."

"Proper pair of leather boots is what you need," Jerry said.

"Like I told you before Jerry, I can't run in boots man! If we come across patrols, I ain't getting picked up 'cos I'm wearing lead weights."

Jerry shrugged. Boss continued.

"Matt put trainers on the list and see what we can find tomorrow. Mikolaj, how about you?"

"Oh I busting for a packet of fags, my mate, but as you don't like me smoke in case it attract attention, I settle for them nicotine patches. And if there's none of them then I like a bottle of good vodka."

"Right, my mate!" Boss chuckled. "Jerry?"

"I'm still after that keg of ale we didn't manage to find this morning."

"Me too," Al said.

"Make that three," Matt added.

"So that leaves me," Boss said. "I'd like a decent mirror, some shaving foam, and a new razor."

Matt continued to scribble notes, then summarised the list for everyone.

"Food list first. We need flour, oats, dried pulses, stock cubes, gravy, and yeast. Added to that we need more plates, bowls, and cutlery. Ideally two sets of stuff.

"Personal hygiene. We need shampoo, soap, washing powder, and loo rolls. Hand cream for Babs. Shaving stuff, including a mirror for Boss."

Al did a small wolf whistle and everyone chuckled. Matt continued.

"Clothing. We need a couple of warm outfits for Josh or Maddie, including pants and socks. Lester needs some size 11 trainers. He'd probably like them to be Nike or Asics, but will perhaps have to settle for Primark."

"Decent stuff man! I got my image to look after," Lester added, grinning.

"Rambo wants some fishing line and a nice sharp chisel.

"For evening pleasures, we have here a keg of ale, and some nicotine patches or vodka. Plus a small tent for Maddie and Josh."

Boss beckoned for the list that Matt had written and looked it over.

"OK. What makes sense to me is that we send out two scouting parties tomorrow. Jerry and Matt head for the pub again to pick up the booze. Correct me if I'm wrong Al, but I think the house with the small tent is in that direction?"

Al nodded.

"So pick that up too and anything else that's worthwhile."

"Yup, got it Boss."

"Al and Lester, you two head for the village by the southern edge of the forest to pick up as much of the list as possible. That way Lester, you can choose your trainers, but don't spend too long fussing.

"Rambo, you check the traps as usual. Mikolaj, you finish the bath. Josh, I'd like you to take up lookout duty for the morning. Maddie, please help Babs around camp."

Boss looked around, checking for agreement. Everyone nodded, including me. I was quite happy spending time with Babs around the camp. A day without being pursued across the countryside was more than welcome.

"So, Maddie and Josh, it's time to hear everyone's story and when everyone's finished, you can tell us all about yours. OK?"

We both nodded and Boss grinned back. He was enjoying this.

Chapter 12: Stories

Story telling began.

"My story first," Boss said.

"I own a successful car repair and maintenance business. We fix cars, service cars, and do MOT testing. Most of my business comes from the villages around this area. My real name isn't actually Boss. However, Jerry and Al work for me and they call me Boss, so it's sort of stuck.

"When the energy wave swept by, I was busy in the office doing the accounts. I felt really rough and passed out, waking up sometime later with my face in a pile of invoices. When I went outside to find out what was going on, I found poor old Bob lying on the ground. Now Bob was one of my oldest employees. He was seventy-two and had spent his entire life working as a mechanic. However, he had heart trouble and although he got fitted with a pacemaker, he was forced to leave his last job in town. Because he lived locally, he came to see if I had any work I could offer him. He couldn't afford to retire, you see. So I paid him to keep the yard in order. He moved cars around, tidied up, swept up and made the tea. Such a nice guy, " Boss said wistfully. "Always cheerful. Customers loved him. Anyway, that energy wave killed him.

"The other lads appeared soon after. They'd all been unconscious for a while but were otherwise OK. Two of them had young families, so I let them go home. Jerry and Al decided to stay with me and see if help arrived. No one wanted to leave poor

Bob like that. We moved him into the workshop and covered him with an old tarp.

"Soon it was dark and we figured we'd be staying for the night. We shared what food we had and made ourselves as comfortable as possible. In the morning, when there was still no sign of a rescue party, we decided to make tracks. We wrapped Bob in the tarp and put him in a lockup where the animals couldn't get to him. Of course, we expected that we'd find help and return, but we never did.

"We set off for the village, which was about a mile away. However, as we drew close we spotted a patrol of those guys in white suits, with guns. Nothing about them looked right. They were pointing their guns at a couple of old women and herding them into a jeep. I mean they were just old ladies. Harmless! So we kept out of sight and watched. They were going door to door, breaking and entering, guns at the ready. Could not believe what I was seeing.

"So we three decided to stay off-grid and headed for the forest. On the way we found Babs, sitting at the side of the road, so she came too. None of us had any food or drink, so we took some liberties and helped ourselves from a house along the way. We also took a tent, some sleeping bags, and a few layers of clothing.

"Not long after we entered the forest, we came across Rambo. He helped us organise a camp, right here where we are now. He didn't really want to stay. He said he'd probably stand a better chance of not being caught without us." Boss laughed, "but he was injured, so in the end he agreed. Since he was an expert on survival, we listened to his advice. We improved the camp and started learning how to survive out here alone.

"So that's my story. Jerry and Al should go next."

Jerry looked over at Al, then began.

"I'm a car mechanic. Started as an apprentice when I was sixteen. For twenty years or so I worked at a Ford garage in town. Everything was going fine until I found out that some bloke was paying too much attention to my wife. I got mad and shouldn't have done it, but I lost my temper. Let's just say that he wasn't so pretty after I finished with him. So I got in some trouble and got sent down for ABH; 10 years, out after six on good behaviour. However, getting back in the trade proved to be difficult, once people found out what I'd done. But Boss here, he gave me a chance. Best job I ever had. Best boss I ever had."

Jerry looked at Boss and nodded.

"And Bob, well he gave me a roof over my head, in exchange for a bit of rent and some help around the house. He never judged me, not once. So like Boss said, when we found Bob dead, I wasn't leaving him there. And the rest you already know."

Well, I wasn't expecting that; in prison for actual bodily harm! No wonder I found him a bit menacing. Six years in prison would do that to anyone. Whilst I absorbed the information, Al started with his story.

"You've probably been looking at me and wondering why I don't speak with an Asian accent. Well, I was born here, grew up here, and probably went to the same school as you do."

He made me feel guilty for being prejudiced but I hadn't expected an accent at all. Plenty of kids at my last school were from different ethnic backgrounds, but most of them spoke just like me. Maybe people around here were more racist. In fact, I realised that there were far more white faces in my new school than coloured ones. Perhaps he had had a tough time growing up here. He went on.

"After school, I started working for Boss as an apprentice. I got qualified about five years ago, and until all this happened, I'd just about scraped enough money together for my own place in town. Anyway, I'm pretty fit, but that energy wave knocked me for six. I thought I'd been struck by lightning or something. When I came round we found Bob and I decided to stay with Boss and Jerry. You see, I've got two brothers and I wasn't worried about my parents. One of them would have looked out for them. When help didn't come, I set off with Boss and Jerry. I was going to make my way home until we saw the patrol. That changed everything. From that point on I knew I was best off with Boss."

Jerry and Al were clearly very loyal to Boss. They had stuck by him and had only nice things to say. I felt that we had really fallen on our feet. Thank goodness we had found these people. It was a relief not to have to worry about everything on our own.

Al looked at Babs. It was like they all knew the order in which to tell their stories. I guess they had done this before.

"I work as a lunchtime chef in a local pub. Most days, after I've dropped my daughter off at school, I go to the pub and I get the prep work done. I peel the spuds, chop the onions, whatever can be done in advance for the menu. There's another chef that comes in to help when the customers arrive and the orders start coming in. Anyway, I was alone in the pub, getting the prep done when the wave struck. I don't remember much about it, except dropping the knife I was using in shock. Next thing I know it's the evening and I'm lying on the kitchen floor feeling really sick. No one else had come in. I was all alone and it was pitch dark. No lights or anything. Luckily my daughter was staying with her dad for a few days of the Easter holidays. I just didn't feel well enough to make it home, so I ended up staying the night there.

"In the morning I felt a bit better and decided to leave but I found that my car didn't work. It was also so quiet everywhere, really spooky. There were no cars on the road and there was just this eerie silence. In the end, I set off on foot. I hadn't gone far when I saw a car wreck by the side of the road. Some guy had crashed into a stone wall and when I got there I realised he was dead. His head was hanging at this really bad angle and his eyes were open, staring. I panicked, jumped the wall and started running across the fields towards my house, as fast as I could. I live two or three miles away and I don't know how far I got, but at some point, I tripped and fell heavily. After that, I slowed down but in the end, I was so tired I just sat down. I'd had nothing to eat or drink and I was still feeling the effects of the wave. I didn't see any of the patrols and they didn't come across me. Luckily Boss, Jerry, and Al did and they took me with them."

Rambo was up next. He cleared his throat. I sensed that he was more reluctant to tell his story.

"I won't say too much other than I been waiting for something like this to happen for years. While most people been living their lives like there's some grand plan for 'em that nothing ain't gonna change, I been waiting and preparing. I taught myself how to survive; how to build a shelter, how to live off the land, and how to keep myself alive without any modern-day inventions. Seems I got it right.

"Some years back I put together a couple of survival capsules; one at my house and one in a shed on my allotment. Those capsules contain enough tools, clothing, and food to keep me alive for days.

"When this disaster happened, I was grafting on my allotment. That first night I had to sleep in my shed but as soon as the effects wore off I got my capsule and headed for the forest. On the way, I nearly got caught by one of them patrols. Hurt my right arm getting over some fencing, which held me back a bit, but I got here and fixed up a camp as best I could. Then Boss and them came along. They did a lot of the work I couldn't do for a few days to get this place running. Well, I decided to stay. Decided to throw my lot in with them."

Mikolaj went next. He was all smiles and hand gestures like he was performing.

"I Polish. Been in England for two years and love it here. I live with Polish girlfriend. Very pretty. I very happy. She back home for few weeks to see family. Hopefully she OK back there, away from here. Anyways, I am builder decorator. On terrible day this happen, my boss drop me at house we finishing as there are few snagging jobs to fix up. He go on to next job to do quotes. I work in bathroom to fix small leak, then fill and paint some joints. All going very well and I doing great job when thing happen. I fall down, hit my head on toilet. When I wake up, blood all over floor and I feel terrible. It nearly dark and phone not working. I wait but boss not come back to get me. Peoples who live in house not come back neither. So I stay there for night. In morning I feels much better and decide to go home. It long way but I finds small bike in garage, so I think I borrow and give back later. I cycle along road when I see big car and I thinks thank goodness, someone can help me. But people in white get out and point guns. I panic and cycle away. They drive after me but I find small path and they car too big to drive down. I not sure what going on, but I think if they catch me maybe they don't trust Polish and think I stole bike. Anyways, I then finds this bigger track, very long, very straight and I goes fast as possible to get far away."

"I saw you!" I blurted out, suddenly realising why he looked familiar. "You were on a kid's bike, which was much too small and your legs were sticking right out."

"Yes, legs out, very hard cycling," Mikolaj said, laughing. "Anyway, after a bit, bike tyre goes pop. It no good. I hide bike and I run away in wood. I have terrible time. No food, no drink for two days. I very cold but I too scared to leave. Lucky, Boss and boys find me before I dead. They give me huge big question time. I don't think they trust me to start with, but because I builder I help lots with camp. I make kitchen for Babs and I make toilet. Now I make bath. I very happy Boss find me."

I really liked Mikolaj. He was funny, friendly, and easygoing. Next up was Matt, who I wasn't so sure about.

"I was in between decent jobs, so I was doing a bit of work as a supermarket delivery driver.

Horrible job. They don't give you enough time between delivery slots and then you get grief from stuck-up women about being late, making bad substitutions, and there not being good dates on the fresh stuff. Anyway, I was on my way from one slot to the next, driving along this country lane in the middle of nowhere when the wave hit. I lost control of the van, went through some trees, down a bank, and into a stream. The van hit a rock, triggered the airbag, and I got knocked clean unconscious.

"When I came round it was the middle of the night, pitch dark. I couldn't see a thing. The lights in the cab didn't work, nor did my phone. So I stayed put until the sun came up. Then, I walked back up to the road and hung around for a while hoping to flag someone down, but there was no traffic at all. Eventually, I decided to set off on foot. The sun was rising in the east and I figured I could head directly northeast to reach a more built-up area and get some help. I wasn't sure how long it was going to take me, so I grabbed some food and drink from the back of the van first. I soon found myself deep in the forest, amongst some very tall trees. Then the sun went behind some clouds and I could no longer figure out which way I should be heading. I came across a path, so I stuck to that, but it took me full circle. I literally spent all day walking, getting nowhere. Just as the light was fading, I came across a small den, which was probably made by some kids on a day out. They had leaned long sticks together, either side of a low tree branch to form a sort of tent. I crawled in, ate the rest of the food that I carried and shut my eyes. I had a really bad headache.

"I think it was the worst night of my life. It was freezing cold and really uncomfortable. There were some terrible noises too. It was like being in a horror film. As soon as it was light, I set off again. Luckily I stumbled across Rambo, who was out setting traps. He took me back to the camp to meet the others. I couldn't believe it when they told me what had been going on. I thought I'd had a bad turn in the van, that the crash was my fault. I guess I was lucky not to come across any patrols."

Lester told his story next.

"I work in a gym as a personal trainer, which is the perfect job for me. I get to work out for free and the hours are really good. I have to do some evenin' work, but that means I get time off durin' the day. It's a cool job. Anyway, the night before it happened I'd been out with the boys. We'd had a late night and a few drinks if you know what I mean. So I was in bed asleep when that energy wave hit me. I thought I'd had a bad dream but I felt really ill so I figured it was something to do with my night out. Luckily I wasn't working at the gym, 'cos I'd covered both days at the weekend, so I just chilled out in bed. I fell asleep again and woke up about tea time. That's when I noticed the power was out. My mobile was also dead, but I thought it was the battery. Anyway, I made myself some sandwiches and went back to bed.

"The next morning I woke up real early. Guess I had pretty much slept through the last 24 hours. So, I decided to go out for a run and sweat them bad toxins out of me. I took one of my regular routes, which goes through the forest and I didn't see no one at all. It was early, you know, so I didn't think twice about that. Anyhow, I was just comin' back out the forest when I saw one of them patrols. There were two guys with rifles slung over their shoulders and they was carrying a body bag. Being in them white suits and that, they looked real suspicious. I stopped running and hid 'til they'd gone.

"When I got back home there was a notice on the door, telling me to pack for the next evacuation. I thought, no way man. No way I trust these people. No way I want to end up in a body bag. So I packed some things and I went back to the forest where I know I can hide out. I spent about three nights sleeping rough. I come across Boss and the boys in a village on the south side. They was hunting for food, same as me. They asked me to join them 'cos I had a way bigger haul than they did."

Lester chuckled and beamed at everyone around the room. He was quite an entertainer.

"OK," Boss said, looking across at Josh and me, "you've heard our tales now, so which of you wants to go first?"

Josh nodded at me to start, so I told them all about my adventures up to the point where I met Josh. They were really interested in the part where the patrols evacuated the top road because none of them had properly witnessed how it had been done. When I talked about the chalk markings, the men all looked at one another and nodded. They must have come across these on their foraging trips. I didn't say much about my camp, but covered my trips to find supplies. When I got to the part where I met Josh, I let him take over the storytelling. He briefly covered what had happened to him before we met; how he'd camped at the stables, been spotted, but escaped.

Then I got a bit embarrassed because Josh made a huge deal out of my camp and how cool it was. That part really caught Rambo's attention. He kept looking over at me, raising his eyebrows and nodding. Josh then told them about Chester, our disastrous supply trip, the escape to the river, and the miserable night under the bridge.

"That's an impressive story," Boss said. "You did well to escape the patrols and not leave a trail. I can see that you'll both be a real asset here. Also sounds like Rambo could learn a thing or two from Maddie." Boss winked at me and there were smiles and murmurs all around.

That first night sleeping in the big tent was unpleasant, to say the least. Matt had suggested that I sleep in between him and Josh, to keep warm. However, I didn't fancy that at all and one glance at Josh and he knew. So after some insistence on both our parts, Josh put himself between me and the rest of the men. I was really tired after our last unsettled night, but I just couldn't sleep. Every time I thought I was about to drift off, someone would shuffle, sigh or groan. Then one of them, Jerry I think, started to snore and someone else joined in. And I was cold laying on the outside, just like Matt had suggested I would be, but not cold enough to switch places next to him. There was something about Matt that I didn't like. I just kept telling myself that tomorrow night we'd have our own tent. Just me and Josh, no one else. Eventually, I went to sleep.

Chapter 13: Mucking in

In the morning, Babs made some porridge and I boiled water to make tea. A mug of tea without milk wasn't particularly nice, but it was hot and sweet. There were so many things that I used to take for granted and having milk in the fridge was just one of them. After everyone had finished their breakfast, our main chores of the day started.

Josh was sent off to keep watch over the camp, taking with him a fleece blanket and my binoculars. I spent the morning washing dishes and helping Babs prepare some food for lunch. We chatted mostly about her daughter, what she liked and what she didn't like. Babs was putting on a brave face, but I could tell that she was really worried and was missing her badly. I guessed that my mum was feeling the same way too.

Jerry and Matt returned to camp at lunchtime, heavily laden. They both had full rucksacks and were carrying a large metal keg between them. Jerry was really out of breath and his face was bright red, but he seemed to be in a good mood. He patted the keg affectionately, like a pet dog. Then, he opened his rucksack and produced two bottles of spirits. They had found vodka and gin. He also unloaded a bottle of water and a huge selection of crisps, nuts, and pork scratchings. Matt dragged a big bundle of material out of his rucksack, which turned out to be the tent that Josh and I had wished for. Other items that had been caught up in the folds scattered onto the floor, which he bent down to retrieve; a couple of boxes of matches, sachets of tomato ketchup, mustard, and mayonnaise. Another bottle of water was set down on the ground.

After Jerry and Matt had eaten, Josh was relieved of lookout duty and came back to camp for some food. I was back on kitchen duty, trying not to feel too grossed out by the skinned rabbits that Rambo had produced for tonight's meal. I'd never eaten rabbit in my life, but I wasn't going hungry. I tried to kid myself that it looked like chicken and would taste just like chicken too. While I was dealing with the rabbit, Josh was sitting nearby eating lunch.

"So what's your morning been like?" he asked.

"Oh not too bad," I replied. "Washing up, cleaning, and cooking basically. Babs is nice though. Hopefully, I'll be doing something different tomorrow. How about you?"

"Well being a lookout is pretty boring and cold, so be careful what you wish for. You have to climb up into a huge conifer tree. There's a small seat up there, which makes it a bit more comfortable than sitting on a branch."

"What can you see?"

"Well, you can see one of the trails that passes the camp. I think it must have been the one we were on when they found us. Otherwise, just forest, although you can easily spot someone approaching the camp from all sides. It's pretty high up, so you definitely need a head for heights."

After lunch, Josh and Jerry put up our new tent and then Josh was asked to help Mikolaj finish the bath. I helped Babs wash clothes. It was a pretty horrible job as the water was cold and my hands soon felt chapped and sore. I could see why Babs had asked for hand cream.

Al and Lester returned late afternoon with a huge haul. As well as the rucksacks they had taken with them, they had also found a couple more. All of them were bursting at the seams. Clearly, their supply run had been very successful. Babs was presented with hand cream, face cream, and lip salve. Boss got a mirror on a stand, with shaving foam, a razor, and even some aftershave. Someone's bathroom cabinet had been plundered! Lester showed off his new Puma trainers.

"These'll do as temporaries," he said, grinning, "but I'm still looking to go a bit more upmarket."

They dragged their rucksacks over to Matt's supply store and unpacked. Matt had his notebook out, adding notes and ticking boxes.

Although it was nice being around camp, by late afternoon I felt a bit cooped up. So when Josh's chores were finished for the day, I was really happy to spend some time with him. Our new tent was set up between the day tent and the big sleeping tent. We went inside. Josh had already moved our horse blankets for a base layer and neatly laid out the sleeping bags on top. We even had a small cushion each as a pillow.

"So much better," I said happily, "although I wish we weren't so wedged in amongst the other tents. Feels a bit claustrophobic."

"I know," Josh said. "Jerry didn't want to move the existing tents around but didn't want us out on an edge where we were more exposed. He said it would be warmer and safer for us to be here, even if it is a little hemmed in. He said that once a couple more tarpaulins go up, we'd look at rearranging all the tents, but that for now, this would do. I couldn't really argue. At least we have our own space."

"No, it's fine, really. It'll be so much better than sleeping in the big tent again."

There was still some time before dinner and Babs didn't need me for a while, so I suggested that we went exploring. Josh took me down to the river and showed me the bath that he had helped Mikolaj finish. It was really cool. Two large rocks could be swivelled; an upstream one to let water into the bath and one further down to let the water flow back out, thereby flushing any dirty water out of the bath area. Move the rocks back in place, and the bath contains a settled pool of water.

"Mikolaj hopes that the sunlight will warm the water a little so that it isn't as cold as the river. Sounds a little optimistic, but he's so positive, you can't help but believe him."

Good old Mikolaj! I wondered what project he'd embark on next.

"Let's take a look at that second exit from the camp," Josh suggested. "We've not gone down that way yet."

We walked back to the main camp area and went straight across to the escape exit. However, we'd only gone a few metres along the path when Jerry appeared behind us.

"Hey," he hissed under his breath, "not this path. This is the escape route and we only use it in an emergency. If you walk up and down here you'll leave a more obvious trail. You might end up getting us all caught." He looked from one of us to the other. "Do you understand?" he said, in a fairly menacing manner.

"Sure Jerry," Josh said, "we didn't mean any harm."

"Get back to camp. Josh, you go and find Matt to see if he needs a hand with supplies. Maddie, go and see if Babs needs help with the meal."

"I already asked her and she doesn't need me for a while," I protested.

"Then go back and sweep the meeting tent instead. It's a mess." He paused, then added, "Go!"

We turned on our heels and headed back to camp, without speaking. Josh went off to talk to Matt and I picked up a broom to sweep the tent. Babs was in there.

"No need for that honey," she said smiling, "I swept earlier."

"Orders from Jerry," I replied. She looked at me sympathetically.

"Come on Maddie, let's check the dinner together."

Before long we were all back in the meeting tent, ready to tuck into our dinner. Boss had arrived clean-shaven, which drew a wolf whistle from Lester.

"Am I getting a little hint of Paco Rabanne there Boss?" he said. "You smell almost as tasty as Bab's stew."

Jerry and Al had installed the keg in one corner of the tent and were rationing out portions of ale amongst the group. I declined. Josh had a sip but pulled a face, which made them all laugh.

The rabbit stew wasn't so terrible. Babs had cooked it with lentils and tinned tomatoes. She'd also added some wild garlic for flavour. The meat was a bit on the stringy side, but being fussy wasn't an option.

After the meal, the meeting time started. First, an account of the day's activities, then a discussion about supplies, and then the wishes list. Although this was only our second night at the camp, the meeting already felt like a routine. It was good. I felt part of something and the mood amongst the community was positive and good-natured.

I decided to make my wish a small one after we'd been given the tent as I didn't want the others to think that I was greedy. I asked for a warm beanie hat to wear at night. Josh followed my lead and asked for warm gloves. The others also wished for small luxuries. It was amazing how many things that used to be taken for granted, were now prized possessions. I also missed having a decent hairbrush and a manicure set. I'm not the sort of girl to be caked in makeup with perfectly applied nail varnish, but I was pretty ashamed about the state of my fingernails; grubby, snagged, and misshapen. I'd seen better on tramps. I'd save that request for another night.

After the wishes were made, Boss handed out jobs for the following day. Josh was to go on a supply run with Al, Matt, and Lester. Rambo was to go out hunting again, which seemed to be all he wanted to do. I guess he had the skills. Killing and gutting animals was certainly not on my preference list. Mikolaj was to help Boss put up two more tarpaulins and create more hanging space beneath for drying and airing the laundry.

I offered to go on lookout duty, but Boss asked me to help Babs again. He said that she had been doing so much for everyone in the camp that it would be nice for her to get a bit more help and take some rest. That was fair enough I thought, but hoped to do something other than cleaning and cooking sometime soon.

Boss asked Jerry to take up lookout duty. I suppose he was less fit than the others, so lookout duty helped him rest up. Climbing up the tree was probably tough for him, but once he was there it was an easy job.

I couldn't wait for the meeting to be over and for everyone to head off to bed. It was going to be our first night in the tent and I was keen to spend time with Josh. After everyone had been offered a couple of glasses of ale, Mikolaj started on the vodka and Jerry passed around the gin. Al produced some lemonade as a mixer, which I settled for on its own. The alcohol seemed to have the desired effect and the group started to break up and make their way to bed.

Josh and I climbed into our sleeping bags and then pulled another blanket across us until it was almost completely over our heads. At first, it was cold, but as we huddled together the warmth slowly started to spread. I wanted to chat about our day, about the others, about our plans, just like we used to in my camp. However, even a whisper felt like it might be overheard. It was a little frustrating and I hoped we could move our tent soon. Annoyingly I could still hear snoring from the neighbouring tent but eventually, I drifted off to sleep.

Chapter 14: Community life

The next day passed uneventfully for me. I helped with breakfast, then cleared up, washing last night's dishes as well as the breakfast dishes. Then Babs and I went through the food stores so that she could come up with a meal plan. We did get a chance to chat in between chores, but I was beginning to feel a little trapped. My world had shrunk to a wall of trees and the occasional glimpse of sky.

Josh however had an exciting day on his supply run and didn't stop talking about it when he got back. They had revisited the village that had been so successful the previous day and carried on exploring the other houses. He had found a beanie hat for me and gloves for both of us. He had also found some better clothes to wear; a pair of heavy-duty cargo trousers that had useful pockets and a black puffer jacket. Apparently, the others had ribbed him about picking out stuff for himself, but they all did it, all of the time. The rule was that as long as they returned with plenty of supplies to keep the camp happy, cherry-picking essential items for yourself was acceptable. Josh had also found two boxes of dried yeast, each containing 5 separate sachets. That made him a hero. Babs was over the moon and the whole camp was excited at the prospect of proper bread.

That evening, we ate what Babs called a Spanish tortilla. Rambo had arrived back in camp with more than two dozen eggs that he had collected from a small holding. The chickens must have been laying every day since the wave came and finding sufficient food in their pen to survive. Rambo also hunted around until he found their feed, which he scattered around, intending to go back in a few days. He also talked about putting chicken on the menu one night, but Babs disagreed. She could do plenty with eggs and if Rambo kept a watch over the chickens, we would have a ready supply.

Spanish tortilla is basically an omelette but with lots of potatoes and other bits and pieces tossed in. Babs cooked it in a frying pan over a low heat, then it was turned out and cut up like a cake. She made two big tortillas, adding onions and sweetcorn to the potato, topping with cheese and then serving with peas. Very tasty.

During meeting time, everyone gave reports on their activities that day, followed by a discussion on supplies. Matt took notes as usual. Then Boss spoke at length about plans for the camp. He was pleased with the success of the foraging trips but concerned for the future. There were only so many villages within easy reach and eventually, there would be no food left to steal.

However, now that the Spring weather had arrived, he thought that we ought to be growing our own vegetables. He had found a spot in the forest that was close to the camp and the stream with enough daylight coming through the canopy to support a few raised beds. He thought that Rambo was best placed to determine what needed to be done and should agree with Babs on which plants were best to grow. Mikolaj would be in charge of constructing the site. Screening would also be needed to ensure that the vegetable plot wasn't too obvious if a patrol stumbled through.

He also thought we should be making more of the farms in the vicinity. Although there was hardly any produce available on arable farmland, there might be some farms with livestock like sheep, pigs, and cattle. Rambo was already looking after chickens to bring in a supply of eggs and Boss thought that we should consider other options too.

"Are you suggesting we start milking cows?" Matt asked.

"Why not," Boss replied. "It's free for the taking if any of you know how to do it."

"I milk goats once in Poland," Mikolaj said. "They belong to my grandmother and she show me how when I was boy. But cow's big init. I not sure how easy it be."

Rambo cut in.

"Well the only cows I know of around here are probably five miles away, so unless we are going to bring one back to camp, it's a bit far for a few pints of milk. However, we could help ourselves to the odd lamb here and there. There's two or three farms I can think of, just outside the forest."

"Mmm, roast lamb," Jerry said. "That sounds more like it."

There were a few awkward glances between members of the group. Taking food from people's cupboards to survive was one thing. Taking eggs from chickens that would otherwise rot was another. But killing farm animals, was that wrong? Then again, many of those animals would be heading off to a slaughterhouse at this time of year anyway, so perhaps it wasn't so terrible to help ourselves.

"I say we do it," Boss said. "Who would blame us? It's just survival. We can't live off venison and rabbits all the time. Rambo? You up for it?"

"Yes Boss, no trouble."

Thank goodness for Rambo! Babs raised her hand and Boss nodded.

"I think we need to extend the kitchen. Those two burners I use are fine, but what I can cook is limited. If Rambo is going to bring us a whole lamb, it will have to be cooked all at once. Can't be done with what we have."

"What do you need?"

"Ideally one of those big gas barbecues; one with a closing lid that allows you to slow cook the meat. So we'd also need a big gas bottle, which might be heavy. What do you think?"

"We should have enough muscle if we send a bigger group," Al said. "We just need to be careful. Sneaking a big shiny metal barbecue back to camp could be tricky."

"Won't the smell from that amount of cooking potentially attract attention?" I asked, thinking back to how paranoid I had been.

"We can pipe the steam through a bucket of water," Rambo said matter-of-factly. "That'll remove the smell. We've got a length of hose pipe lying around already. I'm sure Mikolaj can knock something up."

"No problem my mate."

"Where are we going to find the barbecue?" Boss asked.

Jerry and Al looked at each other.

"The pub!" they said in unison, sharing a look and smiling.

"OK. So let's say we need two people to carry the barbecue, two for the gas bottle, and one to keep an eye out. Jerry, Al, Lester, Matt, and Josh.

"Rambo and Mikolaj. You come with me in the morning and I'll show you the spot by the river.

Maddie, you can do the morning lookout. OK?"

Everyone seemed happy. I was glad to be doing something different and Babs didn't look disappointed to be left working on her own.

It wasn't long before Josh wanted to go to bed. Even though it was quite early, I pretended to be tired too, hoping that we might have some time together. However, Josh really was tired. I guess his day out foraging had worn him out. As soon as he got into his sleeping bag and snuggled up next to me, he nodded off. I lay awake for a while, wondering what would happen in the coming days. It was great being with the community and not feeling so alone and afraid. However, unless something changed, the average day was going to be pretty dull. Could I imagine life carrying on, just like this? *No!* Or would our circumstances change? Perhaps we would be rescued, and reunited with our parents and life would return to normal. *I wish!* It seemed unlikely. At least I was going to be doing something different tomorrow.

In the morning I collected the binoculars, wrapped myself in a blanket and set off to take up lookout duty. As this was my first time, Josh took me to the tree that was used. Just as I was about to climb up, he handed me a flask.

"Surprise," he said. "I found this yesterday and brought it back to camp. Babs has filled it with nice hot tea to keep you warm."

He kissed me lightly on the cheek and headed back to camp. I smiled. He was so thoughtful.

The tree was easy to climb and I was soon sitting on the seat at the top. After the murky shadows of the camp it was so bright up there that despite squinting, my eyes would not stop watering. A cool breeze blew and I could feel goosebumps prickling my skin. However, there was a little bit of sunlight falling on my back and I could just sense its warmth. I pulled the fleece tightly around me and poured myself some tea. I looked around.

To my left, I could see the camp, partly covered by the tarpaulin. The foraging party was assembled, ready to leave. I could see Al and Matt standing to one side, empty rucksacks on their backs. Lester was on one knee, tying a lace in his temporary trainers. The tall frame of Jerry cast a shadow over Josh, but I could just see him, wearing his new cargo trousers. They set off through the exit, weaving between the fir trees until they passed quite close to me. Josh looked up and waved. I waved back.

Next to leave camp were Boss, Rambo, and Mikolaj. Boss was leading the others down the path towards the stream. When he reached it he turned left and started walking upstream, presumably heading for the proposed vegetable plot. I soon lost sight of them and wondered if it mattered that the plot could not be seen from the lookout post.

Taking my duty more seriously, I started to scan the forest in front of me. At first sight, all I could see was the tree canopy stretching all the way to the horizon. Above me, there was a lovely deep blue sky with the occasional puffy white cloud. The forest was huge. As my eyes became accustomed to the scenery I began to pick out a little more detail. To my left, I could see a path, which must have been the trail that Josh and I were using before walking into Jerry and the gang. I lifted the binoculars to my eyes and followed the trail as far as I could into the distance. Nothing to see at all. I scanned to my right, seeing nothing but branches, with pine cones clustered along their length.

After an hour or so, I helped myself to another cup of tea. Glancing towards camp, I could just see Bab's feet, moving around under the tarpaulin. Something caught my eye and I noticed Boss emerging from the pathway to the stream on his own. He must have left the others at the vegetable plot. He sat down near the kitchen and Babs fetched him a steaming mug. I could just hear the murmur of their voices.

Again, I directed my watch back to the areas approaching the camp, which was the whole purpose of being a lookout. If I did the job badly I might never get the chance to do something different again. Nothing had changed. Just deep-green dark forest where nothing seemed to move.

Glancing back to camp again I saw Boss hand back his mug and get up to leave. However, he didn't go back towards the stream. He went down the escape exit. *What!*

So, it was OK for Boss to use that pathway then? I watched as he zig-zagged through the trees and then seemed to disappear. Focusing with the binoculars, I scanned the area for movement and then I spotted him, or at least parts of him. He had come to a halt, part way into the forest and was leaning over, then standing and lifting something, then leaning over again. I lost sight of him for a minute or two but then he reappeared in exactly the same spot. What was he up to? There must be something down there, I was convinced. All this talk about not leaving a trail was nonsense. He was hiding something. Boss and Jerry maybe.

At lunchtime, Mikolaj came to take over lookout duty and I climbed down, cold and stiff-legged from my perch in the branches. I had a bite to eat and then went back to my usual role as Bab's helper. I kept mulling over what I had seen and whether I could find a way to sneak down there and investigate. The trouble is, I'd have to do it when most people were away from camp. Even then, whoever was on lookout duty might spot me. However, perhaps I could do it if Josh was the lookout.

The foraging party returned in the early afternoon. Jerry was the first to appear, carrying just a rucksack. Al and Matt arrived soon after, carrying a shiny black barbecue between them. It was the size of a small chest of drawers with a large barrel lid. They were both panting with the effort.

"We got it, Babs," Al said. "It's not heavy but dragging it through the forest was a nightmare."

Babs lifted the lid to inspect it.

"Looks perfect though. Just what I was after. Thanks!"

Lester and Josh arrived, looking flushed. They carried a large blue gas cylinder between them, which they placed on the ground immediately. Josh was shaking the hand he had used to carry it and Lester grimaced, tucking his hand under his armpit.

"Never knew they weighed that much," Lester muttered.

"Come and have some lunch," Babs said. "You all look like you need a rest."

The foraging party had a long lunch, then spent the afternoon around camp. It was too late in the day to go out again, so they found the odd job to do. Everyone except Jerry that is, who just sat around watching everyone else work.

Al and Josh moved the barbecue into the kitchen area and connected the gas. It worked perfectly and soon the whole camp was talking about the possibility of having roast lamb the next day. Tonight, however, rabbit was on the menu again.

Before the evening meal, I got the chance to talk to Josh without anyone else in earshot. I told him about Boss and the escape path. Josh was intrigued.

"I wonder what he's got down there?" he said. "You know, Jerry was so quick to call us back the other day."

"Yep," I agreed, "and he got angry too like he was seriously warning us off. Next time you're on lookout duty, I'm going to sneak down there and take a look."

"That's a bit risky, isn't it? Maybe he's just got a secret stash of food or something."

I thought there was more to it, but decided to drop the discussion for now. At least I'd told him and that meant we'd both be noticing when Boss wandered off.

After helping Babs serve up the meal, we all settled in the day tent to eat. Tonight's rabbit had been turned into a curry with rice and flatbreads. Soon after, Boss called a start to the meeting.

"Jerry. Can you say a few words about your trip to the pub?"

"Not much to tell really. The journey there was uneventful. We knew exactly what we wanted, so didn't spend much time at the pub. The lads got the barbecue and gas bottle from a shed in the beer garden. I went into the pub and grabbed a few bottles of booze. The journey back was slower but we didn't see any patrols."

"You did well. Anyone else have anything to add about that trip?"

None of the others did. They just shook their heads.

"Maddie. How was your first watch?"

"Good thanks. Nothing to report though," I lied.

"Mikolaj. How are we doing with the veg plot?"

"It going to take a few days Boss and we going to need some stuff. Me and Rambo mark out area for beds, then I spend some time making green fence to hide bits that show. Now we need logs to make sides and then put some decent soil in. Rambo say soil down there rubbish, so we need get some."

"Any idea where from, Rambo?" Boss asked.

"Yeah, there's a few gardens around with decent soil we can nick. A few allotments too. Ain't gonna be that easy mind. I expect we'll have to do it a bit at a time."

"Fair enough. Anything else to report?"

"Well the traps turned up a few more rabbits and I collected some more eggs from the chicken farm. That's about it really. No sign of any patrols."

"And Babs?"

"Just the usual. I know you were all hoping for proper bread today, but I couldn't get the dough to rise, hence the flatbreads! I don't think it was the yeast. I just couldn't keep it warm enough to work. However, if we can finish getting that barbecue set up, I'm pretty sure I can get it warm and then let the dough rise inside."

"Sounds good," Boss said, turning to Mikolaj. "Mikolaj. I'll let you figure out how we're going to pipe the steam from that barbecue into a bucket of water. Think you can get that done in the morning?"

"Yes, my mate."

I was waiting for Boss to tell us about his day, wondering how he might account for the time he spent on his own, but he didn't report his activities at all.

During the discussion about supplies, it seemed we were running low on drinking water. So it was no surprise that Boss set a foraging trip for the next day, with water as the priority. I offered to help, hoping for a chance to leave the camp.

"No, thanks Maddie," Boss said. "It would be too dangerous if we come across a patrol."

"I can handle myself fine," I argued. Josh backed me up.

"Yes, she can. We were out there together for days. Look, the first time I met Maddie was on a sports field. She was doing circuits and putting most of the guys to shame. I reckon she could outrun quite a few of you too."

Boss raised an eyebrow and looked back at me.

"I'd like you to stay in camp and help Babs. We want to keep you safe. No argument."

I looked around. Jerry was sitting there, arms folded, staring aggressively at me. Matt had a smirk on his face. Mikolaj gave me a little sad look. Josh just stared at the floor. I could feel the anger rising and fought back tears of frustration too. Was this my new life now? Stuck in a forest, cooking and cleaning for everyone. Forever? This was modern-day slavery. This was so sexist. I was furious.

"OK, I think we're done," Boss said, bringing the meeting to a close without covering wishes. I got up and walked straight out, fists balled. Josh followed me back to our tent.

"Maddie I'm sorry," he whispered. "Look, I'll work on Boss. I'm sure I can persuade him to let you do more. I can see that being stuck here is getting to you."

I tried not to raise my voice.

"Getting to me? Too right it is. I want to go back out there, help with the foraging, stand in the sunshine, enjoy the countryside and the villages. I don't want to spend my life holed up here doing all the dirty work. It's not fair."

Josh wrapped his arms around me.

"I'm sorry. Listen, I'll work on Boss. I'll get him to change his mind. Trust me."

I was shedding angry tears. I wanted to shout. I wanted to scream. Eventually, I managed to calm down. I hated this. If it wasn't for Josh, I'd leave. The forest was closing in on me.

Chapter 15: Shady discoveries

Heavy rain had fallen overnight, collecting on the tarpaulins that stretched above the tents. Each one bowed in the centre, a darkened area marking the pool of rainwater above. Josh helped Lester get rid of the water before it found its way through. They were both quite tall and held a long straight branch between them, pushing up the tarpaulin and moving from the inside edge to the outside edge. Sheets of water cascaded into the bushes. Although it was no longer raining, the sky was dark grey, suggesting it might return. Beneath the forest canopy, the camp was almost dark. Everything was damp and no one felt much like doing anything. Getting soaked to the skin without being able to light a fire and dry off was no fun at all. However, Boss rallied everyone and sent a party out to get the much-needed drinking water. Jerry got lookout duty. Rambo went out, intent on bringing back lamb. Mikolaj started work on the barbecue.

My first chore of the day was to wash up the dishes from last night's dinner, but Babs wouldn't let me do it. I guess she felt bad for me.

"I'll do it," she said. "You make us both a mug of tea and then I'll find us a little treat."

I poured two mugs of drinking water into a pan and turned on the stove. Babs put her hands into the cold bucket of water to lift out the dirty plates.

"Damn," she said, "that was stupid. I've cut myself on something."

It wasn't a large cut, but it was bleeding. I poured a little tap water over the wound to clean it.

"Do we have a first aid kit somewhere?" I asked.

"I think there is probably something in the store, but Matt hates anyone going in there to rummage around. There's a box of plasters in my tent though, left over from my last clumsy accident. They're in the box by my bed."

I unzipped Boss and Babs's tent and went inside. It was a little gloomy but I spotted the box and opened it up. As soon as I looked I realised that I'd opened the wrong box. This one must belong to Boss as I could see a man's watch. But there wasn't just one watch, there were at least three and as my eyes grew accustomed to the light I could see that it wasn't just watches in this box. There was jewellery too: gold necklaces, bracelets, and rings. Also a big roll of cash. *Wow!* Boss had a box that was almost full of valuables. I was stunned. I stood staring at the contents, mouth open. I didn't have to ask myself where this had come from. So much for Robin Hood and his merry men taking only what they needed to survive. Boss was helping himself to other people's valuables.

"Have you found them, Maddie?"

Bab's voice snapped me out of my daze. I quickly closed the lid and looked around, spotting another box on the other side of the tent. That was obviously her box as it had a hairbrush on top, next to the hand cream she had wished for. My mistake. I found the plasters and left the tent quickly.

"Got them. Sorry, took my eyes a moment to adjust to the light."

Babs gave me a slightly quizzical look, but then shrugged and smiled.

"Yeah, it's gloomy today. Miserable weather."

I tipped a few plasters from the packet and picked one that looked about the right size.

"Here," I said, tearing the paper envelope, "you should really have some antiseptic on that too. Maybe Matt can find some later." I wrapped the plaster around her finger, pressing gently to seal the sticky part. "I'll get the washing up done and you can tell me what needs doing next."

"Thanks, honey," she said, giving my arm an affectionate squeeze. "How did I manage before you arrived?"

I carefully lifted the dishes and cutlery from the bucket, trying to look calm while my brain processed what I had just discovered. That was some jewellery collection! Where his stash had come from was obvious, but had he taken it himself? That seemed unlikely because I'd never seen him join a foraging party. So were they all in it together? Did they all help themselves and share the proceeds? Or maybe just Jerry and Al? The shine was starting to come off this community. I had looked up to Boss and admired him at one point. But now? I couldn't wait to talk this through with Josh. He'd been out foraging a couple of times now. Maybe he'd seen something.

Babs produced a bar of chocolate.

"Look what Lester brought for me. He said it was a special treat for keeping his belly full, bless him."

We had a mug of tea and shared the chocolate, which tasted amazing. Babs let Mikolaj have a few pieces too. He was almost finished with the barbecue. Connecting the hose had been quite easy because the lid already had a sliding vent. All he had to do was cut a circular hole in the vent and insert the open end of a tin can. In the bottom of the can he made another small hole into which he inserted the hose.

"I need find something to stop it slippin'," he said, wiggling the hose, "so be careful when you open lid. I think it work though." He grinned at us, clearly very pleased with himself.

"Great job," Babs said. "Hopefully we'll have bread in time for lunch!"

"And hopefully we'll have roast lamb in time for dinner." I turned to see who had spoken. Rambo walked into view with something slung over his shoulder. He walked up to the kitchen area and hung the package on a hook. "Gave me a right runaround, but I caught it. Prepared as best I could Babs."

Mikolaj rubbed his hands together.

"You all amazing. Now I going down to veg plot, but I back for lunch."

"I'll just have a cuppa," Rambo said, "and then I'll follow you down there."

Because of Bab's sore finger, making the bread was down to me. She gave me instructions and once I had formed the dough, she showed me how to knead it using her good hand. We fired up the barbecue until it was nice and warm and then turned it off. The dough was placed on the top shelf in a glass bowl that was covered with a tea towel. We closed the lid and left it to rise. It worked! Forty-five minutes later the dough was twice its original size. I divided it into ten pieces and shaped each one to look like a miniature loaf.

Babs fired up the barbecue again and I placed them all on the rack. The hose went into a bucket of water and twenty minutes later we lifted the lid to find freshly baked rolls. They smelled amazing.

"Shall we have an early lunch?" Babs asked with a giggle.

Babs and I stood on either side of the makeshift kitchen counter. We had just finished eating our rolls, which were so delicious. I hadn't had fresh bread for so long I had forgotten just how amazing it tasted.

"That was fantastic," Babs said, smiling. However, as she looked at me I noticed her refocus on something behind me and her smile dropped, replaced by a look of shock. "Don't move! There's a huge dog next to the tent. Oh God, it's coming towards us."

She picked up a knife, holding it blade down, like a dagger.

I turned around very slowly, swallowing hard and trying not to show any fear. Then I gasped. It was Chester.

"Chester! Chester!" I shouted happily. "You found us!"

Chester's ears, which were laid almost flat against his head, suddenly popped upright. He bounded over to me, his tail wagging so hard that his back end swayed. He ran around me in circles, licking my hands and rubbing against my legs. I was so pleased to see him. He must have found our trail and followed it.

"What a clever dog you are," I said, scratching just behind his ears, the way he liked it, "and I bet you are a hungry dog too!" I looked over at Babs. "What have we got that Chester can eat? He must be starving."

"I think we have some corned beef," she said. "I've been trying to work out how to cook it to make it edible!"

"Perfect! I know he likes spam. I'm sure he'd love it."

Babs shuffled through the contents of a box underneath the counter and produced a tin of corned beef. She pulled out the key from the side of the tin, inserted it back through the hole from the other direction, and then turned it to peel back the lid. I grabbed a bowl from the counter and Babs used a fork to pull out the contents and roughly chop the meat. It smelled disgusting but Chester was drooling.

"Here you go, Chester."

I think I managed to count to ten before he had completely cleaned the bowl.

"I don't know what Boss is going to say," Babs said with a troubled look.

"But he'll be great for the camp," I replied. "He'll be like a guard dog. Nothing will sneak up on us here without Chester knowing."

Babs bit her lip. She came around the counter, ruffled the fur on Chester's head, and removed the bowl.

"You'd better take him down to the river," she said. "Corned beef is very salty. He's going to need a drink."

Chester happily followed me to the river and drank a lot of water. I sat on a tree trunk and watched him. When he'd had enough he came over and lay down next to me. The poor boy was worn out. He must have been looking for us all this time.

When Boss, Mikolaj and Rambo returned to the camp, Chester was lying on the ground next to the kitchen. Before either Babs or I had heard them, Chester jumped to his feet, growling.

"It's OK Chester," I said gently to reassure him. "These are friends."

"Where the hell did that come from?" Boss asked angrily.

"This is Chester," I replied, "the dog who saved Josh and me from the patrol. He must have found our trail and followed us. He's such a good dog Boss, honestly. He'll be no trouble."

"Last thing we need is another mouth to feed."

"That's no trouble," Rambo said curtly, walking straight up to Chester. He dropped to one knee and offered Chester his hand to sniff. "I'm always leaving bits of kill behind that we don't eat. I'm sure this boy ain't so fussy. Eh, Chester?"

Chester licked Rambo's hand and then Rambo made a huge fuss of him. Chester loved it.

"I used to have a German Shepherd," he said. "His name was Lucas and he was my best friend. Fantastic dog. Clever. Loyal. The day he died was the worst day of my life."

I looked over to Boss, who was still frowning. Mikolaj stood behind him, looking slightly nervous.

"OK," Boss said reluctantly, "but he's your responsibility, Rambo. And if he causes any trouble, he's out. Understood?"

"Sure thing Boss."

I breathed a sigh of relief. Rambo found a low stump to sit on and called Chester over. He trotted across and sat by his side. After some more fuss from Rambo, he lay down at his feet. Rambo was beaming. I'd never seen him smile properly before. His eyes disappeared behind a web of creases. To be honest, I felt a little jealous of Rambo as Chester had clearly taken to him. However, I doubt that Boss would have let Chester stay without Rambo's intervention and at the end of the day, he was best placed to find food for him.

When the others returned to camp, laden with tap water in large plastic containers, Chester put on a similar display. However, the moment he saw Josh he stopped growling and rushed over to greet him. Josh laughed with surprise and slapped his knees.

"Come on boy!"

Chester knocked him clean off his feet and then pinned him down to lick his face. The others looked on, stunned. After he had finished greeting Josh, Chester walked over, tentatively sniffing at the men. Matt pulled his hands away as if Chester might bite, clearly not comfortable around dogs. *Why aren't I surprised?* Chester viewed him suspiciously and returned to sit at Rambo's feet.

"Got to share our food with that now, have we?" Matt said.

"Already discussed," Boss said calmly. "Rambo's responsibility."

Nothing more was said.

Josh had been really pleased to see Chester, but when that moment passed I caught his eye and he looked troubled. I called over to him.

"Josh, can you help Babs and me for a while, please? Babs has hurt her finger. We need to make up these rolls for lunch and then we need a hand to get this lamb on the barbecue."

"Sure. Happy to," Josh said, walking over to the kitchen. He was looking at me every step of the way and I could see that there was something up. Behind him, Al took Boss to one side for a chat. The others wandered off, glancing over at Josh, then glancing away. Something must have happened on the foraging trip.

I started on the rolls while Josh took some instruction from Babs to prepare the lamb for roasting. As soon as it was in the barbecue with the pipe immersed in the bucket, I picked up the vegetables for the evening meal and asked Josh to help me wash them in the stream. He started telling me what had happened the moment we got there.

"We came across an old man while we were out who needed help, but Al sent him on his way."

"What?! Why?"

I couldn't believe it.

"Al said that he was basically another mouth to feed with nothing to contribute. I tried to argue and he got really funny with me. That poor old man was cold, hungry and desperate. Al just pointed at the hills and told him that he'd find help up there."

"Well, it's all beginning to fall into place for me," I said. "When they came across us they decided we were useful. They've got me cooking and cleaning up after everyone and you bringing in supplies. We might be getting fed but we're basically slaves. All this rubbish about Robin Hood and his merry men. Do you know what I found this morning?"

"What?"

"Boss has a box in his tent that's full of gold jewellery, watches and cash. Either he's stealing it or someone else is and they're sharing the bounty. Have you seen anything suspicious while you've been out with them?"

"Wow! Well no, I don't think so." Josh furrowed his brow. "Except, I thought I saw something in

Jerry's hand when we were at the pub yesterday. He went inside while the rest of us were in the beer garden, getting the barbecue. As he came out of the pub, I think I saw him pushing something shiny into his pocket. I didn't think any more of it."

"I bet they've been helping themselves all along."

"Now we're going to have to find out what Boss has got in the forest."

"I've been thinking about that," I said. "We need to do it when one of us is on lookout duty and the camp is empty."

"I bet I get put on lookout tomorrow," Josh said, "or digging the veg patch maybe. I'm not sure Al trusts me out on a supply run anymore."

"OK. Let's see who gets what. If you get given the veg patch, I'll volunteer for lookout duty."

We finished washing the vegetables and returned to camp. Boss immediately summoned Josh to the day tent. He asked me to go in as well.

"Right," he said, "Al told me what happened today with the old guy and I'm betting Josh already told you, Maddie?"

I nodded.

"This community is finely balanced. We have a lot of people to look after and a lot of mouths to feed. We can't afford to take in people that can't pull their weight. Now from what Al told me, that guy was pretty frail and I doubt he would have been able to contribute anything at all. Now I know it sounds mean and it's not what we normally do in society, but this is survival of the fittest. Understood?"

We both nodded. There was no point trying to argue with Boss.

"Now I don't want anyone bearing a grudge. Not you, not Al. So any further discussion about it ends here. OK?"

We nodded again and Boss walked out. I looked at Josh and mouthed the words, "I don't want to be here anymore." Josh mouthed back, "Me neither." He took my hand and we walked out of the tent.

Meal time was a little subdued, which was a shame, considering that we had roast lamb. Babs had even managed to roast some potatoes and cook carrots and tinned peas on the side. The events of the day had clearly been circulated amongst the community and everyone was behaving a little awkwardly around us. The saving grace was Chester, who put on his best behaviour in the hope of getting some scraps and got the focus of everyone's attention. He sat silently, watching every mouthful of food that got consumed. Everyone parted with a little bit except for Matt, who said he was a cat person and didn't like dogs. *Well, Chester doesn't like you either!*

Boss barely covered status. Everyone had heard about the patrol and it didn't need to be brought up again. So he moved swiftly on to talk about supplies, focusing on input from Matt and Babs. When it came to jobs for the following day, Boss wanted two foraging parties. One was tasked with bringing back soil from an allotment, plus any seeds that might be found in the sheds. The other was tasked with reaching a village on the north side of the forest that he considered might be fruitful. As Josh had already guessed, he was not in either party but was tasked with helping Mikolaj at the vegetable plot. I volunteered for lookout duty and much to my surprise, I got it.

Soon afterwards, Josh told everyone that he was having an early night as he wasn't feeling too good. I went with him. If they did a wishes list, we missed out.

Back in the tent, I asked him if he was really OK. He whispered quietly.

"Didn't want to spend a moment longer in there. Did you see the way Jerry was looking at me?"

"I thought maybe you were starting an excuse to get out of work so we can find out what Boss has in the forest."

"What's the point if we are going to leave anyway? Do you really care?"

"Hmm, no I guess not."

"Best not talk about it anymore tonight in case someone overhears."

Josh hugged me, whispering even more quietly, "I'll get us out of here, I promise."

Chapter 16: The search party

As soon as it was light, Josh made a lot of noise getting up and rushing across camp to the toilet. He came back noisily too, causing Chester to growl and Rambo to stir and settle him. Twenty minutes later, Josh repeated his trip. When he came back this time, both Rambo and Jerry had emerged from their tent.

"Sorry guys, didn't mean to wake you. I'm a bit delicate this morning."

Back in the tent I caught his eye and mouthed, "are you OK?" He grinned back at me, raising a thumb.

I made apologies for Josh at breakfast, saying that he wasn't too good. Babs was worried that it was something to do with her cooking but everyone else was fine. I told her it was probably the mini pork pie that he had taken from someone's fridge when he was out foraging. I told Mikolaj that Josh would join him as soon as he felt a bit better.

The foraging parties set off and I climbed up to the lookout post with my blanket, binoculars, and flask of hot tea. Down below Mikolaj was collecting his tools for the vegetable plot and Chester followed Rambo out to the trail, his tail wagging furiously. Babs was busy clearing up after breakfast and as far as I knew, Boss hadn't even emerged from his tent. Having a lie in maybe.

I wasn't sure what Josh was planning to do. Last night he didn't seem too interested in discovering what Boss might have stashed in the forest, so perhaps he was hoping we would get a chance to discuss an escape plan. Or maybe he was planning that we would escape today? The idea panicked me a little. I wanted to go, but we needed to figure out what to take and how to leave without anyone seeing us.

Twenty minutes or so passed by. Then, down in camp, I watched Babs head down the path that led to the stream, clutching a bag of laundry and some soap powder. That washing was going to keep her busy for a while. A few minutes later, Mikolaj reappeared for some reason but I had no idea why. Then, he came back into view followed by Boss and they headed back down towards the stream and vegetable plot. The camp was empty, which was a perfect opportunity for Josh and me to have a quick chat or for Josh to take a look down the escape path. I craned my neck, trying to see if he might emerge from our tent, but it was hidden beneath the tarpaulin. For a moment I wondered whether to come down from the lookout post and find him. Suddenly he appeared, waving up to me. He pointed to the escape path and gave me the thumbs up, then immediately set off. I swivelled around slightly, to get a better view, then trained my binoculars on him. My heart started to beat a little faster. We should have had a plan. What if Boss reappeared and I needed to warn Josh. How could I do it without drawing attention to myself? I retrained my binoculars on the path to the stream, watching for Boss. The minutes ticked by slowly. I glanced over to the escape path now and again. Josh was taking his time. Maybe he couldn't find anything. By now, my heart was racing. Then, my worst fear was realised; Boss came into view, back from the stream. *Damn!* I looked back to the escape path and to my horror, I could see Josh coming back towards the camp. I thought about throwing something in that direction, but that might make Boss look towards him. Instead, I leaned back, hoping to get out of Boss's view and started waving my arms around frantically. Josh was still moving towards the camp. *Look up! Look up!* It was almost too late. I had to do something. So I dropped my flask, which hit about ten branches on its way to the forest floor. Boss stopped dead in his tracks and looked over, then advanced into the camp where he could see me and looked up. I held both hands up in surrender and mouthed, "Sorry". He shook his head with disappointment. It worked though; with relief, I could see Josh backing away up the escape path. However, my relief was short-lived. I realised that Josh now needed to get back into camp before he was missed. *Oh God!*

I waited another nail-biting ten minutes, perched in the tree, praying that Boss would leave camp again. However, Josh walked back into camp from the path to the toilet and I breathed a sigh of relief. He must have worked his way there through the forest. He slowly walked across the open space rubbing his stomach, as if he was still suffering a little. He stopped midway, partly obscured by a tarpaulin. Then I saw a pair of feet, Boss's feet, in front of him. They must be talking, although I couldn't hear what they were saying. I swivelled back around and resumed my lookout duty. The rest of the morning passed slowly.

By lunchtime, the dark sky had cleared, leaving patchy white clouds. Al and Lester were returning from their trip to the allotment, each carrying something long and heavy over their shoulder. As they got closer I realised that they were grow bags, the kind that gets used in greenhouses for tomatoes or cucumbers. Weaving their way back through the trees was quite comical. Lester was in front and as he pushed branches aside they flipped back, slapping Al. I could hear Lester muttering 'oops' and giggling but not really making any attempt to avoid doing it. When they made it into the camp, they dropped the grow bags by the entrance to the stream and found a couple of logs to sit on. Al looked irritated.

To my annoyance, I got relieved from lookout duty by Josh. Now he was going to be spending the afternoon up the tree and we would have little time to talk. However, as I reached the forest floor he hugged me, holding me close. We held a rapidly whispered conversation into each other's ear.

"You had me really worried there. I thought he was going to catch you."

"You and me both! Luckily I found a route around to the loo. Got away with it!"

"So what did you find back there?"

"He's got a stash of weapons: shotguns, knives, baseball bats, and some gas canisters."

I gasped, my reaction obscured to anyone watching because my face wasn't visible.

"Wow! Didn't expect that!"

"We'll try and talk more later."

Josh took the blanket and binoculars and started to scale the tree. I looked around and retrieved the flask, which didn't look too bad for all the branches it had hit on its way to the forest floor.

I went to the kitchen where I found Babs. An omelette was waiting for me.

"Thanks, Babs. It gets cold up there. This is just what I need."

"You're welcome, honey. Everyone else has eaten except you, Jerry and Matt. Al and Lester are down by the veg plot, helping Mikolaj."

Just then, Jerry and Matt came rushing back into camp, red-faced and breathing heavily. Boss was immediately on his guard.

"Danger nearby?" he asked, but Jerry shook his head. Boss beckoned them to join him in the tent. Babs and I looked at one another, slightly alarmed. I ate my omelette and Babs busied herself, clearing the kitchen surfaces down.

A short while later they emerged and Matt disappeared down the path to the stream. Babs looked at Boss for an explanation.

"Nothing to worry about. They spotted something. I'm going to go out and take a look."

Al arrived back in camp looking concerned. Then he, Jerry and Boss all walked out of camp. On the way, they called Josh down from the tree and took the binoculars.

"Do you mind if I take Josh some tea, Babs?" I asked, waving the flask. "He's still feeling a bit rough."

"No problem. Rambo hasn't come back yet so I'm not sure what he might bring for dinner. I'll give him a little while longer before starting on something."

Happy for the unexpected chance to chat with Josh, I made some tea and hurried to the lookout post. He was surprised and pleased to see me, shifting himself over to a branch so that I could sit on the little seat.

"What's going on?" he asked.

"Not sure. Jerry and Matt have seen something, so Boss wants to take a look. He sent Matt down to work on the veg plot with Lester and Mikolaj. They all looked pretty serious. Anyway, gives us a chance to talk, make some plans maybe?"

"Yes, sure. So, I've been thinking. Best time for us to get away is in the morning when most people are not around. Then we can get as far away as possible before dark. We'll need to find somewhere safe and warm to camp."

"Any idea where to go?"

"I think we head south. It's sort of the right direction from the escape exit and an area that I don't think they've explored much. To be honest, I don't know it as well as the places we've been, but if they come after us, I reckon they'd assume we are going back to where we come from."

"Do you really think they'll come after us?"

"I don't know. No point taking any chances though."

"So I guess we need to pull together some stuff to take with us. Keep it hidden in the tent. Sleeping bag, clothes, a bit of food and drink. What else?"

"Ideally we want those binoculars back. Also, if we leave by the escape route, we'll help ourselves to a couple of knives from Boss's stash. We lost your hunting knife during the chase and it was useful."

"So what's the escape route like? Can you see where it goes?"

"It's heavily wooded! I mean really heavily wooded, and dark. The ground starts to rise, too. I could just catch a glimpse of daylight in the far distance. I'm hoping I'll recognise where we are at some point and then I'll know where to take us next."

"What if they want you to go out with them tomorrow?"

"To be honest, I don't think they will. They don't trust me much after yesterday. Maybe I can carry on making myself unpopular this evening." Josh laughed and I hugged him awkwardly across the gap between us.

"Can't wait to get out of here."

"Me neither."

I climbed down from the lookout post, feeling excited and nervous all at the same time. Maybe tomorrow would be the day we'd escape.

When I got back to the camp, Rambo had returned, carrying four dead chickens. He'd gone to the chicken farm to collect eggs, discovering that a fox had got in and run riot. Lots of chickens had been killed and mutilated by the fox and these four had been wounded in some way. He decided it was kinder to put them out of their misery, but wasteful not to bring them back for us to eat. But it wasn't all bad news because some of the chickens had survived unharmed. Rambo mended the fence, cleared away the carcasses, and threw down some more seed to keep them going. Apparently, Chester had behaved himself very well, despite being faced with all that food, so Rambo cut the breast meat from a few of the mutilated chickens, which Chester then feasted on. Rambo then told us that Chester had done his business right outside the fence, which should deter the fox from having another go. Babs and I giggled about this for quite some time afterwards.

Babs decided that we should roast the chicken on the barbecue, so we plucked them, then removed the breast meat, then separated the legs and wings. She created a BBQ sauce, marinating the meat to tenderise and add flavour. She was such a clever cook and I realised that I had learned more from her in the last few days than I ever had at home. My mum would be proud.

Towards the end of the afternoon, Matt, Lester and Mikolaj returned from the vegetable plot. Mikolaj was looking dejected.

"I tell you my mate that you're wasting your time," Matt said, huffing heavily. "I bet the badgers will be back at it tonight and all our hard work will be wasted."

"Ah," Rambo said, overhearing and looking serious, "I had a feeling that might happen. We're probably better off growing our veg in an allotment somewhere and looking after it there. At least those places are fenced to keep the wildlife out. Got to be careful, of course. Probably got to find the right place and make it not too tidy, so it ain't obvious."

"I spend much time already," Mikolaj said, shaking his head sadly. "Boss very keen."

"I'm sorry Mikolaj," Babs said, "I think this is my fault. I was talking to Boss about how useful a vegetable garden would be for the kitchen. I imagined myself being able to potter around down there and choose vegetables for our meals, without relying on what was brought back from a foraging trip. It was a bit of a pipe dream."

I felt sorry for Mikolaj and for Babs. She must be feeling trapped, just like me. Cooking and cleaning, day in, day out, without ever leaving the camp. I could see that a vegetable plot was appealing; a chance to do something a bit different.

When Boss, Jerry and Al returned from their trip, Josh was called down from the lookout post.

Then, Boss called an extra meeting, ahead of the evening meal. We all filed into the day tent, looking apprehensive.

"OK," Boss said, "what you need to know is that today, we've seen patrols. However, we're not talking about two or three guys with a Jeep, we are talking about a full-on search party.

"There's a long, long line of white suits about five miles north from here, systematically searching. They are moving towards us, in tandem, poking every bush and turning over every stone. We are going to need to monitor them and we are going to need to come up with a plan, in case they decide to search the forest. That's all I am going to say for now. I want every single one of you to think about what we might do ahead of tonight's meeting. I want ideas. I want opinions. OK?"

Boss scanned the room, giving everyone a direct look, one by one. Everyone nodded.

"Dismissed." Boss got up and walked out. Josh and I looked at each other. He raised an eyebrow.

Outside, small groups had gathered to talk in whispers. Al was talking to Lester and Matt. Jerry was talking to Rambo, although Rambo didn't seem to be listening. He looked deep in thought. Mikolaj had wandered over to Babs, looking dejected. His shoulders drooped and he kept rubbing his forehead. Babs made him a cup of tea and he sat down. Boss retired to his tent. Josh and I took the opportunity to head for the stream for a chat.

"Guess it makes no difference to us," I said.

"Hmm. Yes and no. Yes, because when we leave they know we won't be heading north, which is what I thought they'd suspect. No, because they're going to be so distracted by the search party that they probably won't try and find us."

"That's true. It could make escaping easier."

"Listen, we're going to have to go along with this planning session later on though, so we need to come up with some ideas. What shall we say?"

"How about a plan to hide somewhere in the forest? Make the camp look abandoned and find a way to get around and behind the search party. Then move back in when it's all clear."

"That's good thinking! I'm sure they'll have plenty of ideas about where to hide. We can make the rest up as we go along."

"OK, so back to our escape. Are we going to get ready to go and then see whether we can do it tomorrow?"

"Yep. All I have to do is avoid becoming part of the team that watches the search party."

We went back to camp and helped Babs get the dinner finished. Before long, we were all in the day tent again with meals perched on our knees. Everyone tucked into the BBQ chicken but there was tension in the air and no compliments were forthcoming. The discussion started as soon as the plates were cleared away.

"So as I told you all earlier, the search party is headed in our direction and we have to come up with a plan. The two options that jump out at me are flight or fight."

"Fight?" Josh asked, a look of astonishment on his face. "Are you kidding? Don't these people have guns?"

Boss snapped back at him.

"I'm looking for suggestions, Josh, not criticism. If you've got nothing positive to contribute, I suggest you shut up."

An awkward silence filled the tent.

"Well," I said, trying to placate Boss, "we could make the camp look abandoned, hide out somewhere and then work our way around the search party. Get behind them and move back in here afterwards?"

"You see Josh. That's the sort of thing I'm after! Positive thinking. Well done Maddie. So for me, this option fits with flight. We're not exactly running away, but we're avoiding any kind of standoff."

"Do you think we could mount some sort of decoy?" Lester asked. "Lead them away from us somehow, so they don't come near the forest."

"I guess that's a possibility, Lester. It could be something we try first. To me, their search looks to be very systematic. So a decoy might just be a temporary measure that buys us some time. They might still retrace their steps and carry on where they left off."

I could see several heads nodding. Lester's idea seemed a sensible option.

"So how would we achieve this decoy?"

Silence.

"Could we leave a false trail?" Al said. "Something that forces the search east or west. We could leave something that makes it look like it was dropped by accident. A rucksack with some food in it? Something like that?"

"Hmm. That might work if it was fresh food, something that couldn't have been dropped before the wave hit. Getting it close to the search party might be risky though. OK, so let's work on that as plan A. Al, you and Lester can put your heads together later and come up with something more concrete.

"So Rambo. You know this forest better than anyone. If we hid like Maddie suggests, do you have any idea where?"

"There's a few places we could lay low but I think we'd have to keep on the move. I don't see how we could hide and let a search party sweep right past us, especially if they use dogs."

"We didn't see any dogs today, but we can't rule that out. We know they used them to track Josh and Maddie. OK, Rambo, what we need is a map of the forest. Where we are, which routes we might use to move around, and how we'd get behind the search party."

Rambo nodded. Boss continued.

"OK. Raise your hand if you know how to use a gun."

Boss, Jerry, Rambo and Matt raised their hands.

"Jerry's done clay pigeon shooting, that I know. What's your experience, Rambo?"

"I done some hunting in the past. Birds and rabbits, that kind of thing. So I can handle a shotgun."

"How about you Matt?"

"Guns, rifles and shotguns. I was in the Explorers in my teens. We did a lot of target shooting. Even went on some big camp a couple of times; some national rifle shooting event. Scout groups used to come from all over the country. Never got to use live rounds though. Shame."

Matt smiled to himself, deep in thought. *Thank God no one ever gave him real bullets!*

"Excellent," Boss said confidently. "Tomorrow I want you to show the others how to handle a shotgun."

167

"What with?" Lester asked.

"We've got a few Lester, don't worry. I had the foresight to create a small stockpile, should the need arise. Plus, we have plenty of live rounds."

Boss seemed to be very pleased with himself. He was scanning the room with a confident smile on his face. Lester looked surprised. Babs and Mikolaj looked worried. Most of the others seemed to be impressed, happy with the knowledge that the community was armed. *Armed! This was madness.* He was seriously contemplating using guns against armed soldiers. We'd all be killed. It would be a massacre. I resisted the urge to look at Josh. The fact that Boss didn't think it necessary to teach Josh, Babs or me how to use a shotgun was no surprise. After all, to him, we were just kids or women.

"About the decoy plan," Al said, "why don't we use gunshots? We could fire at some distance from the search and get away quickly."

"Even better," Lester said, excitedly, "we could fire two shots from different places that draw them in a particular direction."

Lester and Al looked at each other, nodding and smiling. Boss nodded too.

"Great idea. I also want us to lay some traps," Boss continued, "to make it as difficult as possible for them to come after us. I want pits full of sharp stakes, logs swinging down from trees, and snares. I've got a feeling Rambo is going to be a big help here. Right?"

"Sure Boss." Rambo was straight-faced, giving nothing away. I couldn't read him at all. He might be thinking that this was a great plan or that it was completely bonkers.

Boss gave a short summary.

"So I think we have the bones of a plan coming together. We attempt a decoy to buy us some time. We use that time to build some traps and spread some skills. Then we move and hide, attempting to work our way behind the search party. If they track us, we turn and fight."

Jerry clapped Boss on the back by way of congratulation. He was grinning. Al and Matt too.

"Right, I'm calling another meeting after breakfast tomorrow. I'm going to sleep on this tonight and we'll allocate jobs in the morning." Boss got up and left the tent. Babs went to join him. Josh and I took the opportunity to retire soon afterwards.

Back in our tent, we snuggled up together in our sleeping bags.

"He's completely crazy," Josh whispered. "Sooner we get away the better."

"A morning meeting is annoying though, we don't even know what we're doing yet. What if everyone ends up hanging around the camp all day?"

"I know. Perhaps we can at least pack some bags and hope for a good opportunity."

I lay awake, considering endless possibilities until I drifted off to sleep.

Chapter 17: Battle plans

The next morning the camp was awake early and busy. Josh was already up, somehow managing to leave the tent without waking me. When I finally emerged, a hot cup of tea and porridge was waiting for me.

"You were away with the fairies in there!" Josh said, laughing and squeezing my arm affectionately.

"Took me so long to get to sleep last night," I replied.

"I was just about to wake you. Boss wants us all back in the day tent in fifteen minutes. You'd better eat up."

I quickly ate breakfast and headed first for the toilet and then for the bath to wash my face. The freezing water woke me completely. Shuddering, I returned to the day tent just as the meeting started.

Boss was seated with four shotguns lying across his lap.

"OK, I'll keep this brief as we have a lot to achieve today.

"Matt, when we're finished here I want you to teach Al, Lester and Mikolaj how to handle one of these. No bullets for them right now, but they need to know how to load, how to aim, and how to shoot. OK?"

Matt nodded enthusiastically.

"Rambo, I want you to start your day by creating that map. Babs had a good idea last night. She's got a white bed sheet you can use as a canvas. Matt's got a pen but I'm sure you can improvise with something else if you need to."

Babs handed Rambo a folded sheet.

"When you've finished that you'd better check the traps as usual so that Babs and Maddie have enough time to get some food sorted for tonight.

"Josh, you're on lookout.

"Jerry and I are going to take a look at the search party to see where they've got to. We'll be back by lunchtime. OK?"

A mumble of agreement went around the room. I realised that Josh and I were not going to get away this morning. A look at the expression on his face told me that he thought so too. There were simply too many people around camp. Josh gave me a peck on the cheek and trudged off to the lookout post. I gathered up the breakfast bowls and mugs, resigned to my first washing-up chore of the day.

When I got back from the stream, Rambo had gone off to make his map and then to check on the traps with Chester. Babs had set about making some dough for rolls at lunchtime. She tore the ball in two and handed half to me. Then we stood side by side, kneading our sections, entertained by Matt as an instructor.

Matt had got Al, Lester and Mikolaj to sit side by side on a log while he showed them a shotgun. He was acting like a primary school teacher, slowly pointing to different parts of the gun and explaining what they were for. Now, I've never shot a gun in my life, but I do know the dangerous end from the end you hold, as I expect most people do. His students were doing their best to pay attention, although I spotted Lester pulling a stupid face at Mikolaj when Matt's back was

171

turned. That made Mikolaj giggle and Matt spun around, glaring at him. Next, he handed them each a shotgun and demonstrated how to open the chamber. Al and Lester got it straight away, but Mikolaj was fumbling around, cursing in Polish under his breath. Finally, he managed to get it open, whereupon Matt pointed to each chamber, slowly explaining how to load a cartridge and which way round it should go. Boss had let him have just one cartridge for the demo. He put the cartridge in the chamber and showed them how to close it and load the shotgun. Al and Lester were clearly getting bored.

Matt then stood with his back to his students, left leg slightly ahead of his right and brought the shotgun to his shoulder. He peered through the sight at an invisible target in the forest. All the time he was explaining exactly what he was doing. Now they had to try. Al and Lester mirrored him perfectly, but again, Mikolaj got into a mess. It turned out he was left-handed, so wanted to use his left hand on the trigger, which meant his feet were in the wrong place.

"You'll have to stand the other way, with your right foot ahead of your left," Matt said with a slightly sarcastic edge.

"I no good at this Matt. I never use gun before. I think maybe I better off with bat or something."

"You won't be thinking that when some soldier has a rifle pointed at your head!"

Matt had his back to Lester and Al while trying to manhandle Mikolaj into position. Lester jokingly raised his shotgun to the back of Matt's head and mouthed, "Bang," but quickly dropped it to his side again when Matt spun round to face him. Matt was turning purple with rage. He knew something was going on, but was too slow to find out exactly what. Lester appeared to be holding his breath, trying not to burst out laughing. Babs and I glanced at one another, both smiling and trying not to giggle.

"Final part of the lesson," Matt said gruffly.

He stood facing the forest again.

"Look through the sight, make sure your target is lined up in the crosshairs. Then slide off the safety catch here. Squeeze the trigger gently to fire."

Matt suddenly swung the shotgun round, pointing it directly at Lester's head.

"One more funny joke Lester and your brain will be decorating the camp."

Silence. I think everyone took a sharp intake of breath and the smile on Lester's face was replaced by fear and surprise.

"Jesus Matt," Al shouted. "Put that thing down. Now!"

Matt hesitated a few seconds before lowering the gun, a smile forming. He looked Lester in the eyes.

"Just kidding mate. Trust me!"

Mikolaj looked like he might collapse, while Lester and Al were fuming. Matt simply turned and walked off. *What an idiot!*

Babs made some tea to lighten everyone's mood and opened a packet of rich tea biscuits. Mikolaj's despair was instantly replaced with a smile.

"Cheers my mate!"

I managed to slip away to our tent, telling Babs that my feet were cold and I wanted to put on another pair of socks. Once inside I grabbed our rucksacks, folded some clean clothes and pushed them to the very bottom. I folded the sacks and placed them in the openings of our sleeping bags underneath our cushions. There was enough room remaining in each sack for our sleeping bags. I made a mental note of the other things we would need: binoculars, some water, and maybe a little food. We'd have to find a house to break into somewhere for supplies. To escape, we needed to travel light.

It was lunchtime when Jerry and Boss returned. After eating the freshly baked rolls, Boss gave out new orders. Matt was sent to the lookout post to relieve Josh, which I believe was a punishment after he had heard about his behaviour that morning.

"Mikolaj, Lester and Josh. I want you to find some strong straight branches that we can use as stakes. Bring them back into camp."

He then asked Jerry, Al and Rambo to join him in the day tent. Rambo rolled up his map and carried it in. Chester followed.

Babs and I were left with two small rabbits to cook. We were uninspired. All the planning and uncertainty were a distraction. In the end, we cooked a stew with tomatoes and lentils, then made some flatbreads. We saved some rabbit offcuts for Chester.

At meal time, everyone collected their portion of stew and ate quietly, deep in thought.

Afterwards, the bowls were cleared away and the tree stump seating was rearranged in a wide circle. Babs helped Rambo spread a large white sheet in the centre, on which he had drawn a map.

"Move the corner in your left hand a bit more towards Lester. Stop, that's enough. Now we got it properly lined up."

At the edge of the map, Rambo had drawn a compass. He indicated that north on the map was now true north and took us through the main elements.

"So this outline in green is the forest and this here is us, in our camp. We got our entrance here, the paths to the toilet and stream here, and the escape path. You can see the course of the stream through the forest, and I also marked up some of the main paths. Outside the forest you can see the villages in the area, and this over here is the old railway track that almost clips the corner of the forest. Maddie and Josh, this must have been where you came in."

"Yep, that's it," Josh said, nodding. Rambo continued.

"To the north here we have the river, which runs more or less parallel to the track for some distance. Far to the south is the big hill that overlooks the city and the sea. Now, the search party is currently here."

Rambo reached down with a stick and placed it northeast of the forest to represent the long line of the search party. He looked up at Boss for confirmation, who simply nodded and then took over the briefing. He had a long thin stick in his hand, which he used as a pointer.

"At their current course and pace, we reckon they'll reach the edge of the forest in two to three days. So tomorrow we need to use the decoy. We'll fire two shots, one person from this position here and another about two minutes later from here. Then both people need to head for cover and meet up here.

"I've decided to send Al and Matt for the decoy. Al and Lester might have been the best option for speed, but I want at least one person experienced with firearms. Matt, you'll fire the first shot. Lester, I want you and Jerry to monitor the movements of the search party. We need to know whether they react to the decoy. Rambo and Mikolaj will start building the traps, which we'll talk about a bit more now.

"Earlier today, we discussed the types of trap we might easily set up to slow down the search party. We'll dig two pits, one along the path that enters the camp and one along our escape path."

Boss used a stick to point to the position of each pit. Josh raised his hand and Boss nodded for him to speak.

"I was just thinking that if we set a trap along the escape path, they might assume that's where we went and follow. However, if we just hide the escape path and put the pit somewhere else, maybe we can head them off in the wrong direction."

Boss paused, thinking.

"He's right, Boss," Rambo said. "We might keep them off our tail for a bit longer."

Boss didn't look like he wanted to admit that Josh's suggestion was better, but finally, he nodded and moved on.

"So let's say we dig the second pit on the path to the toilet.

"I also want us to rig up a couple of log traps that swing down from the trees when they're triggered. Imagine a log with a long rope tied at each end. We hoist up the log until it's about chest height, creating a pendulum. Then we pull one end of the log up and tie it. The trigger is a trip wire at ground level. The log is released and 'woosh', whoever is standing in the path will get knocked for six. Rambo knows how to set the trip wire and how to use the right knots to release the log. We'll position one log here at the entrance to the camp and one here on the path to the stream."

Again, Boss pointed to the position of each log trap.

"We're also going to set snares all around the camp. They'll be like the snares that Rambo uses to catch rabbits, but when these are triggered they'll close and hoist the victim up in the air. You see, the branches of the fir trees in this part of the forest are perfect. They're strong and they're flexible. For each snare, we'll pull one strong branch down and keep it under tension. The snare gets attached and when it's triggered the branch is released."

Boss looked around the tent, head held high. He was clearly very proud of his plan of defence. It all sounded a bit brutal and unnecessary to me. If they left the camp in plenty of time, there was no need for carnage.

"OK, Rambo is now going to take us through the route he's planned for hiding out and getting behind the search line. Go ahead, Rambo."

Rambo cleared his throat, seemingly a little embarrassed about the attention he was receiving.

"When the time's right, we'll set off down the escape path and make our way east as quickly as possible. Over on this side of the forest," he said, pointing to the map, "there is a forestry commission hut, which is well hidden. It's gonna be quite cosy, but I reckon it's the best place for hiding out overnight. When we can, we'll set off again, moving north. We'll keep to the edge of the forest out of sight until we get to this point here, then we'll be able to head west again to get back behind the search. We'll have to send small scouting parties to keep an eye on where they are and figure out when is the best time to move."

Rambo indicated that he had finished and sat back down.

"Thanks, Rambo. Any questions from anyone?"

"What will we do with the tents and the supplies that we've collected?" Matt asked. "If we leave them behind, they might destroy everything."

Boss answered.

"We'll take the tents down and hide everything as best we can. It's a risk, but we can't carry it all with us. We'll need only food, water, bedding, and weapons. Talking of food, Babs, I'd like you to come up with some ideas about what we can easily eat. Something that can be made and transported at relatively short notice.

"Now let's have a few drinks to toast this plan. It's been a long day and I think we all deserve it."

Matt and Jerry went off to find some drinks. Josh looked up at Boss.

"Do you want me on lookout duty tomorrow morning?" he asked.

"Yes Josh, just for the morning."

"OK, Boss."

Josh caught my eye. He was thinking what I was thinking; tomorrow might be the day to escape. Four out of the camp, two building traps. Boss was bound to get involved in that too at some point. That left us a chance, surely.

We had a couple of drinks out of politeness and tried to look as calm as possible. Then we said goodnight and got ready for bed.

"Maddie," Josh whispered when we were tucked up in our sleeping bags, "that map of Rambo's really helped me understand where we are. I know where we have to go."

In the darkness, I could just make out his face. He was grinning from ear to ear.

"Tomorrow," I said. "It has to be tomorrow."

Chapter 18: Escape

I woke up feeling excited and nervous before I could remember why. Josh was already awake, gazing at the ceiling of the tent. He turned his face towards me.

"Are you sure about this?" he whispered.

"Of course I am!" I replied, panicking slightly. "You're not having second thoughts are you?"

"No, not at all. But I don't want to put you in any danger. We don't know what we'll find out there."

"I don't care. Anywhere is better than here. As long as you're with me."

He pushed a few wisps of hair from my face.

"I'm not going anywhere without you."

"Nor me without you. It has to be today. I don't think I can bear it much longer and we can't get caught up in this ridiculous plan of theirs."

"I was thinking the same. If their decoy plan doesn't work, they might keep everyone here to make traps and start packing up. Then we'll never get away."

"I'll look for a chance to get away this morning. If it looks like we can go, shall I just wave up at you?"

"Yes. I'll have a clear view of the paths to the camp. If I wave back with my left hand, we're safe to go and I'll climb down. If I wave with my right, it means someone is coming back and we need to wait. If they see anything, we can pretend we were just saying hello."

I took a deep breath, trying to calm my nerves.

"OK. I guess it's time we got up then. I'll roll up our sleeping bags after breakfast so that we're ready."

Babs was already cooking poached eggs for Matt and Al, who had a tiring day ahead of them. They had a lot of ground to cover to get into position and needed to move quickly once they had fired the decoy shots. Mugs of tea were also being poured, so I got a pot of porridge going for everyone else.

After breakfast, Jerry grabbed the binoculars and left the camp with Lester to find and watch the search party. That was annoying because they were my binoculars and I wanted to take them with us. However, there was nothing I could do about it. *Two people gone!*

Josh followed them out of the camp to take up lookout duty.

Next, Al and Matt prepared to leave, each with a shotgun slung over their shoulder. Al was given a small box of cartridges, with instructions from Boss to use only two. The others were for emergency use, should they find themselves cornered. *Four people gone!*

Rambo and Mikolaj headed off down the path towards the stream, followed by Chester. They were going to be busy making traps, starting with the log trap at the end of the pathway to the stream. Mikolaj suggested they reuse the logs that he'd salvaged for the vegetable plot, which were close by. *Six people gone, two to go!*

The only people left in the camp were Boss and Babs, who were chatting over a second cup of tea. I was trying to think of a plan that would get rid of Boss for a while. However, I couldn't just stand around, so I grabbed the bucket of breakfast dishes and went down to the stream to wash them. Some ideas started to form. When I returned to camp, Boss and Babs were still in the kitchen area. She was talking to him about her ideas for a meal plan; which food could be easily transported to provide everyone with a decent meal or two while they were in hiding. As I placed the clean dishes on the side, I grumbled about cold hands and said I was off to find my gloves. That gave me the chance to roll up our sleeping bags and stuff them into the rucksacks. Afterwards, I went back to the kitchen and asked if I could make another cup of tea to warm through.

"Help yourself, honey," Babs said kindly. "Just be careful not to heat your hands up too quickly or you'll get chilblains. They're painful," she added, seeing the expression on my face. I had no idea what they were.

"Sounds like fun down at the stream," I said, trying to sound amused. "I could hear Rambo whispering nonstop. Sounds like something is getting lost in translation. Poor Mikolaj."

I smiled innocently at Babs and Boss.

"I better get going," Boss said. "Sounds like Rambo needs some help. I'm just going to grab the rope."

He walked over to Matt's supply store and grabbed a coil of rope.

"See you at lunchtime," he called, heading down the path to the stream.

"I guess we better think about lunch," Babs said. "What can we rustle up today?"

My thoughts were elsewhere. What we might have for lunch was irrelevant as I didn't expect to be here. However, I had to stay calm, go with the flow and wait for an opportunity.

"Oh," I replied, blurting out the first thing that came into my head, "we could make scrambled eggs?"

"I used the last ones this morning."

"Oh yes, sorry I forgot. Erm. How about soup or something."

"I suppose we could, yes, if we used tinned vegetables to speed things up. What could we put with it, to fill everyone up?"

I really didn't want to have to think about this. Normally she just came up with the ideas and I helped out. Picking today of all days to get me figuring things out was frustrating.

"I don't know," I said sharply, regretting it immediately.

"Maddie, are you OK?"

She looked at me intensely, concerned.

"Oh, I'm fine," I said, trying to think how to put things right, "just didn't sleep too well last night. Probably all this talk about guns and traps and hiding. Guess I'm just a bit on edge."

She continued to look at me intensely, which made me feel uncomfortable and nervy. I smiled and looked away.

"It's more than that, isn't it?" she said, suddenly raising her eyebrows in surprise. "You're going, aren't you? You and Josh?"

She lowered her head and shook it slowly, deep in thought.

"The way you've both been behaving these last couple of days. The watching, the whispering."

She looked up at me again. The look on my face must have said it all.

"I'm sorry Babs. We have to. We don't belong here. Please don't say anything, please don't!"

I started to sob uncontrollably. Babs put her arms around me and gave me a big hug.

"It's OK," she whispered. "I know you've not been happy. Josh too. Boss can sound mean at times but he's really trying to protect you. Both of you."

"By planning a war with the soldiers?" I gasped, between sobs. "Before we came here, Josh and I - well, we were doing OK. We'll be OK again, honest. I just can't be here."

Babs started crying too and hugged me even tighter.

"I want you to be safe," she said.

"Then let us go!"

She released me but held me at arm's length, staring into my eyes. Both of us had tears running down our faces.

"Go" she said suddenly, "before I change my mind. I won't say anything."

I looked at her, surprised and unsure, but she meant it. I could see it in her eyes. I walked out from under the tarpaulins, glancing up at the lookout post. Josh saw me immediately. I waved. Then I waited for what seemed like eternity as Josh scanned the forest in every direction. My heart was in my mouth. *Left hand or right hand?* Josh raised his left hand and waved back, then quickly descended the tree.

I rushed back to Babs. She was still standing in the same spot, hand over her mouth, tears rolling down her cheeks. I hugged her quickly, then ran to our tent, pulling out our rucksacks.

As I came back out I saw Josh rush into the camp and then stop dead, staring at Babs in horror. Then he saw me. I was nodding furiously. *It's OK, it's OK!* Suddenly, the expression on Josh's face changed; he relaxed. He smiled, walked up to Babs and gave her a huge hug. She whispered something in his ear, which seemed to surprise him, and then they parted. I ran to her once more and kissed her lightly on the cheek.

"Thank you, Babs. Thank you for everything. Please stay safe."

She touched my cheek but didn't answer me. I could see pain and guilt in her eyes, but hope too. Josh grabbed my hand.

"Now Maddie, now."

We ran to the escape exit, Josh ahead of me. Just as I entered, I turned briefly to look at Babs. She was smiling sadly, but she waved. I waved back, then moved on.

Keeping up with Josh was awkward. The pathway weaved tightly between the trees and I got slapped by a returning branch more than once. Suddenly he stopped, moved to one side and bent over. When I caught up with him, he had uncovered Boss's stockpile of weapons. He reached in and picked up two knives with long serrated blades. He handed one to me and quickly put the other in his rucksack, grinning.

"Think we'll have one of these too," he said, picking up a yellow canister and stuffing it into his rucksack. "Might come in handy. Come on, let's go."

We moved as quickly as possible, Josh leading and me following. The forest was dense, just as Josh had described. We twisted and turned through the trees, clambering over mounds, ducking under overhanging branches, and gaining height gradually. After five minutes or so we slowed. I couldn't take much more at this pace. I stopped, raising my hand in defeat. Bending over, with my hands on my knees I gasped.

"I'm out of shape, sorry."

"If you think this is steep, wait until you see the big hill," Josh said, winking. "Come on."

PART THREE

Chapter 19: The hill

The forest that lay behind the escape path was really tough going. The trees were densely packed and it was very, very dark. As we moved, I got whipped by the branches of the fir trees and scratched by their sharp pine needles. The ground also rose with each step and we kept sliding backwards as we tried to get a foothold on the thick bed of dry pine needles. The air was musty and I was gasping for breath when we finally approached the ridge. Thankfully, the darkness of the forest started to recede and dappled light filtered through from above. The trees here were further apart and soon, small gaps in the canopy revealed the blue sky overhead. We kept moving, keen to put as much distance between us and the community as possible. Luckily the ground started to drop away on a gentle slope, making the going much easier. Slowly, I managed to get my breathing back under control and the knot in my stomach started to ease. I smiled to myself, noting how easily we adopted our old pattern of movement; Josh pausing as lookout while I moved ahead, then me pausing as lookout while he caught up. Before long, a brick wall came into view on our left. I pointed and Josh nodded confidently.

"There'll be a road on the other side," he whispered. "We'll follow the wall but keep some distance, just in case there's a patrol."

We must have been approaching the edge of the forest because the trees were thinning out and in some places, the conifers were replaced by deciduous trees such as horse chestnut and silver birch. Holly bushes and rhododendron bushes also sprang up here and there. The woods were starting to resemble those around my first camp. I was surprised to see that the leaves had now come out on the big trees. How long had I been stuck in the forest? Over the wall, I could see a line of detached houses bordering the other side of the road. We needed to get some food, but it was too soon to stop and explore. Eventually, the road reached a T-junction onto a bigger, more major road.

"Where now?" I asked.

"Straight over," Josh replied, pointing, "into the woods on the other side."

We cautiously peered over the wall, looking left and right. The road was very straight and there was nothing to be seen. Josh cupped his hands together to give me a leg up over the wall. I stepped on and he heaved upwards. As I straddled the top, he jumped up beside me and slid over, descending to the grass verge. Then he helped me down and we quickly ran across the road to the woods on the other side. My heart was hammering. I'd forgotten quite how nerve-racking it was to be exposed in the open.

"We'll go left here," Josh said. "These woods run more or less all the way to the base of the hill. Then we'll work our way up to the top. We'll probably have to stop and camp out somewhere on the way."

"Is that the hill on Rambo's map?" I asked. "The one that overlooks the sea?"

"Yep, that's the one. It also overlooks the city and dockyard and I want to see what it looks like now. Thousands of people live there. I can't imagine how the patrols would have dealt with them all. Anyway, I know there are houses between here and the top of the hill, so we should be able to find food and shelter. We'll also be a good distance away from the community and that search party."

I tried to imagine what might have happened in the city when the energy wave struck and was curious to see it too.

We turned eastward, sticking to the woods that ran beside the main road. Josh was less sure about this area, but knew the roads and where they led. However, the wooded areas were relatively small and interspersed with fields. We found ourselves turning to the south for some distance to remain undercover before we could turn east again. In some places, we had to use the hedgerows around fields to move from one wooded area to another. That made the journey a lot longer but it felt safer. We wondered whether all the patrols were involved in the search and whether we could take more chances, but it wasn't worth the risk. It was late morning and I was already hungry. I had got used to three square meals in the camp, thanks to Babs. I hoped she was OK.

"What was it Babs said to you when we left?" I asked, remembering the exchange between them. He laughed.

"Well, she said that if I didn't take care of you she'd track me down, even if she had to do it from beyond the grave. You mean a lot to her, you know."

"Poor Babs, I really like her. God knows what she sees in Boss though. He's such a bully."

"I think she made a choice to keep herself safe. You know, a woman on her own like that."

"Makes me feel so bad about leaving without her."

"I know Maddie, but she wouldn't have come with us."

At that moment we heard the familiar whir of a helicopter. Not one but two, heading rapidly towards us from the south. We were three-quarters of our way across a field, hugging a hedgerow that was no more than five feet high.

"Quick," I shouted, then pointed to a thicket of trees ahead. We ran as fast as possible, bent forward to maintain the cover of the hedgerow. We dived into the cover just as a helicopter came into view. I held my breath, arms wrapped around Josh in the undergrowth, face buried in his chest.

"Did they see us?" I asked, my voice muffled by Josh's sweatshirt.

"No, I don't think so. Relax. They're flying in a straight line over the forest. Hmm. Could be that Matt and Al have fired their decoy shots and they've been sent to investigate."

"I guess the timing is about right," I agreed, "but if they are using helicopters to investigate, it doesn't sound like the decoy plan will divert the search party."

"You may be right. Let's rest up for a while in case there are more to come."

We sat up and looked at one another. We were both covered in sticky weed: stems, leaves, and little seeds. I started to remove them from Josh and he started picking them off me, laughing. I thought about a wildlife documentary I had seen recently; two apes grooming one another. Josh must have read my mind because he made a little monkey noise. I laughed. It was such a relief to be away from the community.

After some time had passed with no further sightings, we set off. The thicket we had rested in was the thinnest section of a new area of woodland that gave us good cover for the next stage of our journey. I began to relax, knowing that with every step we were further from the community and the search party. As we neared the edge of the woods, Josh stopped me and pointed to the south.

"There's the hill Maddie. We'll find somewhere to take cover for the night. I can picture a few properties on different roads over that hill, so I'm sure we'll be able to gather some supplies too."

I looked at the green expanse ahead of me, feeling a little nervous. The occasional copse could be seen, but there were a lot of open fields too. Josh read my thoughts.

"I think we'll have to weave our way up there, using whatever cover we can find."

I nodded.

The next few hours were tense. Time and time again, we were forced to take a few chances covering open ground. Knowing that the helicopters might return at any minute kept us anxious and alert to the smallest of sounds. Eventually, we came across a stream that was lined with trees and followed its course eastward, grateful for the canopy overhead. As we rounded a bend, the hill came into view once more. Josh stopped ahead of me, staring.

"I think I've spotted something familiar," he said. "Look, do you see that church steeple? It's just poking up above those trees."

I followed his gaze, searching and finally focusing on the tip of a brown steeple. He continued.

"There's a few houses there plus a large farm. They've got sheds and barns that we can probably camp in tonight."

"Sounds good."

We followed the stream until the church steeple stood directly south of our position. From there we were able to climb up through woodland, before veering east along a hedgerow to find another copse of trees. The copse took us north again until we were almost level with the church. We then cut east across a field, taking the biggest risk yet with a sparse section of hedgerow. Finally, we found ourselves just below the church. I turned to look back at where we had come from. We had climbed quite a long way up the hill and had far-reaching views of the countryside. The sky was partly cloudy but the sun shone through the gaps, illuminating bright green spaces. Everything looked so new and fresh, such a contrast to the constantly miserable gloom of the forest. Brown and dark green, everything in the forest was either brown or dark green and damp.

"Come on," Josh said, "we need to get to the farm and find some proper cover. Wish we had those binoculars!"

Moving slowly, we approached the farm buildings. We stopped every few steps to survey the area, looking for signs of movement. Other than a few ducks, happily swimming in a pond, there was nothing to see. The first building was an open barn with a large corrugated roof. We had just walked in when we heard the helicopters returning south.

"Phew! Just in time," Josh said, laughing and wiping his brow for effect.

Luck was definitely on our side. We sat down on a bale of straw, waiting until the sound of whirring blades had disappeared over the hill.

The open barn led to a small courtyard at the side of a farmhouse. We crouched, looking for signs of life and signs of an alarm system. We found none. The back door was locked but Josh spotted a small window that had been left slightly open on a window lever above the larger, main window. Using a stick, he pushed the lever up off of the retainer and swung the window outwards. Then he looked across at me.

"Sorry Maddie, think this next job is yours!"

The window looked impossibly small and I was not sure I could get through it. Josh dragged a large bale of straw under the window and helped me onto it. I looked in. Underneath the window was a kitchen sink and draining board. I had no choice but to go head first but at least I didn't have to drop straight to floor level. I removed my rucksack, my coat, and reluctantly my sweatshirt. I shivered. Squeezing myself past the window fixture was going to be painful but it looked pretty rotten. Josh passed me his knife and I dug out the knob that retained the window lever.

First, I got my arms partly through, then one shoulder, then my head turned to one side, and then the other shoulder. Josh climbed up on the bale and lifted my lower half to a horizontal position, gently pushing me forward. When I could reach the sink I was able to support my weight and start wriggling the rest of me through the gap. I got as far as my hips before I panicked. There didn't seem any way that I could pass through. Josh tried tilting me diagonally to see if that might help, but it didn't. Trying to remain calm, I looked around. The larger window below me had a handle and window lever, which I thought I could just reach. First, I released the handle. By straining with my fingertips, I just managed to reach under the lever. I flipped it up, then pushed the window slightly open with my elbow. Josh dragged it wide open from outside. Popping his head through the opening, he looked up at me and grinned.

"Well done! Guess I better try pushing you back out before the next helicopter passes by."

"That's not very funny!"

Josh climbed through the open window and knelt on the draining board. He supported my upper body, helping me to wriggle back through the window. He guided my shoulders and my head until I was finally clear of the opening. When I climbed through the large window to join Josh, he was holding out a much-needed glass of water.

I glanced around at the large farmhouse kitchen. A dark green range cooker stood against the far wall, with a display of old blue and white plates on a shelf above. One row of pine cupboards supported a work surface with more cupboards on the wall above. The centre of the kitchen was occupied by a huge farmhouse table with three chairs on each side and one chair at each end.

We wasted no time looking for supplies. Josh started at one end of the kitchen and I started at the other. We opened cupboard doors, sifted through the contents and placed anything of use on the table. By the time we had finished, we had amassed quite a selection of food and drink, together with some plastic picnic plates, a tin opener, matches, knives, forks and spoons. Our rucksacks were already full of our sleeping bags and spare clothes, so Josh went into the adjoining hallway to see what he could find. I followed cautiously. A cupboard under the stairs revealed several bags from which he selected two large rucksacks. We packed them and retreated through the kitchen's back door into the courtyard.

Behind the farmhouse stood a single-storey flint building with small windows. The door was locked but I remembered seeing a row of keys by the back door. After retrieving all three sets, we tried the keys one by one until we found one that worked. The building was some kind of workshop, with a large workbench and tools hanging from the wall. A ladder leaned against what looked to be a loft space, much like you'd find in a barn. Josh went up the ladder to take a look.

"Perfect," he said. "If you can find a broom I'll give it a sweep. We can sleep up here. There's also a little window, so we can keep watch or escape if necessary."

I found a broom, a dustpan and a brush. I also spotted a pile of large cushions that must belong to garden furniture. When Josh had cleared up, I passed these up to use as a bed.

"It's going to be dark before long, let's get all our stuff up here and figure out what to eat."

I locked the building from the inside and passed up the rucksacks, then went up the ladder to see our bedroom for the night. It was a bit dusty with a few cobwebs but the cushions made a good bed and would keep us off the floor.

We sat opposite each other, grinning from ear to ear. We had certainly landed on our feet. We emptied the borrowed rucksacks to figure out what to eat. We settled for a packet of cheese sandwich biscuits, some plain crackers with peanut butter, and a tin of peaches with evaporated milk. After finishing a large bottle of fizzy orange drink between us, I felt full and content.

While Josh repacked the borrowed rucksacks, I unpacked the ones we had brought with us. Putting the weapons and canister to one side, I dragged out our sleeping bags and laid them on the cushions. The rucksacks now contained only spare clothes and could serve as pillows.

Josh picked up one of the knives he had taken from Boss's pile, turning it over in his hands. It was quite an ornate hunting knife with what could be a bone handle. The blade was immaculate and looked like it had never been used. I picked up the yellow canister.

"So what do you think this is?" I asked.

"Not sure really. Maybe CS gas. I guess you pull out that pin just there and throw it, a bit like a grenade. Might come in useful if we get cornered."

I shrugged. It seemed a bit pointless to carry extra stuff that we might not need but if he wanted to weigh his rucksack down, it was his choice.

"What's the plan for tomorrow then?" I asked, climbing into my sleeping bag.

"I was thinking about that while we were eating. I'm a bit worried about how much cover there is as we go up the hill. It's mainly fields and farmland, so all we'll have is hedgerows. The other thing I've been trying to remember is what's on top of the hill directly above us. There's a road that goes all the way along the top of the hill and there are a few old forts. I must have been driven along there hundreds of times but it's hard to remember which section is right above us."

"Forts? What sort of forts?" I asked.

"Old forts, from a long time ago, before the First World War even. They were built to protect the city and the naval base. One is now a museum. I went there on a school trip years ago. There's another one that has a summer camp in the school holidays and a riding school, I think. My uncle used to tell me stories about them. He was into all the history but not much of it stuck."

"I wonder if we can find some binoculars in the house? Sounds like we might need some."

"Yeah, let's have a good look around in the morning."

Josh climbed into his sleeping bag and cuddled up to me. Compared with sleeping in our tent, this was luxurious. Soft padded cushions beneath us and a proper roof over our heads.

Chapter 20: A shocking view

We both woke early, just as dawn was breaking, to the sound of a cockerel. If he had crowed just once I might have gone back to sleep, but he repeated his call over and over and over again. After several minutes, Josh covered his face with his hands and groaned.

"Fancy cockerel for breakfast?" he said.

"Well if there's a cockerel there might be some chickens and eggs," I replied, thinking that eggs might go down well for breakfast.

"Come on then, let's have a good look around."

Outside it was bitterly cold. The sky was clear and a frost lay on the ground. Although it was going to be a lovely day, right now it felt like Winter. We went back into the house, which was cold and damp.

"Look, that oven has a gas hob," I said, spotting the hob for the first time. "If we can light it, I'll boil some water."

"Good spot. I guess they must use gas cylinders as there's no mains gas around here. My mum used to get them but she got fed up with them running out at the worst possible time. In the end, she got an electric cooker."

I opened a drawer next to the hob, found some matches and lit a ring on the hob.

"Great stuff Maddie! I'll leave you to it and have a hunt around the house."

Before long I had water on the boil with some cups and tea bags at the ready. If we could find some eggs I could use the same pan to cook them.

However, from the kitchen window, I could see no sign of a chicken coup.

Josh came back into the kitchen looking pleased with himself.

"No sign of binoculars so far," he said. "Look what I found though. It's an ordnance survey map of the area. It will help me remember what's up the hill from here."

He spread the map on the kitchen table and we both pored over it. I couldn't make any sense of it at all. It could have been Belgium for all I could tell, but Josh soon honed in.

"Here's where I live. There, that's where your house is. So, do you see the river?"

"Yep."

"OK, so we entered the forest here and we will have left it down here. That means we're up here somewhere."

He paused, searching for a clue.

"Could that be the church," I said, pointing to a cross.

"Yes, well spotted! So we're in one of these little brown squares. Now, if we go straight up the hill following this road we get to the top road here. Hmm, it's quite close to the first fort, where we might get a good view of the city. Further along, there are car parks and picnic benches. We'd get a much better view from there."

"So do you think we need to go further that way then?" I asked, pointing east on the map.

Josh was silent for a moment, deep in thought.

"I think it's too far."

He moved his finger across the top of the hill, reading as he went.

"OK, this first fort here, the one closest to us, is the one that's a museum. See the 'M' on the map?

I have some vague memories of standing on a platform and looking out to sea through a telescope. You know, the sort of telescope that's fixed to a pole in the ground. Trouble is, I don't think there's much cover on the way up there and we've got a lot to carry."

"Well, why don't we leave most of our stuff here and just go up for a look and come back?" I said. "It feels pretty safe here and if the patrols are mainly on the other side of the forest, busy searching, perhaps we can stay another night?"

"Sounds like a plan," Josh said, grinning. "You're too smart. I'll go search for chickens and see if I can find some eggs for breakfast."

As Josh headed out the back door, I stayed, studying the map. I followed the road that ran the length of the hill. I could see four forts altogether. Looking at the area behind the hill I could see the odd copse, but no more woods. We'd have to be really careful. I heard a commotion outside and looked through the kitchen window. Josh was waving his arms at something, then quickly ran for the door.

"Vicious!" he said. "That cockerel has no fear whatsoever!"

"Did you find any eggs?" I asked, laughing.

"I only got two before he spotted me."

I poured some boiling water into our mugs for tea, then popped the eggs into the pan. They sank straight to the bottom.

"They're fresh!" I said, topping up the water and turning on the gas. Once boiling, I counted five minutes and removed them from the heat. Josh found some egg cups and teaspoons and we dined on soft-boiled eggs. Sadly, no bread soldiers to dip in.

We decided to travel light, wearing rucksacks that carried only our knives, the map, a bottle of water, and a packet of biscuits. After locking the house and outbuilding, we set off to find the fort. By zigzagging up the hill we were able to pass through small copses and skirt around arable fields via the hedgerows. The route was high risk, so we moved fast through the open spaces, pausing to catch our breath when we were well hidden. As we neared the top of the hill we found ourselves adjacent to a small lane and Josh spotted a road sign. Checking the map, he confirmed that we were northeast of the fort and would soon approach it if we crossed the field ahead.

We moved cautiously, edging our way along a low hedgerow, bent almost double. Ahead of us, the fort crept into view above a tree line. It looked like a huge grassy mound with the odd patch of brickwork. The barrel of a black cannon could be seen above a wall near the top. The closer we got, the taller it loomed.

"I don't remember it being that big," Josh said, "but I guess I would have been inside, looking out. Hope we can find a way up."

The fort was surrounded by a narrow strip of woods and bushes from which we had a good view. As I studied the fort I realised that there was a gully around it, like a moat. I couldn't see how deep it was but it was a big enough drop to force us to stop. On the other side of the gully, the tall flint and brick walls of the fort looked impenetrable. The grassy mound on top towered over us so that instead of a view of the city, all we could see was the sky.

"Well, we can't get in or see over it, so we better go around it," Josh said.

We slowly started to make our way around to the east side, following the edge of the gulley from the safety of the trees. Eventually, we approached a car park next to the main road, which had a dense stand of trees that gave us cover. We found a good spot with a view out onto the road and surveyed the scene in silence, stunned.

On our side of the road was a barbed wire fence, the sort that you would expect to find around the courtyard of a prison. It must have been well over two metres high with reels of razor wire along the top. On the other side of the road, there was another barbed wire fence of the same construction. We peered east and west. The fences seemed to run the length of the road for as far as we could see. Josh grabbed my arm and pointed. I followed his line of sight, spotting a surveillance camera behind the outer perimeter, pointing directly at us. It swept slowly east and west, keeping watch. We took several steps back into the undergrowth.

"What the hell?" Josh said with alarm. "We're trapped. What's going on?"

But I was looking beyond the fences, down to what I could see of the city and I pointed.

"Look," I said, faintly. "You can see the city."

Without binoculars, we couldn't see that well, but beyond the barbed wire fences, at the bottom of the hill, the city looked normal. I had imagined burned-out buildings and smoke drifting in the skyline, but no, it was untouched. I could even make out small vehicles moving on the roads. In the harbour, a ferry was moving away from the docks. I was speechless.

"I can't believe it. That's normal life out there Maddie. People waking up, going to school, playing football, watching Netflix. I just don't get it."

"No, me neither," I said. "We've been separated, fenced off. We're being hunted by armed patrols wearing suits to protect them from something. Some sort of contamination?"

"What contamination though? We're fine, aren't we? I mean we're not sick or anything!"

Josh spread his hands in front of him and then turned his palms upwards as if looking for rashes or sores.

"It has to be something to do with that energy wave though," I said. "It can't have reached the city or they wouldn't be driving their cars."

"So they're afraid of something. They've fenced the area off and they're removing everyone from it. Are they really saving people though?"

"They could be. Maybe those evacuation centres are real and they're looking after everyone until it's safe to go back."

"Or maybe they're killing people off," Josh said, sounding nervous. "They're afraid we've all got something that's a threat. You know, better to sacrifice part of the population to save the rest. Maybe that's why they've started a full-on search. They're combing the area to get every last one of us!"

"But surely that couldn't happen in this day and age? There'd be an uproar."

"Yeah, there would be, unless," Josh paused, rubbing his forehead. I finished the sentence for him.

"Unless they told everyone that we'd all been killed anyway."

We looked at one another.

"Exactly. And there can be no witnesses to tell a different story."

I swallowed hard.

"I prefer the version where they've saved everyone and sent them to an evacuation centre," I said, feeling a knot form in my stomach.

"Me too, but do we want to take a chance? I say we try to escape to the city where we can find out what people are being told."

"How on earth are we going to do that?!" My voice was starting to waver.

Josh grabbed my hand and pulled me further back into the trees, putting a finger to his lips. The sound of an engine grew larger. I held my breath, watching and waiting. A black Jeep appeared, driving on the road between the barbed wire fences. It moved slowly, the occupants in no hurry. The windows were down and I could see the barrel of a rifle sticking out, propped casually against the frame. My biggest fear was that the camera had spotted us and that the car was sent to investigate. However, the jeep moved at a steady pace, passing the fort and disappearing towards the east.

"Regular patrol maybe?" I asked.

"Come on," he said gently. "Let's get back to the house and figure out what to do. We're a bit exposed here."

We made our way back around the side of the fort. Josh was silent, deep in thought as we slowly retraced our steps to the farm.

We had a late lunch, enjoying a large tin of tomato soup. I blew on a spoonful to cool it a little, glancing across at Josh. He was motionless, staring at the table with his spoon halfway between his bowl and his mouth.

"What's up?" I asked.

"I've got it," he said slowly. "This is going to sound a bit crazy but I think I know what we should do."

He took a deep breath, placing his spoon back in the soup bowl.

"Remember I told you about my uncle, the one who was into the history of the forts?"

I nodded.

"Well, one of the forts has a deep network of tunnels beneath it. They were created during the war as a top-secret command centre, where the people were safe from bombs. I remember him telling me that there are three long staircases from one of the forts down into the tunnels and three escape exits somewhere below that come out on the hillside. If we can find one of the staircases, we can go under the fences and escape."

I laughed out loud because it really did sound crazy. Josh just looked at me, a serious expression on his face.

"Honestly, it's true. I think we have a way out."

He grinned at me, looking excited.

"Are you sure it's all still there?" I asked, wanting to believe but feeling distinctly dubious.

"Yeah, it's all still there but I don't know how easy it'll be to break in. We have to try though. It's the only idea I have."

We spent the rest of the day planning. Josh studied the map once more and decided that the fort with access to the tunnels was the next one along the hill, travelling west. We decided upon a route, based on the woodland areas shown on the map. For the best cover, we needed to go down the hill, travel east, and then climb back up the hill to the rear of the fort.

We hunted around the outbuilding for some tools that might come in useful if we had to break in. Josh came across a claw hammer and some pliers. I found a couple of screwdrivers. We also found a coil of rope that might come in handy if we had to climb. During the search, we also discovered an old oil lamp. It had a small oil reservoir at the base that fed a rope wick, which was housed inside a glass lantern. The lamp hung from a small wire handle. Although it was fragile, the reservoir was full of oil and we decided to take it with us. The tunnels would be dark and we didn't have access to any working torches. The talk of dark tunnels gave Josh a flash of inspiration and he raced back into the house to retrieve a compass that he had spotted when he found the map. The compass, he explained, would help us find the tunnel exits, which would be to the south. While he was gone, I added a box of matches to the pile. Our sleeping bags would be essential, plus at least two days of food and water.

As we lay in our sleeping bags that evening, Josh was excited and optimistic.

"We can do this Maddie. I know we can do this. We're going to make it to the city and get our lives back."

I wasn't so sure but it felt good to have a plan and something to hope for.

Chapter 21: The fort

We woke even earlier than the cockerel and packed our rucksacks. I wrapped the lamp carefully in my sleeping bag and Josh packed the tools separately. We treated ourselves to a couple of tins of baked beans for breakfast, warmed on the stove. Compared with other places that we'd stayed, the farm was almost civilised. I was going to miss this place.

Locking up carefully behind us, we set off down the hill towards the main road. The map showed a long stretch of woodland, which extended nearly all the way east to the point where we needed to climb back up the hill. The woods were made up of tall fir trees with red-coloured bark. The branches of these trees were quite high off the ground and the trees themselves were evenly spaced. The ground was covered in rust-coloured bracken. Small coils of new growth could be seen emerging here and there. You could see through the woods in every direction, but luckily the trunks were big enough to provide cover. We moved quickly in short bursts, pausing behind tree trunks here and there to catch our breath. We heard and saw nothing of the patrols, which were probably involved in their big search on the other side of the forest. At length, we came to a dairy farm, with cattle grazing in the fields. With no one to milk them, their udders had shrunk, which made them look fitter and more agile than normal. We made a short detour to avoid their field, picking up a tree line by the side of the main road for cover. After following a sweeping bend, Josh beckoned to me to follow him away from the road, where we paused for a drink.

"There's a roundabout just ahead and the last exit goes up over the hill. It's a road my mum uses a lot to visit my aunt. It goes further west than we want, but if we follow it part way up, we can work our way across the fields to find the fort. I reckon we could be there in an hour."

I felt excited but nervous. Reaching the fort was just the first step and we might find it just as impenetrable as the last one. Josh stood up and offered me his hand, dragging me upright.

"It's a steep climb!" he said with a smile.

We walked through a stretch of woodland on a small incline before meeting the road that went over the hill. From here we stayed close to the hedgerow, which was mostly gorse and bramble. In places, the gorse was in bloom with bumble bees visiting the bright yellow flowers. It was so nice to see colour after our stay in the forest. Josh was right about the hill. It was a steep climb and the cold air pierced my lungs, but we stopped at regular intervals to catch our breath. When the road veered west, we crossed over and made our way through a copse that bordered the fields above. As the ground levelled out, Josh grinned at me.

"I think we're nearly there."

We crept through the bushes, eager to get our first sight of the fort. However, the first thing we came face to face with was a mesh fence.

"This must be the perimeter," Josh said. "Do you think we can get over it?"

The fence was as tall as me with a double row of barbed wire at the top.

"Look," I said, "barbed wire. That's not going to make it easy. Do we have any tools that will cut through it?"

"Pliers might work. Let me try."

Josh rummaged in his rucksack, pulled out the pliers and started working on the lower strand of barbed wire. He used both hands and wiggled the pliers back and forth to try and cut through. He paused to check his progress. I could barely see a dent.

While Josh continued working on the wire, I moved along the fence, looking for a possible weak point. My luck was in. A short distance away I found a small split in the mesh next to the bottom of a fence post. The hole wasn't very big but it looked like a small animal track passed through it; big enough for a rabbit but not big enough for us. I knelt and took hold of the broken link in the mesh. Without too much difficulty I was able to work the wire upwards through the loops that held the mesh together to increase the size of the hole. Eventually, I created a gap that I thought we could get through. I went back to get Josh, feeling pleased with myself. His face was red from the effort he was putting in but he still hadn't managed to cut the first wire.

"Problem solved," I said, "follow me!"

Josh looked up, surprised but pleased.

Getting through the gap I'd created wasn't easy but with one of us pulling back on the mesh the other was able to lay flat and squirm through. Once we were both on the other side with our rucksacks, we edged forward towards the fort. From behind a gorse bush, we finally had our first view. After yesterday, I wasn't too surprised at what I saw. In front of us was a massive drop, easily as tall as a house. However, I could see to the bottom and this gully wasn't entirely empty. Trailers and lorry containers were parked here and there. On the other side, the fort reared up on top of a red brick wall, standing much higher than where we were crouching. The car park stretched around the fort as far as I could see.

"Wow, it's even bigger than the last one!" I said. "Looks like that gully goes all the way around."

"It's a dry moat. The gun emplacements would have been over there on the fortress wall."

"I thought the guns would be at the front of the fort, overlooking the city."

"No, the forts were built to defend the city from the north. Imagine if the invaders had landed further up the coast and travelled inland to attack the naval base from the hill."

"I didn't think it would be this way around at all. How odd. So how are we going to get down?"

"Looks like they've made it quite easy for us. See?"

Josh pointed further up the dry moat where some blue lorry containers were parked against the wall.

"Reckon we can drop onto those but we'll have to get closer to see."

"Hope we can find a way to climb up the other side or we're going to be stuck down there."

"I'm sure we will. We'll just have to walk around to figure it out."

We set off towards the containers, bending low and winding our way through the shrubs that bordered the edge of the moat. When we got there we lay flat on our stomachs and inched up to the edge. It looked more than a short drop to me, but Josh was confident.

"I'll lower a rope down so we can measure the drop."

Josh removed the rope from his rucksack, uncoiled it and lowered an end until it touched the top of the metal container beneath.

"Put your hand there to mark the top and I'll pull the rest up."

Holding the length of rope between us, we figured it was about a three-metre drop.

"I'm only one metre sixty centimetres," I protested. "That means I've got to drop nearly twice my height, without falling off the container."

Josh laughed.

"I'll lower you down on the rope," he said. "I'm almost two metres, so if I hang from my arms I'll have less than a metre to drop when I join you. It'll be fine, trust me."

Josh looped the rope around a tree trunk, passing me one end and taking up the slack. He sat on the ground, facing away from the moat with his legs braced against a rock.

"Are you sure about this?" I asked, nervously.

"Lay on your stomach with your legs dangling over and I'll slowly lower you from there."

I did as he asked. Josh let the rope out slowly, taking my weight as I went over. It was a bit uncomfortable as my shoulders went over the edge, but once I was hanging I was soon on top of the container. The rope disappeared upwards and reappeared lowering our rucksacks, which I untied. I watched as Josh lowered himself off the edge. He had looped the rope around something and was descending with an end in each hand. Hanging fully extended, he was not far from the container and as he dropped I stepped forward to steady his landing. A loud metallic thud echoed up and down the moat. He pulled the rope, which quickly snaked down to join us.

"Yikes, let's get off this quick. Do you want me to lower you again?" he asked.

After that noise, I was in a hurry.

"No, this looks easier. There are some footholds. We can climb."

I smiled, then disappeared over the edge, determined to take cover quickly. I descended as far as I could before dropping to the ground. I dusted my hands off on my trousers and looked up, smiling. After lowering the rucksacks, Josh joined me and we crouched between the containers for a few minutes to see if the noise had attracted any attention.

Satisfied that we had got away with it, we set off, looking for an easy way to climb up onto the fort. Just like the last one, the wall looked impossible from the ground. We walked around the west side, scanning the wall as we went, looking for anything that might help us scale it. Near the end of the moat, we came across an entrance to the fort; a huge pair of solid wooden doors. They fitted neatly into a frame in the wall. I couldn't even see a gap that I might look through let alone squeeze through.

"I guess that's how the containers get down here," Josh said, sounding disappointed.

We walked on, soon reaching the west end of the moat. With no obvious way of getting into the fort, we turned around and walked back the other way.

At the northernmost point of the fort, we found what looked like our best bet. A large square section stuck out from the fort, which the moat swept around in an arc. Some more containers were parked against it, right up into the corner. The brickwork on the wall looked pitted where some bricks had been eroded by the weather. A few cracks were visible too.

"We climb here," Josh said confidently, clambering up the side of the container. I followed, grabbing his hand so that he could pull me up the final section.

"I used to go to a climbing wall sometimes. My mum used to take me and my brother there when the weather was bad. We had harnesses, but I got pretty good at it. I'll go first and then I'll drop the rope. We'll get the bags up and then I want you to tie it around your chest before you climb. I won't let you fall, OK?"

"OK," I agreed, taking a deep breath.

Josh took a moment to study the wall, working out the route he needed to take. He slung the coiled rope over his head and put one arm through, then set off. I watched, my heart in my mouth, but he made it look easy. Finding good handholds in the wall above, he lifted his left foot and jammed his trainer into a crack. He pushed up, then reached out with his right hand, searching for a new hold. His fingers found a recess, and then he raised his right foot, pushing the toe of his trainer into a space where there had once been a brick. He pushed up again, then reached above his head with his left hand to find another hold. It took him no more than 60 seconds to scale the wall. He disappeared over the top, then reappeared looking down at me with a broad grin on his face. The rope snaked back down and I tied both rucksacks to the end, which Josh hauled up carefully. The rope snaked back down again. I looped it around my back, under my arms and tied a reef knot at the front. I had memorised the first two hand holds that Josh had found but they were too high for me. I was going to have to work this out for myself. I looked down, spotting a weathered recess at knee height. I lifted my right foot into the hole, held on to a shoulder-high crack with my left hand, and then propelled myself up until I could reach the hand holds that Josh had used. I then tried to spot the place where he put his left foot, but again it was too high for me to reach. Suddenly I was jerked upwards, losing my foothold completely. My feet scrabbled around on the wall as I tried to find somewhere to take my weight. However, Josh kept pulling me up. I tried to help by grabbing at gaps above my head, but I got yanked away again, this time swinging sideways to collide with the wall. My shoulder banged hard against the brickwork and I swore loudly. He pulled again and again, each time giving me little opportunity to steady myself or take my weight. I realised that there must be something wrong. As soon as I could reach, I put my hands over the top of the wall. My right foot caught on a ridge just long enough for me to push up as Josh hauled me over. I looked up at him. He was glancing left and right, a terrified look on his face.

"Come on," he hissed, "we need to take cover."

Grabbing both bags and me by one arm he pulled me over a grassed area and down into a narrow brick recess where we were hidden. I sat on the floor, my back against the wall. Josh sat across from me.

"Are you OK?" he asked rapidly. "Sorry, I'm really sorry, I just panicked."

I rubbed my shoulder where I had banged into the wall. Josh stared at my hand and then took it gently, looking at a long graze across my knuckles. Bubbles of blood had surfaced here and there. It looked angry and raw. He leaned across and hugged me, holding me tight.

"I didn't mean to hurt you. I'm so sorry. When you started to climb I looked to my left and I could see the road. I thought about yesterday, about the cameras and the patrol and realised how exposed I was. I just panicked. I wanted to get you up as quickly as possible so that we could get out of sight. I'm such an idiot."

"It's nothing," I said, my shoulder throbbing and my hand smarting. "I'm fine. Let's find somewhere more comfortable and have a bit of a rest. Maybe have something to drink."

We peered out of the recess to take a proper look at the fort's interior. It was a huge semi-circular shallow bowl, with multiple levels. The long southern edge of the semi-circle ran east to west beside the road and was taken up almost completely by a large brick building. It was at least two stories high with a long row of arched windows. The wall of the dry moat swept all the way around, enclosing the fort. Most of the central area was marked out as a car park, with a few buildings, one of them modern.

Between us and the central area stood a ring of large circular blocks, which must have been gun emplacements of some sort. Each seemed to have a short central post that might have been used as a pivot to turn the gun towards its target. The area between the gun emplacements and the outer wall consisted of a series of grassy levels and bunkers. There was a lot to explore.

"Three tunnel entrances here somewhere," Josh said with a sigh. "Guess this spot is as good as any for lunch."

I opened Josh's rucksack, finding our bottle of water, some crisps and some biscuits. The crisps were so battered that we would have been better off with a spoon. In fact, a spoon was what I needed. They were salt and vinegar, which made my grazed knuckle sting. I left them for Josh and moved on to the biscuits.

When we had finished we packed up and started exploring.

"I reckon the tunnel entrances must be in the lowest part of the fort," I said. "It would be a waste of time and effort to dig down from up here."

"Good point. Let's head down."

We ran down the bank, past the gun emplacements and hid behind a large modern building close to the centre. From this position, my eyes were drawn to a grassy mound that had a flagpole on the top. On the south side, a pair of white railings ran on either side of some steps that led down into the mound.

"Surely it can't be that easy?" I said, pointing.

"Well, let's find out."

Chapter 22: Tunnels

A short flight of steps led straight into the mound where they curved into a spiral staircase that descended clockwise. We were both amazed and excited that we had stumbled upon a possible entrance so soon. I unpacked the oil lamp, which was thankfully still intact and lit it. Josh went first carrying the lamp in front of him and we slowly descended the stairs. The concrete steps were damp and a little slippery, so I held on tightly to the stair rail. We went round and round in a tight spiral, finally reaching the bottom. Already I had no idea which direction I was facing. As Josh moved the lamp around, our surroundings were revealed. We were in a space with a concrete floor and brick walls. A rusty ladder stood next to the bottom step, disappearing upwards into the centre of the spiral staircase. The walls were painted white but the paint was old and flaky. I reached out to touch the wall beside me. It was deathly cold and gritty. In the lamplight, we could see four arched entrances leading off into the darkness in different directions.

"Do you think this is it?" I asked, my voice echoing eerily around me.

"I don't think so. I remember my uncle saying that there were hundreds of steps to descend. The tunnels are deep in the hillside. I don't think we're that far under the surface. Here, hold the lamp and I'll find the compass."

Josh dug around in his rucksack, finding and opening the compass. In the light from the lamp, he rotated it to line the needle up with the symbol for north.

"South is through that tunnel straight ahead."

We went through the arch into the tunnel, which smelt damp and earthy. As the darkness swallowed us I could feel a rising sense of panic and grabbed hold of Josh's hand. He led the way, holding the lamp ahead of us. The sound we made as we walked seemed to disappear into the distance and then return, dulled and flat. I had the horrible sensation of there being something behind us and repeatedly looked over my shoulder. The hair on the back of my neck prickled. Josh halted, moving the lamp from side to side. There was another tunnel on the left, going off at an angle. Josh checked the compass and walked past the tunnel entrance. After a few paces, the tunnel opened into a large room with a high arched ceiling. Something scurried across the floor in front of us and I let out an involuntary gasp. Josh grabbed my arm.

"Rats!" he said. "I can't bear them. Let's get going."

The lamp cast an eerie glow across the room. Strip lights hung in rows from one end to the other and the walls were a creamy colour. Other than a long dusty table, the room was unfurnished. Some old cardboard boxes were stacked in one corner; the rat's nest maybe. The room looked like an old office of some sort. We moved cautiously, hugging the left-hand wall to discover that the tunnel continued through a doorway at the other end. Almost immediately, another tunnel entrance joined on the left, this one leading back in the direction we had come. I had the feeling that something was watching us and gripped Josh's hand more tightly. We walked on. In the distance, I could see a faint light, which grew as we approached.

"The exit," Josh said, whispering.

He extinguished the flame and we hurried forward to reach the daylight. The tunnel entrance had green doors, with flaky paint. One side had been left open. We peered out. Opposite the exit was a brick wall and as I looked up I recognised the long brick building at the southern end of the fort with the row of arched windows. What had looked like a two-storey building was actually three stories. The tunnel had simply led us under the main area of the fort. We were in a gully, no more than three metres wide between the building and the car park.

"I guess those are original tunnels, built at the same time as the fort," Josh said. "The soldiers would have been able to get to their firing positions from this building. In fact, I suspect those other tunnel entrances we saw go to other firing positions around the edge."

"Makes sense. So where now? This looks like the lowest place inside the fort, so shall we start at one end of the building and work our way along?"

Josh nodded, leading me out of the tunnel and heading east. As we walked along the gully, we passed under a short footbridge that connected the car park to an entrance in the building above. The brick walls on this lower level were painted white, but much of this had flaked off or turned green with algae. The building definitely looked its age. At the end of the gully, we came across a single-storey square block that was connected to the side of the main building. The door to the block was behind a black cast iron gate with a heavy lock. The door itself was made of thick steel. Josh shook the gate as hard as he could, but it didn't budge.

"Well if that's a tunnel entrance, there's no way we can get in there. Not without a bulldozer. Let's see if we can find the others. They might be less secure."

We walked back along the gully, peering into the barred windows as we went. However, they were so dirty that I could barely see in. Most rooms appeared to be empty.

At the west end of the gorge, we found an underground storage area. Wooden crates were stacked against the wall beside the entrance, some containing metal pipes. A few chairs were piled in a corner, next to some rusty ironwork. The floor was gritty, the walls were green and the furthest recesses disappeared into the darkness.

"Guess we ought to check this out," Josh said.

We relit the lamp and walked towards the end. A huge rusty cabinet stood against the wall, one door slightly ajar. I pulled it open, revealing a row of old paint pots and metal containers. Josh pulled the other door open, then moved the lamp around to get a proper look at the interior. A box on the top shelf caught his eye and he passed me the lamp to hold. Reaching up, he pulled the box towards him, releasing a few decades of muck and grit straight onto his head. Cursing, he ran his hands through his hair and wiped his face with his sleeve. Then he lifted the box down to the floor and opened the lid. I crouched down, placing the lamp on the floor beside it. The box contained lots of old tools: screwdrivers, a hammer, a rusty hacksaw, and various nuts and bolts. Nothing of any real interest, but Josh continued to poke around. Suddenly the lamp caught my eye. The flame was flickering. Concerned that we were running out of oil, I lifted it slightly and shook it. I could feel the weight of the oil swirling around inside the base. The flame became solid again, so I placed it back on the floor. However, the flame started flickering again. I placed my hand behind the lamp. A cool breeze was flowing from under the cabinet.

"Josh," I said slowly, "I think there's something behind this cabinet. I can feel some air flowing from somewhere."

Josh stopped, stared at the flame and then held his hand under the gap between the cabinet and the floor. He looked up at me, smiling.

"I think we might have stumbled on something here. Let's try and shift the cabinet."

Josh stood on one side and I stood on the other. As hard as we tried, we couldn't budge it an inch.

"Let's empty it," I said.

Between us, we emptied the cabinet, stacking the contents against the opposite wall. There was so much stuff in there. It was no surprise that we couldn't shift it. With the cabinet empty, we tried again. It was still heavy but we managed to drag one end away from the wall, which made a terrible screech. Josh lifted the lamp and we peered through the gap, staring in silence.

Behind the cabinet was a large arched doorway, with a mesh gate across the entrance. Through the mesh I could see a staircase, disappearing down into darkness. *Bingo!*

I couldn't quite believe it. The idea of secret tunnels under the fort seemed like a fantasy. I'd gone along with Josh's plan because I didn't have any other ideas, but I wasn't convinced, until now.

We really did have a chance of escape. I turned towards him laughing and we hugged, jumping up and down with excitement.

Josh shook the gate a little and powdery mortar tumbled from a hinge.

"This one's not as secure as that other door," he said.

"Probably why they hid it!"

Josh picked up a screwdriver and jammed it behind the top hinge. I grabbed one too and started working on the lower hinge. Years of decay had left the brickwork in a poor state and the screws were also worn and rusty. Little by little, I managed to work the first screw loose. Josh was already on his second and passed me some pliers, which I used to grab the head of the screw and wriggle until it came free. The next one was easier but the last one wouldn't shift. Josh had removed all the screws from the top hinge, so he took over. After ten minutes or so had passed he gave up on the screwdriver and rummaged around in the box for the hacksaw. Luckily it just fitted through the gap between the hinge and the wall. He started to saw through the screw, but with awkward movements because the hacksaw kept getting stuck. Eventually, with sweat dripping from his brow he made it. However, the gate still took some effort to open. Although the hinges were free from the wall, a heavy chain and padlock hung from the other side. Josh used a claw hammer to lever up the latch and luckily, there was just enough length in the chain for us to push the gate partially open. Josh squeezed himself through the gap and beckoned for me to follow. I passed through the rucksacks and the lamp and joined him at the top of the steps.

Chapter 23: Deep and dark

A steep staircase led down through an arched tunnel of corrugated steel, with a handrail on either side. I took a deep breath, shouldered my rucksack, and held Josh's hand. My earlier excitement was replaced by fear and anxiety. From what Josh had been told, these tunnels were extensive. I imagined us getting lost, not finding a way out or a way back.

"Hope there's plenty of oil in the lamp," I whispered.

"The faster we move, the quicker we get out, come on."

We started our descent in the eerie silence, our footsteps echoing as the darkness closed in behind us. A draft of cold air rose from below, smelling a little damp and musty. We could see only a few metres ahead and with each step we took, more and more steps appeared relentlessly before us. Eventually, we reached a flat section where the tunnel continued for a few metres before ending in a brick wall. However, from the light cast by the lamp, I could see that the staircase had turned at ninety degrees and continued down. After a shorter flight of steps, we reached another flat section, the same as before. Again, the tunnel ended in a brick wall but the staircase continued at ninety degrees to our right. The next flight of steps seemed to go on forever, broken occasionally by a metre or so of flat ground. It reminded me of a slide at a swimming pool that cascaded in sections into the water.

Eventually, hundreds of stairs later, we reached the bottom. We were now deep down under the fort and the thought of all that earth between me and daylight made me shudder. I could feel my heart thumping inside my chest. Josh looked at me, a faint smile on his face, but he looked worried too. A piece of green tarpaulin hung from the ceiling, blocking our path. Josh pulled it to one side and held out the lamp. A long tunnel stretched ahead, its walls clad in corrugated steel. We cautiously stepped into the entrance, letting the tarpaulin swing back into place behind us. Josh moved the lamp from side to side, revealing another tunnel that ran across the one we were standing in from left to right. Josh pulled out the compass, turned it to identify north and then pointed to the tunnel on the right.

"That way is south. That's the way we need to go to find the exit."

However, the tunnel heading south ended in a brick wall, just a few metres in. Disappointed, we went back to the first tunnel and started to walk along it. I reached out to touch the surface and small flakes fell into my hand. The gritty grains were sharp and smelt metallic. I realised that it was rust. It seemed like the tunnels were rotting from neglect and that maybe some tunnels had been sealed off because they had collapsed. The idea of collapsing tunnels did nothing for my state of mind. I tried to put the thought out of my head.

After twenty or so paces, we came across another tunnel that crossed this one, also running north and south. This tunnel was much narrower than the first one but still clad in corrugated steel. I spotted a small gap between the metal sheets. Underneath was white rock and a little had tumbled out onto the floor. I picked up a small piece and rubbed it, leaving creamy white marks on my fingers and thumb. The tunnels seemed to be hewn from chalk.

"Let's make marks on the wall as we go in case we get lost."

"Good idea."

I drew the number one onto the corrugated steel wall as we headed south into the narrow tunnel. After several metres, we found a wider tunnel that crossed the one we were in, heading east and west. This place was like a maze. Holding up the lantern, Josh revealed that the tunnel heading west was also bricked up a few metres in. We continued south. I was about to ask Josh why he thought the tunnels were blocked when we both froze. I could hear a voice, a man's voice somewhere nearby. Terror rooted me to the spot. Josh quickly extinguished the lantern, plunging us into darkness. Terrified, I grabbed his hand. We stood very still, trying not to make a sound. Another voice could be heard that was distinctly different from the first. I couldn't make out what was being said, but we then heard laughter. The voices were coming from the tunnel on the east side. Josh was squeezing my hand so tightly that I nearly cried out in pain. He pushed the lantern onto my arm and whispered,

"Hold the lantern in your left hand and keep hold of me with your right. I'll feel my way along the tunnel wall."

I did as he asked, my hands trembling badly. My heart was beating so loudly that I swear I could hear it. Slowly, Josh led me down the narrow tunnel. In the pitch dark, I could see a faint glow ahead. As we got closer we found yet another, wider tunnel. This one crossed the one we were in, running from east to west. A glow was coming from the tunnel heading east where more voices could be heard. Josh turned into the tunnel that headed west, wanting to get us further away from whoever was down here. I was trying to walk as quietly as possible, but without being able to see anything I stepped on Josh's foot. He had stopped.

"Another dead end," he whispered. "We'll have to go back."

I was starting to panic. I didn't want to go back but what choice did we have? He felt his way across the dead end of the tunnel, gently guiding me along. Then he started to feel his way back along the opposite wall. The murmur of voices became louder as we reached the thinner tunnel once more. All kinds of thoughts were running through my head. I thought perhaps we had come across another community who were using the tunnels for shelter. But if that was the case, surely they would have found an exit. I couldn't bear the thought that there was no exit down here. We continued south along the thinner tunnel, away from the voices. Suddenly, Josh pulled me to the right and I realised we had entered yet another tunnel that ran west. I prayed that this one would not end in a brick wall too. After a few minutes, Josh stopped.

"The wall ends here and turns a corner back north. Maybe it's another tunnel running north and south. Let's cross to the other side and see."

Josh led me slowly into the darkness across the tunnel. He edged, bit by bit into the darkness until he reached the other side.

"Yep, there's another corner that turns south."

We turned into the tunnel and edged a few metres along the wall. Josh stopped.

"Let's put the lamp on low to see what's here."

I handed him the lantern and rummaged in my rucksack for the matches. As I struck a match the noise it made echoed horribly and I almost shook the flame out. *Stupid!* In the light from the flame, Josh quickly opened the lantern and lit it, turning the flame as low as possible, without letting it go out. I blew on the match, the acrid odour wafting in the air as the flame died. In the gentle light from the lamp, I could see that we were in another tunnel, wider than the one before, but still clad in corrugated steel. I drew a small number two on the wall and we started our journey south again. Having a little light to guide our way calmed me a little. It was fortunate too because this tunnel had old boxes piled up here and there. Without the light, we would have been stumbling into them and making a terrible noise.

"I can't believe it," I whispered. "Who can be down here?"

"I don't want to think about it. Let's just get out as quickly as we can. Come on."

We moved more quickly, careful to weave around the clutter as silently as possible. A tunnel entrance loomed on our left, presumably joining back up with the thinner tunnel that ran parallel to this one. I realised that the tunnel network was a bit like a grid, except some tunnels were blocked off, perhaps because they were unsafe. Josh whispered.

"Look. There's no tunnel entrance opposite that one, so we could be right at the edge of the tunnel network."

Hopefully, we were as far away from the voices as we could get.

We walked past the tunnel entrance as quickly as possible, Josh shielding the flame with his hand, and continued our journey south. After a short distance, another tunnel entrance appeared, again heading back east.

"Damn," said Josh, pointing ahead. Our tunnel was blocked off. We were going to have to head back towards the thinner tunnel. Josh passed me the lantern and put his right hand on the tunnel wall. I extinguished the flame and reached out to hold his left hand. Slowly, we edged forward, wary of any junk that might be stacked against the wall. As we neared the entrance to the thinner tunnel, the sound of voices returned. This time, a man was talking in a loud bossy voice. I heard the word 'dismissed', followed by another voice saying, "Yes, sir." *Oh no!*

Josh must have heard it too because he came to a halt and gripped my hand more tightly. I could feel his breath on one side of my head. It came in rapid puffs, much the same as mine. We were both terrified. The voices had to be soldiers. It dawned on me that Josh had described these tunnels as some sort of command centre in the Second World War. Clearly, they were still in use. What if these were the same soldiers that had fenced us in and were searching, hunting us down? I couldn't believe that we might have walked right into their camp. Josh tugged on my hand and started to move south along the tunnel.

We inched along the thinner tunnel, pausing now and then to listen. I could hear a murmur of voices just on the other side of the tunnel wall. How many soldiers were down here? There could be a whole squadron. Part of me wanted to go back, but what then? Josh pulled me on, then to the right. He had found another tunnel entrance. I felt him jump slightly and curse under his breath, then move on. I stepped on something hard, my foot tipping to one side awkwardly. I let go of Josh's hand to steady myself against the wall, grazing my knuckles. The wall was rough rock, cold and unforgiving.

"You OK?" Josh whispered.

"Yeah. Think we have to light the lantern."

The fizz of the match filled me with dread, but without light, we were going to be making more noise by stumbling around. As the lantern cast a faint light, I took in our surroundings. The tunnel had once been a room but was now in a very poor state, with torn plasterboard peeling from rusty metal hoops that arched across the ceiling. Behind the plasterboard, roughly hewn rock was revealed. The floor was littered with debris. We quickly picked our way to the far end, where a wooden door stood ajar. Beyond was a tunnel, running north to south. The lantern revealed a blocked-off wall a couple of metres north but the south was clear.

"Must be the same tunnel we were in earlier," I whispered. "Guess they had to brick up a damaged section."

Josh turned the lantern up a little, revealing a long tunnel heading south.

"Come on," he said, taking my hand, "let's get out of here."

At regular intervals, tunnel entrances appeared on our left, running east. Each time, we shielded the light and passed quickly on. Soon after passing the third entrance, the light revealed a brick wall ahead and the tunnel turned east at ninety degrees. This place was huge. In our hurry to escape the voices, I had not been writing on the walls. I felt slightly sick, fearing that we would never find our way back to the staircase.

"Maybe we're near the exit now," Josh said hopefully.

Creeping cautiously along the tunnel we soon found ourselves back in the thinner tunnel that ran north to south. I could not hear any voices now, just silence. Josh stepped into the tunnel, holding the lantern in front of him. Peering around the corner, I could see that the tunnel extended a short way south to a doorway. Above the door was a sign 'FIRE EXIT'. Josh was grinning in the lamplight with the flame flickering over his face, which made him look a bit scary. We were finally getting somewhere. I grinned back, feeling a little relieved.

At the doorway, we peered through. To our right was a room of some sort and to our left was another tunnel heading east. However, straight ahead was a wide tunnel entrance.

"This has to be it," I whispered excitedly.

We walked into the entrance and Josh held up the lamp, revealing a solid wall of concrete blocks a few metres in. My heart sank.

"Well, if it was an exit, they sealed it up!" he said bitterly. "Come on, we'll head east along the tunnel, and see what we find. The soldiers had to get in here somehow."

"What if the exit is guarded?" I asked.

"I don't know, but we'll think of something. Come on, let's just take a look."

The tunnel heading east was huge with a very high arched ceiling, clad in corrugated steel. Large

231

rusty pipes were anchored to the walls but whatever they had been connected to was removed, leaving only the impression of a large round object on the concrete floor.

We passed another wide tunnel with a lower ceiling that ran north. At the end we found the entrance to a thinner tunnel that was almost identical to the one we were in earlier, also running north to south. The only difference with this tunnel was that pools of artificial light could be seen in the distance, marking the areas that must be occupied by the soldiers. We moved back into the shadows, hiding the light from our lantern. It dawned on me that the two thinner tunnels were like corridors, crisscrossed with wider tunnels that must have been used as rooms. Some, it seemed, still were. I looked over to see what lay at the southern end of this corridor. A short section was visible that ended in a wall of concrete blocks.

"Bet that was an exit too," I whispered. "What now?"

"There's got to be another one and it must be in that direction," Josh said, pointing east. "Trouble is, we're going to have to go up this tunnel until we find another way across."

"But what if a soldier walks into the tunnel while we're in it?"

Josh was silent, thinking.

"Let's go back to the wide tunnel we just passed and head north. I bet the first tunnel we come to heading east will cross this thinner tunnel further up. These tunnels are laid out like a grid. Then, we only have to quickly dash across to carry on."

If he was correct, that was a much safer option. I nodded but felt very uneasy.

Before long we found that Josh was right. We walked only a short section north through the wide tunnel before finding an entrance on our right, heading east. A doorway had been built across this tunnel, but the door was no longer there. Inside, the tunnel was divided into two halves with a brick wall down the centre. It was mucky and dusty. Lumps of iron protruded from the wall forming the shape of a large rectangle. Something may have been fixed to the wall long ago. At the end of the room, another doorway led through to a similarly shaped room. Again, just another empty space. However, the doorway at the end of this room led onto the thin tunnel, which we knew to be correct by the same pools of artificial light in the distance. Straight over was another tunnel with a doorway, heading east. *Bingo!*

I extinguished the lantern and we stood hand in hand for a second before walking quietly but briskly through the doorway into the tunnel opposite. Once inside I breathed deeply, my heart hammering in my chest. I relit the lantern, my nerves jumping once more at the strike of the match. The room we were in was narrow and very dirty, with black inky walls. It led into a much larger section of tunnel with a high arched ceiling. I made the flame in the lantern larger and held it forward. I caught my breath. Boxes and crates were stacked against the wall. However, not old dusty boxes but pristine cardboard boxes, sitting on pallets. We had walked into an area used by the soldiers for storage. I could see big plastic bottles of water, still shrink-wrapped in their packaging. My stomach reeled as I turned to look at the opposite wall, finding a long row of white protective suits hanging from numbered hooks. Beneath each suit was a pair of black wellingtons.

Josh grabbed my hand and pulled me through the tunnel, past all the white suits.

"The entrance has to be near here. They wouldn't carry pallets of water too far inside."

"Slow down, we ought to be careful. There might be guards."

The tunnel curved gently towards the south. We crept along the tightest curve of the wall, Josh in front of me. Suddenly he stopped.

"There's a breeze," he whispered. "Can you feel it?"

I couldn't, but that was because I was behind him. As soon as I peered around Josh's side, I felt my fringe blow to one side.

"Yes," I replied, "and it looks lighter ahead."

Josh extinguished the flame and in the distance, we could see a faint light. Moving more quickly, we rounded the curve and straight ahead was a tunnel-shaped patch of fading daylight. By now we were almost running, all caution lost as we saw the exit up ahead. I could see light blue above and green below. Yes, sky and bushes. *Freedom!* The only thing separating us from freedom was a gate with vertical iron bars. I could see two sliding locks, top and bottom, and a latch in the centre. Suddenly, from behind a voice bellowed.

"Stop where you are!"

We spun around to see a soldier in a khaki uniform. He lifted a radio from his belt.

"Two intruders at the front entrance. Possible escapees from the zone."

Josh and I looked at one another. We had no time to waste. I turned around and started to unbolt the gate while Josh quickly slid the rucksack from his back and rummaged around, pulling out the yellow canister. The bolts were stiff, but I managed to slide the top one across, and then quickly moved on to the second.

"I said stop where you are," the soldier yelled.

"He's not armed," Josh said urgently, holding the canister in front of him where it could be seen. He had one finger through the ring of the handle, ready to pull.

The second bolt slid across much more easily, leaving only the latch. At that moment, five more soldiers appeared, all in white suits with rifles. I gripped the circular handle with both hands and twisted to lift the latch. It snapped open and I pushed, then pushed again. Panicking, I shook the gate, but it wouldn't budge.

"Stop right now!" one of the soldiers shouted. "You'll not get out. It's locked."

They whispered amongst themselves urgently, one soldier running back up the tunnel from where they'd come. Then another soldier spoke, this time more calmly.

"Now, both of you calm down. We're not going to hurt you."

They lowered their rifles but remained where they were, just staring at us.

"You," he said. "You with the canister. I want you to lower that very gently to the floor. OK?"

Josh looked furious. I'd never seen him so angry.

"Just let us go," he yelled, gripping the canister more tightly as a threat.

Four of the soldiers took a step back, wide-eyed. The fifth soldier stood his ground.

"You don't know what you've got there mate. You pull that ring and we're all done for."

He whispered to the others and they all gently lowered their weapons to the floor. From behind them another soldier appeared, walked slowly forward, and then stopped beside the fifth soldier.

"Good evening," he said calmly. "Josh and Maddie I presume? Now let's take this very slowly.

"You will come to no harm, I promise. Josh, please place the canister on the ground very carefully and step away from it."

Josh looked at the canister in his hand, then back to the soldiers. I swallowed hard, staring at the canister.

"Please Josh," I said, with growing alarm. He removed his finger from the ring and gently lowered it to the ground.

"That was a good decision, Josh," the soldier said. "Now please come towards us, away from the canister."

I grabbed Josh's hand and pulled him to one side. He looked at me and nodded. Very slowly, we walked towards the soldiers. The group parted and the soldier who spoke last led us back into the tunnels.

Chapter 24: Revelations

Josh and I were taken to a small room and asked to sit side by side at a table, facing a glass window. Refreshments were brought in by a soldier in a white suit. I stared at the tray in front of us. Two cans of cola and a selection of biscuits were arranged carefully on a large oval plate. The last thing I felt like doing was eating. I swallowed hard, gripping Josh's hand. Neither of us touched the food. I didn't trust anything or anyone any more. Thoughts raced around my head. We were far underground. No one knew we were here. They could do anything to us. *No one will hear me scream!*

Suddenly the dark window opposite lit up, revealing two men and a lady, all wearing military uniforms in an adjacent room. The man on the right had grey hair and a moustache, the man in the centre was bald. The lady had very short-cropped hair and wore a serious expression.

"Good morning Maddie and Josh," the bald man said, his voice coming from a speaker above the window in our room. "Forgive us for not all sitting around the same table, but we have to follow protocol. Please, allow me to introduce myself and my colleagues. Then I'll tell you a little about what has been happening."

His voice was authoritative, but not menacing. I acknowledged that these must be British soldiers but I still didn't trust them. They had fenced us in for some reason and they were hunting us down.

They might still want to get rid of us. The bald man continued.

"My name is Lieutenant General Palmer, head of command for the response force in cooperation with the Ministry of Defence. On my left here is Lieutenant Colonel Golding, who is the commanding officer for our soldiers and on my right is Colonel Grieves, who is acting as staff officer.

"Now, if you have any questions I want you to ask, OK?"

Josh and I looked at one another, then nodded. I took a deep breath and waited for him to begin.

"On 10th April, a nuclear device exploded high in the atmosphere, releasing an electromagnetic pulse, an EMP for short. The pulse came directly down over an area of the countryside that's roughly eighty square miles, with your local villages at the epicentre. Now an EMP destroys electrical circuits, so not only did you experience a full power outage from the national grid, but anything electrical was destroyed. So that's everything from mobile phones to landlines to toasters. If you think about it, everything we use these days contains some sort of electrical component. So even petrol cars and oil-fired boilers don't work any more. Now an EMP was not thought to be dangerous to humans unless, of course, you are unfortunate enough to rely on a pacemaker. Indeed, many scientists thought that an EMP could not even be felt by a human. This event has proved that theory wrong."

My mind was racing as I tried to absorb what he said. A nuclear explosion, a pulse of energy of some kind. Anything electrical being destroyed.

Yes, it was all plausible. And yes, we had definitely felt it too. Josh piped in.

"We both felt something and lost consciousness. Other people said so too."

"Quite so," the general said. "Nearly all the evacuees that we've spoken to have reported similar experiences. However, most recovered within a few hours. Sadly, there were a few heart attacks and deaths as a result of pacemaker failures. We also lost a few people through car accidents and the like."

I felt a slight wave of relief when he implied that the evacuees were safe but I remembered the body bags, the crashed cars and the plane. Surely there were more than a few people dead.

"I saw a plane come down and a huge fireball. Did the passengers survive that?" I asked sceptically.

"Ah, yes a plane too. Luckily it was a cargo plane and was not carrying passengers. It came down on a golf course, so no other casualties but sadly the pilot and co-pilot were killed. We recovered the black box, but that was also destroyed by the EMP.

"Where the nuclear device came from is still a mystery. No nation has claimed responsibility. Indeed most of the usual suspects have come forward to deny any involvement and condemn the action. Now, our defence department monitors radar from several bases in the UK and abroad, but this device just appeared in the skies above us. We've looked at the data from every angle and there is no trajectory recorded. One theory is that this device entered the atmosphere from space."

"Aliens?" Josh asked with a look of horror on his face. The general chuckled.

"No, we don't think so. We've long suspected that certain nations that have satellites orbiting the Earth might also be storing nuclear warheads up there. We think this might have been an accident, a malfunction of some kind that caused a warhead to be deployed. We think that it was deliberately destroyed high in the atmosphere to avoid the consequences of a nuclear detonation on land. If that had happened, we'd probably be in a full-scale nuclear war. A nuclear explosion high in the atmosphere poses no threat in terms of radiation at ground level. The EMP that was emitted, however, would have been unavoidable."

I couldn't believe it. The whole thing sounded like something from a film. And yet it made some sort of sense. However, it didn't explain why the military acted the way they had. I'd seen soldiers threaten people with guns and even fire shots. And they'd set dogs on us. I folded my arms across my chest and stared at the general. He raised his eyebrows a little, then continued.

"Now our defence department and security services have plans for handling all kinds of scenarios. Believe it or not, we have one for managing an EMP attack.

"We were able to figure out the area that was affected by the EMP quite quickly by looking at real-time data; electricity networks, mobile phone networks, and radio. We could see the extent of the black spot, so to speak. Teams of military personnel were then deployed to secure the area and create an exclusion zone. We picked this old command centre to coordinate the plan as it's conveniently situated on the boundary, although most of it is uninhabitable, as you'll have seen. Now, all types of plans following an attack on the

United Kingdom cater for the possibility of biological agents being released. Agents that might cause disease in the population. Although we think it's unlikely to happen in modern times, we still take precautions. Hence all military personnel were supplied with Level A Hazmat suits for their protection. We then set about evacuating everyone in the affected area and moving them to quarantine facilities for monitoring. Luckily, with it being a rural location and a small population, we achieved the evacuation quite successfully."

"Are they still there?" I asked, thinking about the people I had seen boarding the coach.

"Yes, they are, although we believe they're all perfectly healthy. There's no evidence of any infections and no lasting effects of the EMP. However, our protocols require four weeks of quarantine, so they all have just under two weeks to go. As do you two, hence the glass barrier between us." He smiled apologetically.

"We both saw people being removed at gunpoint," I said. "Was that really necessary? I mean, it made us think you were the enemy!"

"Well I can see how you might think that," he replied, "but we needed to get everyone out of there straight away and that meant the use of force if people resisted. The trouble is," he went on, "history tells us that disasters such as this always result in lawless behaviour. People need food, so they find it, even if that means breaking and entering. Then there'll be some people that can't resist helping themselves to more than just food. Suddenly, you've got looters, you've got people making up the rules, forcing other people to bend to their will. Violence usually follows. That's the human species for you. Despite hundreds of years of civilisation and a firm understanding of right from wrong, if you put us in a tight spot, we start to unravel. Just like that."

He snapped his fingers to make his point. Josh and I looked at one another. He was absolutely right. We'd witnessed it all first-hand.

"So, we did everything we could to evacuate everyone from the area. We had the data to know who lived where and we slowly started to account for every single person. We ended up with a list of the missing. Actually, it wasn't a terribly long list, but both your names were on it and considering your ages, we were keen to bring you in. We even used thermal imaging from a helicopter to try and locate you, but you must have been well hidden. We nearly got you though, right?"

"Right," Josh said, shaking his head. "That patrol with dogs scared the hell out of us."

"No harm done though," he said evenly. "Those were rescue dogs not attack dogs. If they had caught up with you, the worst you would have suffered was a nasty lick.

"What about the old man with the shotgun?" I asked. "Did the soldiers kill him?"

The general paused, then turned to the grey-haired lieutenant, looking for an explanation.

"No they didn't," the grey-haired lieutenant replied. "Shots were fired to control the situation but the man was unharmed."

The general smiled and continued his explanation.

"As far as the EMP goes, our mission here is more or less complete. The defence department will continue to work on what caused the EMP and why, but otherwise, the plan we implemented has pretty much run its course."

He laughed, wagging his finger at us.

"You certainly gave us the runaround. Those soldiers were furious at being outsmarted by a couple of teenagers. Anyway, you're here now, safe and well. Your families are being notified as we speak."

"Are they OK?" I asked, starting to feel relief but also emotional at their mention.

"They've been very worried about you but I'm sure they'll be fine once they hear that you're safe. Your parents aren't in a quarantine facility though, Maddie. They were intercepted trying to return to your house and have been staying in a hotel at the government's expense."

"What about my mum and brother?" asked Josh.

"They were safely evacuated to a quarantine centre. You'll be able to speak to your families soon.

"Before any of that though, we need to discuss that little yellow canister. It's actually quite old, so we are all very lucky that it's still in one piece."

"What is it then?" Josh asked. "I thought it was CS gas or something but it must be much worse because everyone looked terrified."

"I'm afraid it's very bad. Have either of you heard of anthrax? Or to give it its full name, Bacillus anthracis."

I gasped.

"Yes, yes I have. I learnt about it in Biology. It's deadly, isn't it? Didn't they want to use it as a weapon years ago?"

"That's correct, Maddie. There's a particular strain, called Vollum 14578 that was developed as a biological weapon during the Second World War. Fortunately, it was never used. Some British scientists from the biology department at Porton Down tested it on a small island in Scotland. They observed the subsequent unpleasant death of all the sheep that lived there. The strain was so virulent and the spores so indestructible that the island had to be closed off for decades."

I looked at Josh. He was deathly still, eyes staring and mouth open. He swallowed, then spoke, his voice wavering slightly.

"So that explains the writing on the canister. There was the letter V with a number next to it."

"That's right. You might also have noticed the letters BDP, which stands for Biology Department Porton Down."

"But how did the canister find its way to this area?" Josh asked, clearly distressed that he had been carrying something so deadly and had come so close to releasing it.

"Well long story short, an ex-scientist from the Porton Down biology department lived locally. It seems that he was sacked for repeatedly ignoring safety procedures and left with a grudge, plus a case containing three anthrax canisters. For some reason, those canisters were never missed but have been sitting in that case inside a garden shed ever since. The current owners bought his estate after his death and knew nothing about the case. Sorting out the shed was something on their to-do list.

"Anyway, one of our patrols noticed that the shed door was open and went inside to investigate. The place had been looted. However, he spotted the case and became suspicious. It was a military-grade security case that had been broken open. The case contained three moulded compartments, two were empty but one contained a canister, just like the one you had. He brought the canister back to base. The writing on the canister rang alarm bells and we've since launched a detailed search to recover the two that are missing."

"So that's what you're searching for," I said. "The community thought you were after them."

The general sat bolt upright, staring at us intently.

"OK, let's slow down a moment. First of all, I'd like you to tell me where you found the canister and then I'd like to hear a little more about this community."

I looked at Josh and nodded. I wanted him to tell them about Boss's stash of weapons since he'd been the one to pick up the canister. Josh paused for thought before explaining.

"The two things are sort of tied together. You see, we spent some time with a community in the forest. We came across them after we'd escaped from that patrol with the dogs. Although we were a bit suspicious of them at first, they seemed really genuine. The community was all about helping one another survive off-grid. They planned what was needed from day to day, we helped out and in return we got food, somewhere to sleep, and some security.

"However, the thing you said earlier about human nature and how some people take advantage during times of disasters. Well, that's exactly what happened. We learned some unpleasant truths about some of them and before long we wanted to leave."

Behind the glass, all three were listening intently.

"What happened?" the general asked.

"Basically, they were happy for us to join the community because we were useful. They put us to work. Maddie was treated like a slave, doing all the washing and cleaning and never getting a chance to leave the camp. I was part of a foraging team, sent out to get supplies. One day we came across an old man, desperate for help, but they quickly decided he was of no use and sent him on his way. That was the start of it. Then Maddie found a hoard of watches, jewellery and money. Their claim to be taking only what they needed to survive was clearly rubbish. Then we discovered a stash of weapons, just outside the camp.

"The final straw was when your search party was spotted. A few of them started to talk about taking you on. Unbelievable! We had to get out. We planned our escape and ran at the first opportunity. Our way out passed by the stash of weapons, so I helped myself to a couple of knives and that canister. The knives were to replace ones that we'd lost. The canister, well I didn't really know what it was, but I thought it might be useful."

All three were staring at Josh.

"Josh, was it the only canister in the weapons stash?"

Josh paused.

"No, there were two."

The room was silent while everyone processed this information.

"OK," the general said, "we are going to need a plan to get it before someone tries to use it. If that canister releases anthrax, we are going to have a really, really big problem on our hands. One that will be on a national if not international scale.

"I'm going to need to know everything about this community. The people, their roles and personalities, the location of the camp, access points, and any plans you think they have concerning our search party. Anything else that might be relevant, no matter how small. Do you think you can both help with that?"

Josh and I looked at one another, realising the enormity of the situation. We both nodded. I swallowed hard, feeling slightly sick.

"OK, I'm going to call a thirty-minute comfort break. Josh and Maddie should have an opportunity to freshen up and then I want a decent meal in front of them as soon as possible.

"Colonel Grieves, call an immediate halt to the search party. Get them to pretend they have found something and stop. No one continues without my order."

"Yes, Sir!"

After a little while, the door opened and Josh and I were led down a series of corridors by a soldier in a white suit. We were each shown into a room and given towels, a toiletry bag and a change of clothes. In my room, I found two large bowls of hot water and wasted no time getting cleaned up. I changed into a pair of grey joggers and a sweatshirt. When I opened the door to my room, I found Josh and our guard waiting for me.

"Mmm, his and hers matching outfits," I said jokingly as we were escorted back to the briefing room.

A jug of water had been placed on the table, with cups and cutlery at the ready. Two soldiers walked in, each carrying a tray and we were presented with a full English breakfast. Sausages, bacon, hash browns, scrambled eggs, baked beans and grilled tomato with toast on the side. Josh's eyes literally popped out of his head. Another soldier appeared carrying a tray with hot drinks and an electronic tablet, like an iPad.

"Tuck in you two," the loudspeaker announced. "We're just getting a few things set up before we start."

I glanced through the window to see the three army officials sorting through some paperwork whilst someone in the background was sitting at a laptop with a screen hanging on the wall above. Another screen hung on the wall behind us too.

We ate in silence, enjoying every morsel. Ordinarily, I would have turned my nose up at sausages because I've heard too many tales about what's in them, but I was over that. Perhaps all fussy eaters should spend a couple of weeks in the forest.

I poured myself some tea and Josh some coffee and our plates were taken away.

"OK, let's make a start," the general announced.

"First, we need to establish where the canister is. Now, you have control of the screens from your tablet. Can one of you approximate its position please?"

Josh turned the tablet on. A Google map of the area appeared that was also projected onto the screens. He moved the position of the map and then zoomed in. Finally, he clicked on the map to create a marker.

"I think that's where the community camp is," Josh said, "but I might be a bit out. It's hard to know for sure, as distances are difficult to judge in the forest."

"That's OK. Now, how are the weapons hidden?"

"There's a brown tarpaulin hanging over a branch and the stash is underneath, protected from the weather. But if they've left the camp, they'll have taken it all with them."

"What makes you think they'll have left the camp?" the grey-haired lieutenant asked.

"They had a plan," I explained. "First they were going to try and lead the search party away by firing guns from a different location."

"Ha!" the general said triumphantly. "Well that didn't work. We sent a couple of helicopters to take a look, but the search party continued."

Josh went on.

"So, if that didn't work they were going to leave the camp and work their way around, behind the search party."

"Damn," the general said, shaking his head. "So they might have left the camp already.

"OK. We need to know about the people. That'll help us figure out what they're capable of and how to deal with them. How many people are we talking about?"

"There are eight altogether," I answered.

"Hmm. That shouldn't pose too much of a problem then. Who's the ringleader?"

"It's someone called Boss," Josh said. "We never knew his real name but he owns a local garage, if that helps."

The three conferred amongst themselves, looking at a list.

"Put up number three, please?" the lady instructed.

A photograph of Boss appeared on the screen. He looked younger, with shorter hair, but his piercing blue eyes were the same.

"That's him!" we said in unison.

"His real name is Derek Chambers. No criminal record, but the tax man is watching closely. They suspect he's doing a lot of undeclared trade.

"So he's put himself in charge of this community has he?"

"Yes," Josh said. "There are two other guys who work for him at his garage that are very loyal. They do anything he says and one of them has been to prison."

"Ah," the general said, "that'll be Jerry Jones. Put up number one please."

Two photos of Jerry appeared on the screen, like the ones they take at a police station. One was facing the camera and the other was a side shot. His face looked thinner and a lot younger. He even had a bit of hair.

"He's quite a scary guy," I said. "He'll do anything Boss says."

"OK. Tell us about the others. What do you think they're capable of?"

"Al is the other guy that works for Boss in the garage. I don't think he's a bad person, but he does what Boss tells him to do," Josh replied.

"There's a guy called Matt that I don't trust at all," I said. "He's got a mean streak in him and he knows how to use guns. If Boss decides to wage a war, I think Jerry, Al, and Matt will be the ones who support him."

"The others are really nice," Josh said. "They just go along with what Boss says, because it's easier to do that than challenge him.

"Oh and there's a dog called Chester," I added. "He helped us escape from the patrol and then he found us in the forest by following our trail."

"Hmm, a dog could be a problem. It will know we're coming before we can surprise them.

"These other four people, what are their names?"

"Babs, Mikolaj, Lester and Rambo," Josh replied. "They're all good people."

"Rambo," the grey-haired lieutenant said, laughing, "what's he like?"

"We never knew his real name either," I explained. "He knows all this stuff about survival though, so that's what they called him. Boss had him building all sorts of traps in the forest."

"Traps?" the lady asked, sounding alarmed. "What sort of traps?"

"Nasty traps for the search party," Josh said. "Hidden pits full of stakes, tripwires to release swinging logs. Boss was putting together a full-on battle plan. It all got a bit crazy."

There was silence for a moment while they considered what we had told them. Then Lieutenant General Palmer cleared his throat.

"I think we have a bit of a problem. This Boss person sounds crazy enough to take us on and has some support at least. If we risk a confrontation, he'll likely use everything at his disposal, including that canister."

He was right. Josh and I looked at one another. I had a sinking feeling. A possible course of action occurred to me and to Josh too, who put it into words.

"We have to go back. We have to get the canister."

The grey-haired lieutenant and the lady both looked at General Lieutenant Palmer who studied us, pursing his lips. Finally, he spoke.

"I don't like it much, but I agree. However, we will be on hand to intervene. Your safety is a priority."

The conversation continued for another half an hour or more. Eventually, a plan was agreed upon.

The following day, Josh and I would be dropped close to the camp in a safe area and attempt to retrace our steps back to the community's camp. If possible, we would retrieve the canister unseen and return it directly. If we were spotted, we would pretend that we had made a mistake in leaving and ask to rejoin. If the community had left the camp we would track them. Either way, we would then have to find an opportunity to retrieve the canister. Our movements would be tracked by a tiny device, inserted into the soles of our shoes and we would also carry small microphones. An elite group of soldiers would be on hand at a discrete distance and would intervene if necessary.

Chapter 25: Back to the forest

I slept well in a camp bed, which had a proper mattress and a pillow. When I woke up, I couldn't remember where I was. Rubbing my eyes, I looked around the windowless room and spotted Josh in a camp bed next to me. I took a long breath, remembering that I was deep beneath the surface and that today, we had to go back to the forest. A feeling of dread overwhelmed me.

Following a knock at the door, we were taken back to the washrooms and reunited with our grubby clothes. I pulled them on with a certain amount of disgust but we could hardly go back wearing what we'd been given. A tiny button had been sewn into the neckline of my sweatshirt, which I took to be the microphone but it could easily have been an original part of the top. I studied the soles of my trainers but could see no sign of any tampering.

After a decent breakfast, we were taken out of the tunnels through the gate I had failed to open and ushered into the back of a blacked-out Jeep. We could see out, but no one could see in. The Jeep drove up a small track to a gate in the outer wall of the barbed wire fence, which was manned by a soldier. The gate led onto the road that ran along the top of the hill. We drove past the fort that gave us access to the tunnels, which looked sinister and imposing. After a few minutes, the Jeep pulled up at another gate in the inner wall of the barbed wire fence; an entrance to the exclusion zone.

With a sinking feeling, I looked through the back window, watching the free world disappear before my eyes. An armoured truck followed at a distance, presumably the unit of soldiers that were sent to watch over us. As I turned back to face forward, Josh put his arm around me.

"We can do this Maddie! Then life can return to normal."

We were dropped in a secluded car park not far from the community's camp. I had even recognised the brick wall that we had followed two days earlier to reach the main road. Josh led the way, easily retracing our steps to the dense section of forest through which we had escaped. I looked down the slope, into the darkness, a knot forming in my stomach.

"Come on," Josh said, "with any luck they haven't left yet and we can just sneak in and grab the canister."

I took a deep breath and followed.

Finding the escape path in reverse was really difficult because there was no trail to follow. We were also trying to be very quiet so as not to alert the community. I was especially worried that Chester would give us away. However, he was usually out and about with Rambo at this time of day, checking the traps. Eventually, we came to the stream that ran past the camp and followed until we could see the toilet. From here, Josh led us around the camp, retracing the steps he had taken to avoid being discovered a few days earlier. In due course, we found the brown tarpaulin that had covered the pile of weapons. My heart sank. The tarpaulin had been rolled up at the base of a tree trunk and the weapons were gone.

"They've left already," I said, disheartened.

"Well, we knew there was a good chance that they had. At least we know where they've gone."

"Do you think you can find that building Rambo spoke about?"

"Yeah, I know where it is. Bit of a hike I'm afraid."

Out of curiosity, I took a couple of steps along the escape path towards the main camp. Suddenly, something closed around my right foot and before I could even look down, I was dragged upside down and catapulted up into the tree canopy. I tried to grab branches as I went but all I achieved was friction burns. Eventually, I came to a halt, slowly swinging from my right ankle several metres above the forest floor.

"You OK?" Josh called, sounding alarmed.

"Yeah, yeah. Rambo and his damn traps. So pointless!"

I felt annoyed and embarrassed. My ankle was hurting quite a bit but I didn't want to let on. I reached out and grabbed a branch to my right and pulled, swinging myself closer to the nearest tree. As I swung back, I pulled again, increasing my swing until I could grab the branch close to its trunk. Once there, I managed to pull myself up from one branch to the next until my body was more horizontal. Having created some slack in the rope, I could just about reach my foot with my right hand. Loosening the noose, I slipped my foot out, rubbing the side that hurt. No damage was done, luckily. I climbed down the tree to the forest floor.

"You really OK?" Josh asked, brushing some debris from my shoulder and pulling a twig from my hair. "You gave me quite a fright."

"Just annoyed. I was going to look around but on second thoughts!"

"Yeah, no point. They've clearly left and taken or hidden most things. Look," Josh said, pointing through the trees, "our tent is still there though, collapsed on the floor. Guess they didn't see much point in trying to save it. We might as well start following their trail."

Now that we had found the location where the weapons were hidden, it was possible to see a vague trail of footprints heading off up the slope at an angle. We set off. Some movement caught my eye and I jumped, turning and staring into the forest on my left.

"What's up?" Josh asked.

"I thought I saw something, over there."

Josh stared into the forest where I had pointed.

"I don't see anything. Maybe it was a deer or something. Or it could be one of those soldiers, keeping tabs on us. Come on, let's get going."

We moved on, battling through the dense foliage of the forest, pausing now and again to catch our breath. At length, we came to one of the forest trails. Josh took out his compass, checking that we were heading in the right direction. The going got a lot easier on the trail but we went cautiously. If the community had left the camp recently, we didn't want to stumble across them. After all, there was still a chance that we might grab the canister without giving ourselves away. By early afternoon, we had reached the end of the trail and found ourselves by the side of a tarmac road.

"OK," Josh said, "now I know where we are. We'll follow the road to find the hut. There's probably a more direct route that we could take through the forest, but I don't want to get us lost."

"Let's stop for a drink first," I suggested. "We ought to eat the food they gave us too. Might be difficult to explain how we got hold of decent stuff."

We found a log in a small patch of sunshine and unpacked our lunch. We had ham sandwiches and crisps with bottled water.

"How much further until we get to the hut?" I asked.

"Half an hour tops. We ought to go slower from here and be extra cautious. I really hope we can get that canister without them knowing we're here. I can just imagine the reaction we'll get from Boss."

"I know, but the chances of them leaving their weapons lying around are pretty slim, so we ought to have a good story ready."

"Like the General said, we just pretend that we found it harder than we thought it was going to be away from the forest."

"I suppose we have seen what it's like," I agreed. "Open spaces, little cover, few houses. Staying hidden for any length of time on the hill would be impossible.

"I just can't wait for all this to be over. I want everything to go back to normal"

"What about me?" Josh asked carefully. "Does your version of normal include spending time with me?"

The question surprised me. Did he really not know how I felt about him?

"I want to live in my house and go to our school and I want to spend all my free time with you."

Josh smiled and his eyes lit up.

"Ditto! Every spare moment!"

He hugged me, burying his face in my neck. I hugged him back, feeling so happy that I almost forgot the challenge ahead of us. *Focus!* We had to get that canister. If Boss used it, we might never get a normal day to spend together, ever.

We set off, walking through the trees at the edge of the road and falling into our usual pattern of movement. We came to a junction. Josh pointed to indicate that we should now follow the side road, which rose gently with woods on either side. The trees around us had large trunks and were regularly spaced, providing plenty of cover. We skirted around the back of a large empty car park for forest visitors, sticking to the tree line, each of us waiting, watching and moving in turn.

Suddenly Josh waved and indicated for me to stay put. Alarmed, I looked around to see what the problem might be. He mouthed a couple of words, which I couldn't understand. I looked at him, quizzically. He mimicked someone walking with his fingers and pointed discreetly. Squatting down, I made myself as small as possible, peering carefully around the tree trunk. Then I saw them. Al and Lester were moving amongst the trees ahead, scanning left and right. They walked slowly in an arc, coming closer to where we were hiding and then moving further away. My tree trunk was bigger than the one Josh was hiding behind, forcing him to edge from one side to the other to stay out of view. We waited a good ten minutes after they had disappeared before emerging.

"We must be getting close," he whispered.

My hands were shaking uncontrollably. Josh noticed and held them between his.

"Breathe," he whispered slowly, taking in a deep breath, then breathing out, then in and out again several times. I followed his lead, feeling a little calmer, but not calm enough. I shook my head slowly. I wasn't sure I was up to this. He smiled at me.

"The sooner we get this over, the sooner we get back to a normal life. We get as close as we can to see if we can get the canister without them knowing. If we can't, we pull the 'we're so sorry' card. Then all we need to do is secure the canister and shout for help. The soldiers will be there for us. We can do this Maddie!"

My mind was racing. This whole thing was so unfair. Why did it have to be down to us? What had I done to deserve this? I forced myself to focus on the problem. Crazy Boss had a canister of anthrax that, if released, would certainly kill everyone in the vicinity, including myself and Josh. Worse still, the bacteria would spread. Airborne, the germs might reach the population outside of the exclusion zone, killing my parents, my brother and sister, and all my friends and relatives. All my hopes of returning to a normal life depended on us securing that canister. There was no choice. The burden was ours. Reluctantly, I looked up at Josh and nodded.

"Let's go!"

We slowly edged our way through the trees until we came to a rough track with deep ruts that suggested regular use by some sort of vehicle. The track led back to the road we had been following and I could see a metal five-bar gate at the entrance.

Josh pointed down the track but beckoned me back into the woods. We slowed right down, only daring to move a short distance every few minutes. There was every chance that Boss had someone on lookout duty, probably using my binoculars. Eventually, the hut came into view; a single-storey wooden building with two windows on our side and a green felt roof. A few wooden steps led to a door, located beneath a porch. A sign outside read 'Forestry Commission - PRIVATE'. The hut was partly hidden behind an enormous pile of felled tree trunks, stacked as tall as a house. It wouldn't have been visible from the track at all.

We inched closer, desperate to see any sign that the community was there. From the outside, it looked locked and unused with no sign of anyone on lookout. It was stupid to expect anything else. After all, they intended to hide from the search party and move in behind. They were hardly going to advertise their presence by leaving guns and ammunition in the doorway. They had to be there though as we had spotted Al and Lester a short distance away.

"What shall we do now?" I whispered.

Josh went to answer me but a sudden movement over his shoulder caught my eye. At the same moment, I was roughly yanked backwards. Shocked, I screamed. Looking up, I saw Matt, staring down at me over my shoulder. He forced his arms through mine and pulled them back behind me. I could feel his revolting breath on my face. I never wanted to be this close to him. *Gross!* I twisted my face away to see Jerry with Josh in a headlock. Josh was trying to free himself, but Jerry just tightened his grip, a nasty expression on his face until Josh was gasping for air and gave up.

"Well, well," Jerry said in a dull voice, "what do we have here?"

"Couple of spies, maybe," Matt said, hissing into my ear, "trying to sneak up on us."

Matt pulled my arms tighter behind my back, causing a stab of pain in my shoulder joints. I screamed out in pain.

"Stop, stop," I shouted, "you're really hurting me."

I could see Josh struggling again, trying to free himself from Jerry's grip to come to my aid.

"Leave her alone," Josh said, his voice rasping and his face bright red.

Jerry tightened his grip again, a thin smile on his face. *God, he was enjoying this!* A commotion was coming from the direction of the hut. I looked up to see the door flung open and Chester tearing towards me. He launched himself at Matt's leg, growling fiercely. Matt immediately released me, waving his arms around frantically. Chester let go and put himself between us, a snarl daring Matt to try and grab me again. Matt stood motionless, terrified. Then I heard Babs shrieking.

"What are you doing, you idiots? Leave them alone! Jerry, let go of him."

I looked back towards the hut.

Boss was standing halfway between the hut and us. Behind him, on the porch, stood Babs, Lester and Rambo. I could just see Mikolaj peering around the doorway, looking shocked and scared.

Boss spun around, putting his finger to his lips to quieten everyone but Babs was having none of it. She came racing towards Boss, a look of fury on her face.

"Just stop!" she screamed. "Stop!"

Boss slapped her hard around the face and she fell to the ground. I couldn't believe he had hit her. I was about to run to her aid when Chester charged towards Boss, Rambo now shouting.

"Chester, no! Here boy, now."

Chester obediently went to Rambo's side, looking crestfallen. Rambo patted his head.

"Good boy," he said calmly.

Lester rushed over to help Babs up from the ground. She was holding her cheek, tears streaming down her face. He walked her slowly back to the hut, where she sat on the steps looking sad and shocked. I wanted to go over and hug her but Boss was staring at me, looking furious.

Al appeared in the doorway, carrying four shotguns in his arms. In his right hand hung the yellow canister. I stared. There it was. Such a small object, yet so deadly. Al walked quickly over to Boss, glancing in every direction, and then handed him a gun. Boss also beckoned for the canister, which he placed at his feet. Al then walked over to Jerry and Matt, handing them each a shotgun before disappearing back into the hut. He emerged with three more shotguns, offering one to Lester, who refused to take it. He then tried to give the gun to Mikolaj, who backed away into the hut, wanting nothing to do with it. Finally, he tried to give it to Rambo, who took it but immediately propped it up against the porch railing.

Boss was absolutely fuming. I went to speak but he raised his finger to his lips to silence me, then looked around, staring into the woods. Jerry was also on guard, wondering if the commotion had attracted any unwanted attention. Glancing behind at Matt I was horrified to find him pointing his shotgun at me. My stomach somersaulted and my mouth went dry.

"No!" Josh shouted. "You idiot!"

Suddenly, emerging from the bushes all around, stepped the soldiers. They were dressed in dark, camouflage hazmat suits and armed with rifles. Three had their weapons trained on Jerry, three on Matt, and the rest of the soldiers were targeting either Boss or Al. Jerry looked down at the three red dots from their rifle sights, which danced on his chest. He quickly grabbed Josh around the neck and withdrew a knife from his jacket. He spun Josh around, putting him between the soldier's rifles and himself. *Hostage!* Things were going from bad to worse.

I looked at Matt. He was wavering slightly, maybe wondering if he should give himself up, but he looked at Jerry with Josh, then looked at me and kept his shotgun aimed at my head. *Two hostages!*

Babs started shouting again, getting hysterical.

"Stop! Stop! You're going to get us all killed."

"Shut up!" Boss screamed, then spoke directly to the soldiers. "Right, you lot, back off or they're dead."

Some of the soldiers who had their guns trained on Jerry and Matt now targeted Boss. He looked down, a total of six red dots floating over his chest. My mind was racing. Boss had the canister at his feet. If they shot him they could get it. Maybe Josh and I were now collateral damage. They'd sacrifice us to save everyone else. Time seemed to stand still as we all stared, waiting to see what Boss would do. He reached down and picked up the canister, putting his index finger through the pin. I felt sick.

"Last chance!" Boss shouted.

"You really don't want to do that," one of the soldiers called. "You pull that pin and we're all dead."

Boss stared at him, a slow smile spreading across his face. In a calm voice, he responded.

"I'll take my chances!"

What happened next seemed to be in slow motion. I watched as Boss pulled the pin from the canister. Simultaneously, a volley of rifle shots hit him full in the chest. His body jerked from the impact and he threw his arms up in the air. The canister rocketed skyward and Boss fell to the ground with a thump. Without thinking, without processing the possible outcomes, I started to move, watching the descent of the canister. I wasn't far away from its trajectory. Perhaps I should have run in the opposite direction, but I didn't, I ran towards it, jumping to catch it cleanly as it fell. One of the soldiers shouted.

"Put it down on the floor Maddie, very carefully, then back away."

I placed it on the ground, holding my breath. Josh rushed over, dragging me backwards, away from the canister.

"Has it gone off?" he asked.

"How do you tell? We wouldn't see it, would we?"

I looked into Josh's eyes. I was terrified, shaking uncontrollably. He wasn't doing much better either, so we just hugged one another. If I was going to die, at least we would be together.

I glanced around. The rest of the group were just standing there, dumbfounded. Jerry, Matt and Al had all put their weapons down. Lester was sitting beside Babs with his arm around her shoulder. She was no longer crying, but she couldn't take her eyes off Boss's crumpled body and the pool of blood that slowly spread in the dirt. Rambo was holding on to Chester, preventing him from running over. Mikolaj was nowhere to be seen, presumably hiding in the hut.

One soldier sprinted over to the canister and sprayed it with some kind of foam. The canister became buried in a smooth white covering, resembling a giant marshmallow. At the same time, another soldier ran towards Josh and me, handing us a face mask with a cone filter at the base. Up close, I could see that this soldier was wearing something similar underneath the hood of his camouflage suit. We quickly put them on. Turning around, I could see the other soldiers securing the weapons and also handing face masks to everyone else. Was it too late? Maybe we were all infected. I looked at Babs and Lester, then at Rambo. Mikolaj was being helped from the hut by a soldier, who sat him next to Lester on the step. None of them deserved this. They were all good people. My throat ached and tears rolled down my cheeks.

Jerry, Al, and Matt were handcuffed. While Jerry stood tall, seemingly fearless, Al and Matt were visibly shaken, their shoulders slumped and their heads down.

The sound of a helicopter came from above, the blades whirring, sending debris spiralling around our feet. The soldier who had sprayed the canister was holding a radio and talking rapidly into it. The helicopter moved off, but not far away and the sound it made suggested it was descending to land somewhere. In due course, more soldiers appeared from the track wearing the familiar white suits. Two of them carried a large crate, which they set down near the canister and started to unload the contents. Josh, myself, and the rest of the community were gathered together by the hut. A soldier addressed us.

"Please," he said, "don't be alarmed. We're just taking precautions. We're going to take you all to a safe place. Follow me."

Josh and I looked at one another. Just taking precautions? There was little point in revealing anything that we knew to the community. Although I felt the weight of the world on my shoulders, sharing that weight wouldn't help me. I'd just be burdening everyone.

"I don't want to go," Rambo said firmly.

"I'm sorry, no choice," the soldier replied even more firmly.

"I can't! What happens to my dog? I can't abandon him!"

The soldier looked at Chester, who was sitting obediently at Rambo's side.

"OK, he can come too."

"There you go, my mate," Mikolaj whispered with a wobble in his voice.

Lester linked arms with Babs, leading her gently up the track behind a soldier. Mikolaj and Rambo followed, with Chester at his heel. Matt walked alone, his head hanging down. Jerry and Al waited for a moment longer, staring at Boss. Two soldiers stood on either side of them, each taking an arm and steering them up the track. Josh and I made ready to follow but the soldier who had addressed us all stepped into our path.

"I gather you two know what's at stake here," he said quietly.

We nodded.

"We can't say for sure," he said, "but we're not certain it deployed. Until we know, please don't mention anything to the others. No need to cause unnecessary alarm."

A small wave of relief came over me but quickly subsided. He was probably trying to make us feel better. Help us pretend that we weren't facing a death sentence. We nodded in agreement and he stepped to one side, allowing us to follow the others.

Epilogue

I got off the school bus, pleased to see Josh sitting on a low wall, waiting for me. He smiled and waved. I walked over, aware that people were watching. He gave me a hug and a peck on the cheek, then took my hand and we walked into the school grounds.

The bus ride was fine. Despite getting on last, a girl from my tutor group called out. She had saved the seat next to her. Faces leaned into the central aisle, some just looking, some also smiling.

Josh escorted me to my tutor group, despite it being in a different block from his.

"Meet you by the tennis court at break time?" he asked.

"Definitely. See you later!"

I walked into my tutor group, smiling at everyone, determined to make a fresh start. The blond trio came rushing over to me.

"Hi Maddie," they said in unison. One added, "We hear that you and Josh are an item. He's so gorgeous! Everyone's so jealous."

I wasn't about to become best buddies with these three, but I nodded and smiled.

"Yes, we had quite an adventure over the holidays."

Miss Lacey came into the classroom and we all took our seats.

"Good morning everyone and a special welcome back to Maddie, who has become quite a celebrity!"

She smiled and spoke directly to me.

"Since the school reopened, we've been entertaining each other during tutor time by telling our own stories about the event. Some pupils spent a few weeks in an evacuation centre and some were simply away when it happened, unable to return home. So far, we haven't had any stories from a pupil who lived off-grid and saved the nation!"

She grinned at me, raising her eyebrows.

"If you feel like telling us your story Maddie, I'm sure everyone would love to hear it."

The whole class looked at me intently, some smiling, others looking intrigued. I wasn't enjoying the attention but I couldn't pretend it wasn't happening.

"How long have you got?" I said, smiling. "Maybe I can start tomorrow."

Miss Lacey nodded and winked, then started to take the register.

My thoughts drifted. I had already told my story many times during our imposed quarantine: to the authorities, my family, my friends, and a journalist. They sent us to a quarantine centre for four weeks. It was a long time, but after all those uncomfortable nights off-grid, Josh and I enjoyed ourselves there. We could use a gym and swimming pool, plus watch endless films, television series, and video games. It was great to spend time with Babs, who took a while to recover from her ordeal. She got to Facetime her daughter morning and evening and before long her anxiety was replaced by tears of joy. Lester and Mikolaj were good fun too, becoming a bit of a comedy duo and even making Rambo laugh. Chester, well, he just loved all the attention. We never saw Jerry, Al or Matt again. They were charged with various offences including theft, possession of firearms, and assault.

The centre also provided us with a large pile of newspapers and magazines, covering the time that we'd spent in the exclusion zone. The media had a field day. At first, there was lots of speculation about what had happened. When the truth about the EMP started to emerge, there were sensational warnings about possible war, disease and famine. Then, after the evacuees were released, the media held endless interviews and showed footage of looted houses and crashed cars. But the story they were all waiting for was mine. Well, mine and Josh's, but I got most of the attention because I had caught the canister. Apparently, due to its age, there was a little rust around the nozzle and although the pin was pulled out, the contents didn't disperse. Had the canister hit the ground, they were certain that the blockage would have cleared, releasing the anthrax. I still cringe a little when I remember the headline in one of the national newspapers, 'Anthrax heroine saves the nation!' *Urgh!* Josh and I were even invited to appear on television when we were released but we didn't want any more attention. We just wanted life to return to normal. Except, normal will never be quite how it was. Now that I have Josh, it will be better.

Printed in Great Britain
by Amazon

43754441R00158